my boss's worker

SPOILER IT'S NOT ME

ADRIAN J. SMITH

EREKA PRESS

my boss's stalker

one

THE WINERY

Zoe sipped the red wine, its musky flavor lingering on the back of her tongue. The glass was warm against her lips. She liked it, mostly. Small vials of different flavors were spread out in front of her, and she mixed another concoction, hoping this one was better. She'd been at it nearly three hours already and hadn't found the right flavor yet.

Her boss, the infamous and brilliant Ms. Gwen Fudala, marketer extraordinaire and ruthless businesswoman, had sent Zoe there to create the star flavor for the party they were in the midst of planning. Zoe had no idea why, but when Gwen had leaned against the doorframe and told her she was leaving in ten minutes to make the appointment, Zoe had been so distracted by her long legs and curves that she'd just agreed without thinking or asking questions.

Little did Gwen know, Zoe wasn't an avid wine drinker and didn't fully understand the finer points of what made a good wine. But the event was supposed to be a spectacular one, and Gwen insisted on having her own flavor. Just what exactly was Gwen's flavor?

That question took Zoe down a whole different line of

thought—one she'd been on before and one she'd fastidiously trained her brain away from for years. Or tried to, anyway.

Mixing up another small glass to try a new flavor, Zoe hummed as she swallowed the dark liquid. This one was amazing. At least from what her numbed tongue could tell. How much wine had she had in these last three hours? Scratching her head as she tried to remember, she gave up and went with her gut.

This one was *the* one.

Zoe wrote down what she'd added and how much and handed it to the worker who had been in the room with her on and off for the last few hours. Was his face blurry? She blinked a few times to clear her vision before pushing the chair back.

Whoa.

The room spun slightly, her head felt funny, and she hated to admit it, but she might be a bit drunker than she'd originally thought. *Crap.* She was on the clock. She'd been sent there for work, and now she was drunk at work. Zoe slapped a hand to her forehead. How much more of an idiot could she be?

Heading for the door, she tried to keep the extra sway out of her hips as she made her way toward the front of the winery. She stepped into the main entry area, a place built for extravagance— high ceilings, large glass windows, rustic in feel but modern in touch. Zoe had loved it when she first arrived.

Zoe reached into her purse to snag her car keys, when a gentle, confident, and oh-so-familiar seductive chuckle greeted her.

Fuck.

Gwen stood at the main desk, her thin hand with its perfectly manicured nails flat on the smooth varnished wood. Zoe's heart stuttered. What was Gwen doing there? Did she screw up the entire assignment already? Had Gwen said she was going to join later when she sent Zoe? For the life of her, Zoe couldn't remember.

Panic etched into Zoe's chest. She had to fix whatever she had screwed up. Her voice came out in a rush, her tongue still felt bigger than it should be, slightly numb, and her cheeks burned. "I didn't know you were coming."

"I wanted to taste." Gwen's thin eyebrow rose, her stare intense, and she dropped her gaze from Zoe's eyes, down her body and over her breasts, to her hips, and her toes, and then she slowly dragged her gaze back up.

Zoe could never stop the heat that rushed to her cheeks when Gwen looked at her like that. There was absolutely nothing going on between them. There never would be. Gwen would definitely not be interested in someone like Zoe. Hell, Zoe didn't even know if she was a lesbian or bisexual or liked women or whatever. They never discussed the personal, and Gwen had never mentioned dating anyone. Swallowing the sudden lump in her throat, Zoe folded her hands tightly together and hoped the heat that kissed her cheeks wasn't obvious. "Oh. Um... I just finished up."

Gwen eyed her carefully, her lips slightly parted, and the tip of her pink tongue peeking out before retreating. She may have been the top marketer at Gruzska Publishing, and Zoe may have worked for her for three years as her personal assistant, but that had never stopped her from daydreaming about just what those lips tasted like. And right now, all Zoe wanted was to lean in and find out just where that tongue had gone.

"Zoe?"

"Huh?" Zoe flicked her gaze right up to Gwen's pale blue eyes. She had so been caught. She wasn't going to be able to get out of this one no matter how hard she begged. Oh, begging, that could be—*shut up, Zoe!*

"Are you drunk?" Amusement swam behind Gwen's intense stare for a brief moment before she steeled her look again. Or maybe Zoe just made that up in the hope that Gwen would understand. She'd been sent to a winery for God's sake! Gwen couldn't expect her not to drink anything, could she?

Zoe flushed, embarrassment hitting her hard. She hadn't been able to hide it, and she was sure Gwen had seen everything that flashed through her mind written across her face. All the attraction, all the pent-up sexual energy that she'd managed to hide for the last three years. Zoe pursed her lips and answered, resigned to her fate, "Probably."

Gwen leaned in, her lips inches away from Zoe's ear. Zoe straightened her back immediately and held herself perfectly still, her mind racing to try and figure out what was going on.

Gwen's breath was hot against her face, down her neck. She lowered her voice so it was barely above a whisper, "Silly girl."

Stepping back, Gwen's gaze dropped from Zoe's head to her toes, slowly dragging upward again. A shiver of pleasure coursed through Zoe. If only Gwen meant it and it wasn't all in Zoe's head.

Zoe blanched. She had no idea what to say to that. What did Gwen even mean? Her heart raced as she stood stiffly in front of her boss, hoping that she hadn't revealed too much. Gwen turned to the front counter, her perfect hand still flat on the top of it, and nodded at the worker there.

"Let's taste this wine you've created." Gwen walked confidently to the small room Zoe had just vacated after spending hours there.

What was happening right now? She wasn't fired—yet. So that was a good thing. Zoe had witnessed Gwen firing others, ousting them for small infractions. Somehow, Zoe had managed to stick around for three years—Gwen's longest standing admin so far, and she wore that badge with honor.

Zoe followed dutifully, her chin tilted toward the ground in shame that she had gotten herself drunk while on the clock. She would never let Gwen down if she could help it. She'd worked her ass off for three years to make sure that she was valued and needed.

They brought out the sample of wine that Zoe had mixed in a glass for Gwen to taste. With a single nod, Gwen dismissed the worker and sat on the edge of the table, her hand at the side, and her gaze locked on Zoe's face. Gwen swirled the glass slowly, staring at Zoe over the edge for what felt like forever. The stare was intense and intoxicating.

Zoe wasn't sure how long she would be able to stand there and not fall over. The alcohol running through her system was much stronger than she'd originally anticipated, and it made her head spin—or maybe that was the amused and curious look Gwen had aimed in her direction.

Wait, what?

That was wrong. Gwen wasn't amused or curious. She was probably annoyed that Zoe had gotten drunk, that she had taken so long. Why was she even there? Gwen was supposed to be back at the office, working, which was why she'd sent Zoe to the winery in the first place.

"What are you doing here, Ms. Fudala?" Zoe asked with an undertone of fear, which she was pretty sure she hid with a good dose of happiness. Gwen often chided her for always being happy, but it wasn't quite true. She just used happiness as a cover.

Gwen said nothing as she stared right at Zoe, lifting the wineglass to her deep red lips. Her tongue dashed out against the glass, licking up the lingering drops of wine on the edge before pulling back into her mouth. Zoe had to suppress the groan that wanted to escape her lips. She clenched her jaw and fists, using the tightness of muscles and slight pain to remind herself that this was her *boss*. This was the great Gwen Fudala, chief marketer, who ran the business as if she had her finger on everything.

Zoe's breathing came in short rasps when she finally managed to relax, her gaze still locked on those pale blue eyes as if her entire world depended on this one woman, which she supposed it very well might. Gwen lowered the glass and cocked her head to the side, her lips twitching in the corners before she was able to school the look. Or was that also in Zoe's mind? She didn't even know anymore.

"Is something wrong, Zoe?"

"What? Oh, no, nothing is wrong." Heat kissed her cheeks again, and Zoe found herself unable to look away from Gwen's intense stare.

"Are you sure?"

Zoe couldn't tell if that was fake concern, genuine concern, or amusement. She was going with the latter for now. How often was it that anyone dared to be intoxicated in front of the great Gwen Fudala? Zoe was willing to bet never.

"Zoe?" Gwen stayed evenly in place, that gaze surreal.

Zoe couldn't figure out what to say or how to answer. Was something wrong? Only this massive crush she'd had on her boss for the last three years that she had never managed to rein in, and with the wine in her blood and that damning look on Gwen's face, Zoe very well may be a lesbian with her first girl crush. "Yeah?"

"Are you sure nothing's wrong?"

Shaking her head, Zoe cleared her throat. Her voice was so soft when she answered she wasn't sure Gwen would even be able to hear her. "No, nothing is wrong."

"Hmm."

Gwen lifted the glass to those kissable lips again and finally took a sip, the line of her throat long as the muscles moved while she swallowed. Sweat littered the small of Zoe's back and her palms as she watched Gwen take another small sip of the blended wine. If only Gwen would drink her up like that.

When Gwen settled the glass onto the table and eyed Zoe up and down, Zoe was pretty sure she could come just from that look alone if given enough time.

"How drunk are you?" Gwen asked, her tone precise as always, and any hint of amusement was gone if it was ever there to begin with.

Cold washed through Zoe as she blinked and tried to clear her mind from the arousal coiling in the pit of her belly. "Oh, um, well, I've been here for three hours."

Gwen eyed her again, and Zoe realized too late that she hadn't actually answered the question. Her embarrassment aside, claiming she was intoxicated was probably a good way to get out of anything stupid that was about to leave her mouth—which if Gwen kept looking at her like that, it likely would.

"I'm drunk. I'm really drunk," Zoe confessed, the words rushing out of her mouth before she could stop them.

Gwen drew in a sharp breath as she grabbed the glass again and took another sip before leaving it alone and standing. She stepped to Zoe's side, bending low so her breath washed against Zoe's cheeks. "You're not supposed to swallow."

Zoe clenched her legs together against the pool of wetness that dampened her underwear. Heat from Gwen's body reached hers because they stood so close, the line of Gwen's arm matching with hers as they faced in opposite directions. Zoe's lips parted, but she had no answers. She knew she was supposed to spit, but she'd decided to swallow a few of the flavors when they were good and had forgotten all about it in her distraction over this gorgeous woman.

"I know," Zoe murmured.

"Then why didn't you follow the rules?" Gwen's voice was barely above a whisper, the deep tone of her voice so seductive even though Zoe knew she hadn't meant it that way.

Tilting her chin up in a single act of defiance, Zoe looked directly into those deep light-blue eyes. So many people thought Gwen was cold and aloof, but after working for her for three years, Zoe knew it was exactly the opposite. She had passion underlying everything she did—deeply controlled passion.

If she were a braver person, Zoe would lean up on her toes and kiss Gwen senseless. If she were a braver person, she wouldn't be hiding this massive crush on her boss. She would have quit and left and found a place she could work that would be better for everyone. But she was so weak. She didn't have the gumption to leave and save herself, so she suffered in her attraction in order to stay close to the one person who ruled her world.

"I don't know," Zoe answered, maintaining eye contact until she couldn't stop herself from dropping her gaze to those beautiful red lips. "Maybe I don't like rules."

Gwen hummed again, lingering where she stood only a breath away, her fingers gripping Zoe's wrist and tightening slightly before she let go and released Zoe's arm. "Come along. I'll drive you home. We'll send someone for your car this afternoon."

"Uh...what?" Zoe blinked wildly as she turned around to watch Gwen's perfect ass as she walked out.

"I'll take you home."

Oh, if only Gwen was saying that in an entirely different context. But Zoe wasn't stupid. That would never happen. Gwen was way out of Zoe's league. Gwen didn't even see Zoe as anything more than an office admin who was easily replaceable.

Racing to catch up, Zoe stepped outside into the sunny afternoon and had to squint against it. "You never told me why you showed up. I thought I was supposed to pick the wine."

"And you did a marvelous job." Gwen's tone was back to short and terse, all business. "But we have work to get done. This was only one step that needed to be completed."

"Ms. Fudala." Zoe raced to catch up, but she stumbled and twisted her ankle on the gravel road. She cursed under her breath and winced as she righted her foot. "Ms. Fudala, wait. Did you not trust me to get the job done?"

Gwen turned around, her stare gone from amused to icy. It stopped Zoe in her tracks. Gwen's lips thinned, her cheeks tightened, and she seemed to almost pull in on herself. Zoe had never seen her look like that before.

Opening her mouth to correct her sentence, make it seem less like an accusation and more like a true question, Zoe stumbled again. Gwen caught her, her long thin fingers wrapping around Zoe's upper arm to hold her upright.

"We need to get you home," Gwen said, firmly.

"But I thought you sent me out here to figure out the wine. Why are you here?"

Gwen pursed her lips. "Not because of you, I promise."

"Ms. Fudala..." Zoe trailed off, realizing far too late that she needed to shut up and accept. If she had been sober, that wouldn't have been a struggle to accomplish.

"Don't worry about it, Zoe." Gwen dragged in a deep breath,

her gaze flitting around as she stepped in closer, their bodies about to bump into each other. Gwen hadn't moved her hand from Zoe's arm. "Can you walk on your own?"

"Yeah." Zoe's voice broke. "Why would you think I couldn't?"

"Because you've stumbled twice now."

"I—I'm fine," Zoe stuttered.

"Good." Gwen locked their gazes together. "Let's go, silly girl."

two

THE LONELY BEDROOM

She's so going to fire me.

Zoe sat in the passenger seat of Gwen's new car, every muscle in her body tense. She kept her hands in her lap, her fingers wrapped around the strap on her purse, and her eyes glued to the road in front of her. Her jaw was so tight. When she realized it, she immediately relaxed it, but the ache was already there.

"What's your address?" Gwen glanced at Zoe.

Frowning, Zoe leaned forward and input her address into the GPS in the car. She had Gwen's address memorized. She'd been to her condo more times than she could count, but that was all work related. Gwen didn't even know where Zoe lived, what kind of apartment she had—which was run-down and small and certainly not up to Gwen's standards.

And now she was going to see everything.

Zoe hesitated, almost changing the GPS to another place so she could grab a rideshare from there and Gwen would still be in the dark. But she stopped herself. She shouldn't feel bad about the way she lived. Gwen wouldn't judge her for it because they weren't even on the same level of existence.

Going back to sitting as tensely as possible in the passenger seat, Zoe gnawed on her lip. Her cheeks were on fire, and as much as she wanted it to be from the alcohol, she knew it was from embarrassment. She had to stop thinking about Gwen that way. She really did. Her best friend, Nikki, had told her repeatedly that she had to stop putting Gwen on such a pedestal because it was going to be her biggest downfall. Nikki was right, hands down. But Zoe had found it impossible to do that.

Zoe had met Nikki right around the time she started working for Gwen, so she'd been there through everything, including Zoe's very embarrassing reveal that she had a huge crush on her boss. Nikki had laughed and given her a hug, telling her that it happened to the best of them.

Gwen said nothing as she continued to drive the forty minutes back to town. Zoe kept sneaking glances toward her, but Gwen never took her eyes off the road in front of them. Finally when Gwen pulled up outside of the apartment, Zoe reached for the door handle and tried to leave, but the seatbelt across her shoulder locked her in place and tugged her back inside.

"Fuck," Zoe murmured.

"Zoe, you know how I feel about cursing." Gwen's voice was so cool, so calm and collected.

How the hell did she do that?

Zoe was over here burning from embarrassment, and Gwen was acting like nothing was wrong at all. Zoe couldn't even look at Gwen. She would see everything, and Zoe was never going to be able to go into work again.

"I know. I'm sorry," Zoe rushed the words out. "I won't do it again."

Gwen leaned over, getting closer again. Was this some sort of tease? Gwen hadn't ever had an issue with personal space, but today it was so much worse. It was the wine. Zoe had to keep reminding herself it was all because of the wine rushing through her head. She couldn't stop her thoughts, and she really, really needed to. Gwen got closer.

Was Gwen going to kiss her?

Swallowing the sudden lump in her throat as Gwen's face

moved in closer, Zoe stilled. Gwen's hand reached down by Zoe's hip and pressed the button on the seatbelt. The belt instantly released. Zoe reached for her, her fingers brushing Gwen's accidentally as she leaned closer to the door to put space between them.

"I'll walk you up."

"You don't have to," Zoe rushed. She couldn't stand to have Gwen walk into her apartment building and see everything. It would make her completely unhinged.

"Zoe," Gwen scolded. "You're drunk. I'll walk you up."

Gwen put the car into park and turned the engine off. She was out of the driver's door before Zoe could even manage to find the handle to her door again. It popped open, and Gwen stood on the other side, her hand out for Zoe to take it. She couldn't take it, could she? She couldn't willingly put her hand in Gwen's.

But she found her fingers sliding against Gwen's palm. She found Gwen's hand tightening around her own as she pushed her feet into the ground to stand. She found Gwen standing so damn close that she could smell the subtle perfume she always wore.

Zoe sucked in a deep breath and had instant regret. Gwen didn't release her hand as they walked toward the apartment. When she waited for Zoe to fish out her fob to let them in, Gwen leaned in and whispered, "Don't want you to trip again, do we?"

A shudder raced through Zoe. She was absolutely doomed. Gwen had to know. She was teasing because she found Zoe cute and amusing. Her stupid crush was now out in the world and the one person she didn't want to ever know it existed had found out.

"Nope, but I think I can manage the rest of the way."

"Zoe," Gwen chastised. "I doubt you live on the first floor."

"Fifth," Zoe squeaked.

The look Gwen gave Zoe was filled with something unintelligible. Zoe had never seen it before. Zoe leaned forward and pressed her fob to the door, and the door clicked.

"Perfect," Gwen answered before snagging the door with her free hand and opening it.

The elevator ride was just as intense as the car ride. At least Gwen had let go of Zoe's hand as soon as they got inside. Zoe's heart raced. And when they got to the door and Zoe's hands shook, Gwen took the keys and unlocked the handle.

"You really should have a deadbolt on this."

"Landlord was supposed to install one three years ago, but he's a bit of a slumlord." Zoe bit her tongue hard. She hadn't meant to say that, but when she drank, words just escaped her and there was no coming out the other side with her dignity intact.

"I'll talk to him."

"No." Zoe wrapped her fingers around Gwen's wrist to stop her. "It's fine. I'll remind him."

"At least tell me you have a chain."

"Yeah, yeah, I do," Zoe lied. She couldn't let Gwen know she didn't. Not with that clouded look in her eyes.

"Good." Gwen's face fell as she stood just outside the now open apartment door. When she raised her gaze to meet Zoe's, that clouded look vanished. "Sober up, silly girl."

Was that a smirk on Gwen's lips? No, it had to be sheer annoyance.

"Yes, ma'am." Zoe scrambled into her apartment and shut the door. She pressed her forehead to the wood and closed her eyes before raising up on her toes to look out the peephole.

Gwen stood on the other side, still and motionless, as if she was waiting for something. Whatever it was must have happened, because she turned around and left, her heels clicking as she walked down the hall, her pencil skirt making her ass look amazing through the fisheye of the peephole.

Releasing a breath, Zoe closed her eyes and groaned.

What the hell had she been thinking?

Zoe lay flat on her back in bed, staring at the ceiling. Turning on her side, Zoe buried her face in the pillow and clenched her eyes shut tightly. She would have to walk into the office in the morning, hungover because she was definitely drunk, and act like nothing had happened. Gwen had spared her from as much embarrassment as possible, but still, she couldn't walk in there after today. She would be the laughingstock of the office. Zoe's heart wrenched. She needed to write an apology letter to Gwen, perhaps with her resignation in it, and go from there. It was so inappropriate for her to drink while on the job. Her phone beeped as she received email after email from Gwen.

Well, that at least meant she wasn't expecting Zoe to quit or planning to fire her, so that had to be a good sign, right? Zoe skimmed through them, looking in her declining drunken state to see what she needed to do immediately and what could wait— especially since she'd left halfway through the workday and hadn't completed everything.

The last email that came in surprised Zoe. The subject line read, *For Immediate Action*. Gwen didn't often get that specific when she sent Zoe a list of items to do, but again, with the rest of the emails in there first, Zoe didn't think she was about to be fired for drinking on the job. Her thumb hovered over the email before she finally tapped it while holding her breath. What punishment was she about to face? It wasn't the first time she had messed something up, but she'd never done anything this extreme before. Zoe had tried her best to maintain every boundary line possible while in the office.

For Immediate Action

I will see you in the office in the morning, eight sharp. If I discover you have done any work while you recuperate during your paid time off, there will be consequences to working off the clock.

Gwen

Zoe read it three times over. She wasn't off the clock if it was paid time off, was it? Pulling herself to sit up, she read it a fourth time. Gwen had never chastised her for working from home or after hours before. Nothing had happened to indicate that this was normal for them. Frequently, Gwen would call or email or text after hours and ask Zoe to do something quickly or tell her where a file was.

Zoe read the email a fifth time, her thumb hovering over the reply button. She would be stupid to answer on a corporate email, wouldn't she? Yet, she wanted to. She wanted to tell Gwen she was fine and could work from home on certain projects, nothing that would go out until she was sober enough to double-check her work, but she'd sobered a bit since Gwen had brought her back to her small apartment.

What was she supposed to even say back that wouldn't be considered inappropriate? Zoe pushed her thumb against the reply button on her phone and stared at the blank email. In an instant, she was typing quickly.

RE: For Immediate Action

Ms. Fudala,

I don't believe PTO means I am off the clock.

Sincerely,
Zoe

She hit send before she could chicken out and settled the phone down onto her chest. A smile lingered on her lips. She'd never been so forward with Gwen before, never pushed back on the limits she had set. Perhaps the alcohol still lingering in her bloodstream was giving her the voice she always wanted.

Arousal coiled through her again as she imagined the look on Gwen's face when she read Zoe's response. She wasn't sure when it happened, but she found her hand pressed between her legs, smoothly running her fingers over herself, using the friction of her cotton panties to tease. It had been a long time since she'd touched herself while thinking of Gwen. After the first few times, she had stopped, needing to have more space between them instead of less, and when she did this, she couldn't stop thinking about Gwen touching her instead. Especially with the charged interactions they'd had that day.

Zoe drew in a sharp breath as she eased one finger under the edge of her underwear and brushed the pad against her swollen lips. The moan from her was light. Her eyelids fluttered shut at the barest touch, and she wished it was Gwen's hand instead of hers, those slim fingers, the perfectly manicured but short nails. Still, this was as good as she would ever get from her boss, so she would take what she was given.

As soon as she made the decision, Zoe went all in. She lifted her hips and shoved her sleep shorts to the bottom of the bed along with her panties. Sitting up, she stripped off the tanktop she'd changed into when she'd come home and dropped it to the side of the bed.

"In for a penny," Zoe murmured as she lay back on the bed and closed her eyes.

She started slowly, sliding one finger in a circle around her clit before gently rubbing back and forth. She relaxed into the moment, using the image of Gwen sitting on that table, the direct look, the amusement behind the gaze, the glass to her lips, her tongue...teasing. Zoe was probably just making up that last bit, but she would roll with it for now.

Sighing, Zoe pressed a little harder and slid two fingers inside herself. She'd done this so many times in the last few years that she knew the fastest way to find release. With her thumb moving, Zoe kept her eyes closed and imagined Gwen as the one between her legs.

Normally, she hated thinking of other people, but apparently with enough alcohol in her system in the middle of the day, her brain wasn't thinking clearly. Zoe bucked her hips suddenly, her voice echoing throughout her room.

"Oh, yeah, that feels good." She kept her eyes clenched shut, doing everything solely by feel as she continued to pleasure herself. It would take months for her to pull back from this while working with Gwen in the office, but at the same time, Zoe couldn't stop. She needed it.

Her lips parted as another wave of pleasure rolled through her. The alcohol might be impeding her ability to come as quickly as she wanted, but she would stick through it until she crested through at least one orgasm. She was just about to hit that first edge of the cliff where there was no turning back, when her phone vibrated loudly against the mattress.

Cursing, Zoe reached for it and grabbed the phone hard. She tensed when she saw Gwen's name on the screen. She answered before she missed the call, never wanting to miss a call from the queen.

"Gwe–Ms. Fudala, what can I help you with?" Zoe was out of breath, her heart racing and her head pounding as she tried to decide what to do and say next. She'd been caught red-handed, her fingers still inside her, her thumb still on her clit, and somehow, she had to focus on that sultry voice.

"Zoe," Gwen responded. "I'm calling about your email."

Zoe whimpered. Of all things for Gwen to call about, this was the last one she expected. She knew she'd been petulant in her response, but she couldn't believe Gwen would call over this. "Wh-what about it?"

Why did she sound so out of breath? Her heart picked up speed, and she was sure Gwen would know what she had been up to. She shouldn't have answered. She knew she couldn't hold her tongue when alcohol was involved, and this was only going to make it worse.

"I've put you in for a sick day. Take it. We can survive half a day without you."

Zoe sighed, pushing her thumb into her clit harder. Gwen's tone was always so precise, her words exact. Zoe swallowed and bit her lip as her eyes fluttered shut. "Right. I'll take the rest of the day."

"Good." Gwen sounded pleased.

Zoe wasn't sure what to say beyond hanging up. "Is that everything?"

"Yes. I'll see you in the morning, and I expect you to be at your best."

"Right. See you tomorrow." Zoe clenched her jaw to hold back the moan. Was she actually doing this? She sped up her fingers, the last note of Gwen's voice echoing in her mind. She put her phone next to her and dragged in a refreshing breath of air.

This time she groaned loudly, her hips rising from the mattress as she brought herself right back up to that first edge. Her breathing came in gasps as she flicked her thumb hard over her clit, her body jerking in response. She grunted as pleasure pooled between her legs, faster than she could breathe, as if stacking every nerve ending on fire together was a brilliant idea, but it was. God, it was.

Zoe groaned, her voice ringing in her ears as she pushed her way through her orgasm and kept her thumb moving in slow circles to drag it out as long as possible. As she relaxed onto the bed, she breathed a sigh of relief. It may have been unorthodox, but she was glad she'd done it. Reaching for her phone, she went to check the emails, except—

Gwen was still on the line.

No!

She had ended the call, hadn't she?

"Fuck."

Zoe hit the big red button, triple checked to make sure the call was ended and buried her face in her pillow dominated by embarrassment. She was done for. She would most certainly be fired now.

"Fuck."

three

WALK OF SHAME

"I can do this," Zoe murmured to herself as she stood in the elevator with several other people from the building and only one person from Gruzska Publishing.

She hadn't told anyone about what had happened last night. Normally she would have told Nikki, but Zoe couldn't even bring herself to swim through that level of embarrassment. Maybe in a few years she would be able to bring it up. Unless she got fired, and then she really wouldn't have another choice, would she?

Surely, Gwen wasn't going to fire her, right?

Zoe dragged herself into the office suite she and Gwen shared at seven forty-five in the morning. Hitting the lights as she stepped in, Zoe immediately looked to Gwen's closed door. She had spent the entire night preparing herself for the explanation of a lifetime, for begging to be spared her job, for groveling at Gwen's feet.

Except when she got to the office, Gwen wasn't in yet. She knew she was early, but more often than not, Gwen was there when Zoe got there and she was there when Zoe left. Sitting at her desk, awkwardly, Zoe started on her morning routine, needing to do something, otherwise she would worry herself to death.

Zoe clenched her thighs together as she sat down, remembering the power of the orgasm from last night. It had been a long time coming, and she knew without a doubt that seeing Gwen in the flesh after something like that—even without the phone call —was going to make it hard to look her boss in the eye.

Her crush on her boss was bad, really bad.

She was halfway through the email list from the previous day when Gwen finally stepped into the office. Gwen kept her long, thin fingers on the doorknob a second longer than she normally did. Her lips were the same deep red they normally were, her makeup perfectly done up, but Zoe detected a hint of pale gray under it.

Was she sick?

Gwen straightened up, putting one foot in front of the other as the door shut with a resounding click. Zoe was about to speak, but Gwen flicked her gaze straight up to Zoe's eyes with a hard stare. She looked gorgeous as ever, the lean lines of her body with the smooth fabric of her skirt suit hugging every single curve. Zoe gulped.

Stepping close to Zoe's desk, Gwen's lips parted as if she was going to say something, but she stopped herself. She nodded once at Zoe, and immediately went into her office, the door shutting as she disappeared inside. Zoe's heart was in her throat, and she hadn't even managed to get out a *Morning, Ms. Fudala* like she did every day. She'd been stunned into silence. Not just by Gwen's beauty but with a resurgence of the absolute embarrassment that she had experienced yesterday.

She was doomed.

Zoe stayed seated, unsure what to do next. Maybe if they just didn't talk about it, then it didn't really happen. Zoe scoffed. That was a bunch of bologna, and she knew it. Of course, it had happened. Not only had she masturbated while on a work call, but on a call with her boss, her boss she'd had a massive crush on for the last three years they had worked together, three years where she had managed to maintain absolute professionalism. Zoe's cheeks were on fire again.

Groaning, Zoe took a deep breath and focused her mind on her work—at least as much as she possibly could. She would wait until Gwen came out to speak with her. Checking Gwen's schedule, Zoe noted she had been late to a video meeting, which was certainly why she hadn't said anything when she came in. That put Zoe's heart at ease.

Yes, it was all because of work. Gwen didn't care about her on the personal level, and Zoe really had to get that through her head. There was nothing more between them than boss and employee. Zoe just had to stop daydreaming where she shouldn't.

The door to the office opened and a mail courier stepped inside. "Is this the right office for Gwendolyn Fudala?"

"It is." Zoe focused on him.

"I have a delivery for her." He set down the thin envelope and held out a device for Zoe's signature. She signed and then grabbed the envelope as he left.

Ripping open the back, Zoe shoved the envelope into the trashcan as she opened a secondary manilla envelope and photos fell onto her desk. She frowned at them.

"What in the world?"

Zoe was used to getting papers mailed in for Gwen, not photos. She frowned as she brushed the photos to fan them out and look at them more closely. They were professionally done photos of Gwen at the winery the day before. Had she been there to take new headshots or promotional photos for something? Surely, she would have had Zoe schedule that, right? It wasn't like Gwen had another assistant.

Riffling through the photos more, Zoe continued to stare at them. Gwen was gorgeous in each one of them, but they didn't quite look like she was paying attention to whoever was taking the photos either. She rarely looked at the camera, except in this one, which was a direct stare and one of those pure Gwen power looks.

Zoe shivered from it as if Gwen was looking right at her through all of it.

There were at least twenty photos here. Zoe gathered them into a pile but stopped on one in particular. It was of her and Gwen, standing outside at the winery, Gwen's hand on her arm. That must have been the second time she'd tripped, when Gwen had helped her to stand up. Zoe shuddered at the memory of those long fingers on her arm, the tenderness in the touch from a woman who was seen as anything but tender by the business world.

But that was odd. Zoe didn't remember anyone being there to take pictures, but the look in Zoe's eyes when she stared up at Gwen was unmistakable.

Lust.

Cringing, Zoe gathered the photos except that last one, which she shoved into the top drawer of her desk. She put the rest back into the manilla envelope and folded over the top to seal it. She would bring those in to Gwen when she was done with her meeting and figure out what she wanted Zoe to do with them then.

Puttering away at more work, Zoe did her best to forget the incident the night before. It was close to lunch before Gwen emerged from the interior office and leaned against the door frame, her legs crossed, and her gaze directly on Zoe as she sat at the desk deep in work. Zoe caught sight of her and stopped instantly, fear ratcheting up in her chest again.

"Ms. Fudala, did you need something?" Did her voice waver? God, she had to get herself under control, but the power this woman had—not just over Zoe but in general, the control she contained—was breathtaking. Zoe wished she could be just like Gwen when she grew up. Now, there was an obnoxious thought if she'd ever had one.

That sly smile Zoe swore she saw the day before was back before it was immediately masked by something else, something she couldn't read other than Gwen's normal countenance. "I need the final edits on the Granular file. They're insisting I go through them."

"Right, I'll get hold of it, and get it to you right away." Zoe's hands flew over the keyboard, but she wasn't looking at her screen. She kept staring at Gwen and her light blue eyes, her lips pulled tightly, her face pinched. Just what was going through her mind?

Gwen stayed put, not moving, staring Zoe down, that same guarded expression as before gracing her features. Zoe had never seen her act like this before. She was always so decisive and direct. But this was Gwen hesitating—it had to be. Zoe stilled her fingers as she looked Gwen over, a frown creasing her forehead.

"Was that all you needed?" Zoe's heart was in her throat again. She hated being in this position, not knowing what Gwen was thinking, if this was going to be the end of her career or if they were even going to speak about what happened. No doubt that was the issue. Gwen knew everything, and she was trying to decide what punishment she deserved.

Gwen's lips pressed together tightly, her expression morphing into one of decision. Zoe tensed as Gwen pushed off the wall and took careful, precise steps toward her. Her legs were long and perfect as she walked, and Zoe couldn't drag her gaze away from Gwen's body, from the fantasies she'd allowed herself over the years, and the ones she hadn't allowed knocking at the door and begging to be let in. The desk. The chair. The wall. Anywhere Gwen would take her, Zoe would allow it to happen.

Zoe couldn't breathe.

Gwen was going to fire her.

If not, then Gwen was going to ream her for what had happened and just how inappropriate everything had been yesterday. From the drinking to the email to the masturbation phone call.

Zoe had been waiting for this moment, when everything would come tumbling out over her own stupidity. She couldn't escape it.

Gwen leaned over the desk, her palm planted on the sleek wood. She reached toward her belly, Zoe's eyes riveted to every movement she made, and she pulled a button on her jacket to release it. Zoe's breath caught, and she had to force herself to drag her gaze upward to Gwen's face, realizing far too late that she had been looking elsewhere. Somewhere way too low.

"We do need to talk at some point." Gwen's voice was pure seduction, that smooth tone filled with depth and arousal that hit Zoe like a Mack truck.

Zoe held her breath. This was it. She was doomed. "Okay?"

"About yesterday," Gwen continued as she pulled the second button on her jacket, her long fingers slowly moving over her clothes. Zoe couldn't drag her eyes away.

Gwen was being so vague about what exactly they needed to talk about. Zoe knew, of course, but she was still left with the question of which was the biggest offense. Being drunk while on the job? Masturbating to images of her boss, to the sound of her boss telling her what to do in her mind? That email that—

"Focus, Zoe," Gwen chided, the reprimand soft and firm at the same time.

"Yes, Ms. Fudala." Zoe flushed, embarrassment slamming down on her again, only this time for something else entirely.

"I don't have time to talk today." Gwen wouldn't move her gaze from Zoe. Just what was she thinking? That Zoe was a complete idiot? There was no way she didn't know what was happening on the phone call.

"Do you want me to schedule it in?" Zoe's voice was so quiet as she asked. She didn't want to schedule her doom into the calendar. That would make it impossible to avoid, and she would know when she'd be fired. She'd essentially be doing it herself.

Gwen hummed, shifting so she was leaning forward on the desk even more, close enough that if Zoe moved upward slightly they could kiss. Though she would never do that. She could never—

"Zoe." Gwen firmly chastised her for losing her train of

thought again, but the confidence in her voice sent a different shiver through Zoe, one she was sure Gwen didn't intend.

"Yes, sorry, Ms. Fudala. I'm focusing." Zoe bit down hard on the inside of her cheek to try and make herself do what she had promised.

"Are you?" Gwen raised an eyebrow and drew in a deep breath, her breasts pushing against the tight fabric of her blouse. "I think we can find time to fit in the conversation around my schedule without putting it into the calendar. Don't you?"

"Whatever you think needs to happen." Elation built in Zoe's chest. She wasn't going to be fired today!

"The Granular file?" Gwen put a single finger on the desk as she leaned forward, her gaze dropping all over Zoe's face, her chest, and then back up to linger on her lips before moving to her eyes again.

"On it." Zoe couldn't drag her eyes away from Gwen as she straightened her back, the flaps of her jacket falling to the sides. Gwen dragged it off, over her shoulders, and folded it over her arm. Zoe swallowed hard, the snake of arousal that had bit her last night coming back to haunt her as her gaze openly roved over Gwen's body.

Gwen cleared her throat, and Zoe immediately looked at her computer and typed out the end of the email she had been about ready to send when Gwen had come to speak with her. Gwen leaned over the desk again, but she stopped short, her gaze falling to the manilla envelope.

"What's this?"

"Oh, I was going to bring it in when you were done with your meeting. It arrived this morning." The words rushed out of Zoe.

Gwen frowned, a deep line creasing in the center of her forehead as she straightened her back and picked up the envelope.

"It's some photos from the winery yesterday. I didn't realize you had anyone doing promotional work for us." Zoe's heart raced with just the memory of what happened there, of what had started there.

"Who brought it in?" Was Gwen's voice tight? Or was that just her usual commanding tone when she wanted information immediately.

Zoe shook her head. "Just some courier. I didn't get his name."

"Him?" Gwen raised an eyebrow at Zoe.

"Yeah, some guy in his twenties, I think." Why was she asking so many questions about him? Gwen had seemed really on edge lately.

Gwen opened the envelope and shuffled the photos out of it. She paled instantly. Zoe was almost up out of her seat, but Gwen stepped back from her. "Nothing else came with it?"

"No, Ms. Fudala. Just the envelope with the pictures." Zoe's nerve endings fired relentlessly.

Gwen looked down at the photos in her hands again. "Okay."

Was she shaking?

Zoe slowly pushed her chair back and stood up. She reached for the photos that Gwen held, but Gwen snapped her hands against her chest, protecting the photos from sight. "Did you look at them?"

"Yes," Zoe answered honestly. "I could have found someone to take PR photos for you if you wanted. That's in my job description."

"It is," Gwen replied, but her voice sounded distant, as if what Zoe had said didn't really make a dent in her head. Zoe had never known her to be distracted. But she was looking at the envelope again, like she could see the pictures inside. "There wasn't a note or anything?"

"No, just the photos."

Gwen nodded slowly. "And the photos...do they look good?"

"You look amazing in them, like always, Ms. Fudala." The tension between them was through the roof. Zoe would take the easier conversation of when she would be fired over whatever this was. She didn't like this.

Pressing the photos to her chest again, Gwen nodded at Zoe firmly. "Thank you, Zoe. I need the Granular file."

"Right. I'm on top of it." Zoe continued to stare at her boss. *What's going on?*

Gwen turned and walked back to her office, the lines of her body exact as she went, but the tension still riding in the room in her wake. It didn't dissipate when she was gone.

What the hell was Zoe missing?

four

LATE NIGHT AT THE OFFICE

"Zoe, you should have gone home two hours ago."

Zoe jerked her head up, finding Gwen leaning against the door to her office, her shoulder resting on the metal frame and her gaze direct. Zoe's stomach churned with arousal in a way it really shouldn't. It had only been a week since the winery incident, but Zoe had yet to figure out what she should do to fix *that* issue, and they hadn't talked about it yet. Even though Gwen had promised they would.

"I was finishing up some work, Ms. Fudala." Zoe raised an eyebrow in a challenge, because if she was supposed to go home for the day, surely Gwen should also have gone home.

With the party coming up, they were in definite crunch time, and late-night hours could be excused. But unexpectedly, Gwen didn't move. She continued to lean against the door, the long smooth lines of her body subtle and perfect. Zoe had dreamed of touching those curves so many times in the last week.

Fuck.

She had to stop that.

"We had to expand the room block at the hotel," Zoe added by way of explanation.

"That's a good problem to have." Gwen sounded almost sad, which was so odd for her.

Zoe had only ever seen her as confident in everything. Sure, she had her off days here and there, but nothing like this. After the odd reaction to the photos and no explanation of them in the last week, Zoe had been keeping a close eye on her boss. She wanted to help in whatever way she could.

"There's also a bad problem. I wasn't going to bring it up until tomorrow."

Gwen's gaze flicked up to Zoe. Her lips pursed, ever so slightly, and Zoe was sure most people wouldn't have even noticed it. But she did. She noticed everything about Gwen. She prided herself in it, actually. But she was left with the problem of what to do about the things she noticed.

When Gwen continued in her silence, Zoe realized belatedly that Gwen was waiting for an explanation.

Still sitting in her chair, Zoe swallowed the lump in her throat. "Amato Literary is pulling out."

"What?" Gwen's voice cracked through the room. She pushed off the door, standing straight and tall in the doorway.

"They pulled out of the event. Or they will. It's just scuttle-butt right now."

Gwen narrowed her eyes, canting her head slightly. "Order dinner."

"Does that mean I'm not in trouble for staying late?" Zoe held her breath as she waited for an answer.

"We'll talk about that later." Gwen disappeared into her office, leaving the door open for the first time all day.

Zoe breathed a sigh of relief. She quickly ordered dinner to be delivered for the both of them, assuming that Gwen would yell at her if she didn't order herself anything, and then gathered up what she knew about Amato Literary and her contacts there. She had a feeling Gwen would want to come up with a game plan to get them back in Gwen's good graces. Zoe, as usual, would be pivotal in accomplishing that.

Gwen's office was different from Zoe's outer one. It screamed more comfort than the sanitized entry with Zoe's desk, but it also was very formal. The lines of the furniture were sleek, the desk and table matched, and the interior wall was lined with a floor-to-ceiling bookshelf and a rolling ladder. Zoe had wondered once how Gwen had managed to convince the executives to put it in there, but she'd never asked. Maybe someday she'd have the gumption to do that.

Setting her notebook and binder on the glass table where they usually worked, Zoe pulled out the chair and sat down. Gwen, however, stood by the bookshelf, staring out the floor-to-ceiling window that her desk faced. A year ago, Gwen had requested that Zoe find someone to flip the desk around so she could look out the window instead of toward the door.

Zoe had thought it odd at the time, but she'd done exactly what her boss had demanded. Now, looking Gwen over, she seemed distracted. That had become more and more common over the last few months, but in the last week, since the winery and the day after, it had really hit home.

"Ms. Fudala?"

"Hmm?" Gwen jerked her head toward Zoe.

"Did you want to talk about Amato Literary?"

"Yes." Gwen glanced toward the window again before coming to the table where Zoe sat. Her long legs carried her smoothly as she walked, and Zoe couldn't help but rake her gaze up Gwen's body to settle on her eyes. But Gwen didn't even seem to notice this time.

Odd.

"I think they're upset because Wade Jameson is going to be there."

Gwen said nothing, but her lips thinned into a line as she stared at the binder on the table. She smoothed her hands under her as she sat down across from Zoe. Again, when Gwen didn't answer, Zoe waited patiently, but her tolerance for waiting easily timed out. This was so unlike Gwen.

"Ms. Fudala?"

Gwen snapped her gaze to Zoe's face. "I'm sorry. I guess I'm more tired than I had anticipated."

"Than you anticipated?" Zoe reached into the binder and pulled out a few pieces of paper, sliding them in front of Gwen.

"Yes." Gwen didn't elaborate as she pulled the papers over and skimmed them. "Wade defected from them, right?"

"She did. It wasn't pretty. Now she's working for Gaudenzi Publishing, in acquisitions." Zoe pulled out another piece of paper. "They just RSVP'd last week."

"And you think Amato feels slighted?" Gwen's face pinched, and it was adorable. It was a reaction that Zoe would normally expect from her, so she was glad they seemed to be getting back to normal.

"I know they do." Zoe pointed to the paper. "When Wade left, she took a bunch of clients with her, leaving Amato in a bind because they lost out on contracts."

Gwen squinted, and Zoe realized belatedly that she didn't have her glasses on. Standing, Zoe walked quickly to Gwen's desk, snagged the readers that sat right in the middle, and went back, handing them over. Their fingers brushed in the process, and Zoe shuddered.

Stop that.

She had chastised herself so much in the last week for doing and thinking inappropriate things about her boss. She never should have masturbated to thoughts of her. It was ruining her ability to keep her head on straight when she was in the office.

Gwen put the readers on and raised her eyebrows, suddenly reading the words on the paper easily. "This is a lot of clients."

"I think the one they're really upset about is Katyana."

"I can see why," Gwen murmured, setting the paper down. "I hadn't known she'd followed Wade."

"She did." Zoe pursed her lips. Gwen was usually far more with it than this, and she was always up-to-date on what was happening with the publishing world, especially movements as

big as this. "Ms. Fudala?" she asked for the third time that
night.

"Yes?" Gwen raised her gaze, meeting Zoe's eyes for the first
time that day.

It was so strange. Zoe shivered at the intensity in Gwen's stare,
her pale blue eyes boring directly into Zoe. Biting her lip, Zoe
continued to watch her. Something was definitely off. Her heart
raced as she debated what to say next, if she could really do this
without getting in trouble. Would Gwen even answer her?

"Is everything okay?"

Gwen's face fell. Her eyes dropped to the papers in front of
her, her shoulders slumping down. She dragged in a slow breath
and looked out the window with longing in her gaze. Gwen faced
Zoe again, shaking her head, her dark brown curls bobbing with
the move.

"No, I'm not."

That hadn't exactly been what Zoe asked, but it gave her more
insight into what she'd observed. Still, delving deeper into this
conversation was outside her comfort zone. They hadn't ever
really moved into a kind of friendship. Zoe knew a lot about
Gwen, but she was pretty damn sure Gwen knew hardly anything
about Zoe.

Zoe's cell phone buzzed, and she glanced down at it.

"That's our dinner."

"We'll talk when you get back." Gwen didn't move.

Zoe hesitated for a moment, and only got up when Gwen
gave her an affirming nod. Zoe skittered out of the offices and
down the long hallway toward the elevator. It didn't take her long
to get to the main level and come back with the food bags in her
hands. It took her a bit to juggle everything, but she managed to
get one hand free to grip the doorknob.

When she entered Gwen's office again, Gwen stared directly at
her, lips slightly parted and stress lines on her face until she recognized Zoe. *That.* That right there was what had been bothering
Zoe. Everything in that single look.

She set the food on the table and shuffled around the papers while Gwen continued to move slowly as if she was in a daze. Maybe she really was tired, but this was so unlike the Gwen Fudala that Zoe knew.

With Gwen's container of food in front of her, Zoe paused. Now how would they get back into the conversation? Zoe leaned over her container and took a bite of her taco. Gwen raised an eyebrow at her, a smirk pulling at her lips as she laughed lightly.

"Tacos? Really?"

Zoe lifted a shoulder in a shrug. "I had a craving."

"For tacos." Gwen said it like a statement, not a question. "If I'd known you liked tacos earlier, I would have had a far better time teasing you."

Zoe jerked her chin up, her eyes wide as she stared at her boss. Was Gwen making fun of her? What was she missing in this conversation that Gwen was finding amusing? "Are you saying you didn't know that I liked women?"

"What may surprise you, since I'm very adept at reading people, is that my gaydar is less than enthusiastic." Gwen lifted her taco and took a bite, but she never lifted her gaze from Zoe.

"You didn't know that I liked women." Zoe still wasn't sure she could believe it. It wasn't like she'd come right out and said it at any point, but she hadn't exactly hidden it either. "When did you figure it out?"

"Do you really need to ask that?" Gwen ran her pointer finger and thumb along her lips, clearing the sour cream from her mouth and then sucking it off her thumb.

Zoe swallowed the lump, unable to tear her gaze away from Gwen's mouth. Her entire body was on fire—if only Gwen would lick her like that.

"Hmm," Gwen hummed, her lips pulling upward. "Exactly."

Fuck.

Zoe really needed to learn to control herself. "Ms. Fudala..." She trailed off, no idea what she was going to say.

"Let's call it a happy mishap, shall we?"

"I'm not in trouble?"

"Hardly." Gwen closed her eyes as she took another bite of food. "But speaking of the other week, who delivered those photos?"

Zoe shook her head, confused by the change in the conversation. "They came in the mail."

"By courier or by post?" Gwen leaned back in her chair, crossing her legs, her charcoal skirt riding high on her knee.

Zoe couldn't tear her gaze away, entranced even through the glass of the table by the lines of Gwen's body. When was she ever going to get over this damn crush? There was no way anything would happen. She didn't want it to.

"Zoe," Gwen chastised.

Jerking her head up, Zoe was confused.

"How were the photos delivered?"

"By courier."

Gwen pursed her lips, a shadow falling over her face. "And that's all that was in the package?"

"Yeah…" Zoe trailed off, thinking about the one photo she had snuck into her desk drawer without Gwen seeing. It wouldn't matter, would it? For promotions, Gwen wouldn't need that photo. Zoe wasn't even sure why it was in there.

"Yes or no, Zoe?"

The firmness in Gwen's voice set Zoe on edge.

"Yes," she answered quickly even though it was a lie. She didn't need to be in any more trouble than she already was, especially with the way that photo had been taken. It had looked so intimate, and with Gwen figuring out she was attracted to other women, surely that would lead in a direction Zoe wasn't ready to go—ever.

"Good."

"Why?" Zoe froze, realizing far too late how strange the question was.

Gwen sighed heavily and pushed her food to the center of the table, only half eaten. She picked up the paperwork again and skimmed over it before throwing it on the table, restless. Zoe watched every shift she made, the struggle clear in her tense movements.

"Ms. Fudala, what's going on?"

"I'm being stalked," Gwen whispered. "Those photos... they weren't PR. They were from my stalker."

"What?" Every muscle in Zoe's body tightened.

Gwen raised her eyes to the ceiling and then lifted her hands to cover her face. "I didn't think it would escalate again, and I'm sorry you've been dragged into it."

Zoe's mind turned to that photo in her desk. She was about to open her mouth to speak when Gwen continued.

"Did you see anyone at the winery?"

"No, but I wasn't...I wasn't exactly in a state of mind to be looking."

"I understand." Gwen gave Zoe a half-hearted smile. "Thank you."

"How long has this been going on?" Zoe wanted to reach out and touch her hand, offer what comfort she could. "Why didn't you tell me sooner?"

"It's been years." Gwen pursed her lips. "And it had calmed down for a while since I hired a private investigator. I don't know why it's kicked up again."

"Do you know who it is?" Zoe desperately wanted to be able to protect Gwen in any way that she could, and the more she knew, the better she would be able to do that.

Gwen frowned. "No, I don't."

"Even with a private investigator?" Zoe's stomach twisted sharply from the news. It was hard to keep up with what she'd just been told.

"Everything has been distant." Gwen looked Zoe over carefully. "I've never seen who this is."

"Wow. That's crazy scary. I'm so sorry that it's happening to you."

Gwen frowned but didn't answer. They fell into a comfortable silence before Gwen broke it. "I thought you should know, since I inadvertently put you at risk."

"You didn't do anything wrong."

Reaching forward, Gwen picked up the paper she'd been reading earlier. "Are you still on speaking terms with Katyana's assistant?"

Zoe wasn't sure why Gwen was going back to the subject of work, but if she wanted to focus on a problem she could solve, then Zoe would give her that. "I can do you one better."

"Which is?"

"Her wife is an acquaintance of mine."

Gwen raised an eyebrow at her. "Is she now?"

"Yes."

"So is the old adage true?"

"What old adage?" Zoe took another bite of her taco, the flavors bursting on her tongue.

"That all lesbians know each other." Gwen pulled her lip between her teeth, amusement dancing in her gaze.

Zoe had missed that look in the last week, and she was so glad to see it again. "It's not quite true."

"Seems you know a fair share."

Laughing lightly, Zoe shook her head. "Except I'm not a lesbian, Ms. Fudala."

"Oh?"

"Oh," Zoe answered with a slight tease to her tone. "But yes, I can call Tiff and see what I can find out."

"Let's do one better than just finding out why Katyana pulled away from Amato Literary." Gwen put a single finger on the paper in front of her before pulling her food back over. Zoe was glad to see that she hadn't completely lost her appetite.

"What's that?"

"Let's win them back a contract."

Zoe's jaw dropped before she let out a wry laugh. "Deal."

five

INAPPROPRIATE CONDUCT

Zoe's phone buzzed on the table, the text from her best friend appearing across the screen. The bakery was quiet, but it was one of Zoe's favorite places to go. She'd already ordered since she didn't have much time for her lunch break. They were still trying to deal with the drama that was Amato Literary, and Gwen had finally gotten her second wind to deal with it. It had taken four days since their impromptu late-night dinner, but Gwen seemed to be more comfortable now than before.

When Nikki slid into the seat across from Zoe with her receipt from ordering, she had an easy smile on her lips. Zoe grinned back. "Hey, how's it going?"

"Oh, it's going," Nikki answered while she shoved the number plaque into the holder so they could bring her food. "You?"

"Busy. We've got an issue that I'm trying to work my magic on."

"Oh?" Nikki hung her purse on the back of the chair and pulled off her jacket. The charcoal skirt suit she wore today looked like the one Gwen had on the other week. Zoe wasn't sure where she'd gotten it, but she was always impressed by Nikki's clothing choices. If only her own style was that good, along with her bank account to be able to afford it. But Nikki had a much higher paying job than Zoe did.

"We had an agency pull out of our PR event that Gwen is planning. I need to work to get them back."

Nikki hummed and smiled as the waitress brought her food over. "Thank you. So when is this event?"

"Um... in three weeks, on the twenty-second. So I have twenty-one days to fix the problem." Zoe was sure she could do it, too. It wasn't the first time she'd had a time crunch like this, and it certainly wouldn't be the last.

"That's plenty of time." Nikki took a bite of her squash soup. "How was that winery?"

"You know, it wasn't all bad." Zoe straightened her back a bit. "Wine's never really been my go-to for drinks, but I found a few that I really enjoyed."

"Good." Nikki smiled at her, her eyes crinkling around the corners.

They'd been best friends for three years at that point, and Zoe wouldn't have it any other way. Moving to the city, she'd needed an ally, and they'd met by chance right here, sharing a table on a busy Friday afternoon while Zoe had tried to sneak in a quick lunch before going back to her secret crush on her boss. At the time, it had been the only and best reprieve from that crush she'd ever managed.

"I'll see if I can snag you some of the wine creation that I made when we have the party. I'm sure there will be extra bottles around."

"Oh, I'd love to try it." Nikki's eyes glittered. She'd dyed her hair a dark brown in the last few months, and it had taken Zoe that long to get used to it. But Nikki had kept up with it instead of going back to her light blonde. Now it was so normal to see her like this. "I'd love to go to the party, honestly. My office never has fun events like that."

Zoe snorted. "Well, we plan them all. I'm not sure how fun

they are for us, since we're running around trying to make sure everything happens the way it's supposed to."

"Maybe you'll have some fun at this one."

"I can try." Zoe grinned as she took another bite of her sandwich. "I did want to talk to you about something though."

"Shoot." Nikki smiled. "I've only got another twenty minutes though. The bossman wants me back early for some meeting."

"Oh, really?"

Nikki hummed. "Yeah, probably wants me to bring him coffee or something, show my pretty ass around so he can act like he's got it good."

Zoe frowned deeply. "I wish you would quit that job already."

"I make good money." Nikki scooped another large bite of soup into her mouth. "What did you want to talk about?"

She hesitated. Gwen hadn't exactly told her not to share, but it was something that was extremely personal, and that photo in Zoe's desk drawer had been weighing on her mind more and more since her conversation with Gwen that night.

"My boss is being stalked." Zoe dropped her voice close to a whisper, not quite sure if she should even be saying these words. But if she couldn't talk to Nikki, who else could she talk to?

"What?" Nikki leaned forward, her brown eyes wide as she stared Zoe down. "Are you sure?"

"Yes, well, she is." Zoe bit her lip and stared at her half-eaten sandwich. She really should bring something back for Gwen, something to make her day easier.

"Zoe..." Nikki frowned. "If she really is being stalked, then it could be dangerous for you."

"What? Why?" A line creased in the center of Zoe's head.

"Collateral damage."

Cold rushed through Zoe. Nikki couldn't have known about the picture in her desk, about the fact that there might already be a threat against her, but she'd looked up stalkers. In fact, she'd spent almost the whole last week researching them. They had one victim that they hyper-focused on. So it wouldn't be her. It was Gwen Fudala who was the real victim here.

"I don't know," Zoe countered. "I didn't even know she had a stalker until the other week, and she says it's been going on for years."

"Years?" Nikki raised an eyebrow. "Why would she tell you now?"

"I don't know." Zoe pressed her lips together tightly, mulling through that question. She'd noticed the changes in Gwen in the last few weeks, her mood shifting from her normal businesslike to withdrawn. Had something else happened that she wasn't aware of? She'd have to find out. "I've just been thinking about it a lot."

"Well, she's your boss, and you like her, so I can see why you'd be concerned." Nikki clenched her jaw tightly.

If Zoe didn't know that Nikki was straight, she'd almost say that Nikki was jealous.

"Just be careful, Zo. I don't need to be losing my best friend."

"No, we don't need that." Zoe smiled, an awkward tension settling into the center of her chest.

She finished her lunch while ordering a second meal to bring back for Gwen. Nikki left before she did, racing back to the office a few blocks over. With Gwen's lunch in her hands, Zoe made her way with a heaviness in her step that hadn't been there before. That damn picture was in the back of her mind, screaming at her. She should tell Gwen about it, shouldn't she?

But she didn't want to worry her boss more than she already was.

When Zoe arrived at the office, there was a package on her desk and Gwen's door was shut. Something didn't sit right in her belly, the package looking exactly like the previous one, only this time Zoe noticed it didn't have a return address or even look as though it had gone through any type of actual mail system. It had been hand delivered. Possibly by the same person who was stalking her boss. Zoe dragged in a deep breath, frozen on the spot.

What was she supposed to do?

"Is that you, Zoe?" Gwen called from her office.

"Yeah, I'm back from lunch." Zoe quickly shuffled around the desk and snagged the package when Gwen opened the door. She didn't want Gwen to see it. Not yet. Not until she could figure out some way to protect her boss from what was going on.

"How was it?" Gwen asked, once again leaning against her door. She'd taken to doing that a lot lately, watching Zoe work silently as though she could hear Zoe's internal thoughts through everything.

"It was good. Too quick, but it was good seeing Nikki again." Zoe forced a smile to leave her lips.

"What's that?"

Zoe hadn't realized that she clenched the package tightly in her hands, holding it against her chest. She met Gwen's gaze, her throat suddenly parched, and the entire lunch that she ate threatened to come right back up. "It was on my desk when I came in."

Gwen stiffened, her entire body straightening as she stood in the doorway and looked Zoe over.

She knew.

Zoe knew.

"I don't know what's in it."

"Give it to me." Gwen swiftly walked over, her long legs carrying her faster than Zoe could ever hope for her own stubby legs. Gwen held out her hand, expecting that Zoe would just hand it over.

Zoe shook her head. "If it's from your stalker, then we should turn it over to the police."

"Zoe, give it to me." This time the command was precise. There was no way that Zoe could ignore it had been there.

She shuddered, continuing to hold onto the package with every ounce of strength she had. For some reason, she didn't want Gwen to do this alone. If Zoe could protect her from just this one thing, then she would. "No."

"Zoe." Gwen raised an eyebrow.

Shaking her head, Zoe held the package tighter. "No."

"You don't even know what's in it. It could be the package I ordered."

"You don't order anything that I don't know about," Zoe countered.

"Fair." Gwen blew out a breath. She stepped over to the side of the desk where Zoe sat, leaning against it with her hip and staring directly down at Zoe. She raked her gaze over Zoe's face, her lips, her breasts.

Zoe sucked in a sharp breath, her heart skittering away in a fury of arousal. Fuck, Gwen knew exactly what she was doing now. Bending down, Gwen reached for the package, her fingers curled around the edge of it and brushing against Zoe's hand. Ripples of anticipation built in her chest.

No matter how many times she told herself that Gwen was using her new knowledge to her advantage, Zoe still wanted her to do it. She wanted Gwen to lean in and kiss, lean in and touch, anything to snap the tension that pulled between them.

"Whose name is on the package?"

Zoe shook her head. She honestly didn't even know. She hadn't looked at it. She gasped when Gwen slid her fingers toward her, the backs of her knuckles brushing the exposed skin at the top of Zoe's chest, the small part not covered by her blouse.

"It's mine, isn't it?"

"Together," Zoe croaked out. Wherever had she gotten that idea? This was stupid, but at least she could still maintain some semblance of control if they did this together.

"Fine." Gwen plucked the package from Zoe's fingertips like she didn't have a grip on it at all. Flipping the package, Gwen stared at the front of it. All it had was her name and address printed on copy paper, taped over completely with packing tape. "When did it arrive?"

"While I was gone."

The mood shifted from the small amount of ease they had

found to tension. Zoe wished she could go back to that soft moment they'd found. "All right, then. Scissors."

Zoe had to pull open the drawer that Gwen leaned against, forcing her to stand up and move straight into Zoe's space. Gwen didn't shift when Zoe had to reach around her and pull out the pair of blue scissors. When she handed them over, Gwen stared directly into her eyes, her lips parted, and amusement in her gaze.

"What?" Zoe asked.

"Nothing," Gwen murmured, her voice dropping as her lips twitched. She cut precisely into the envelope, and just like before, a smaller manilla one was inside. Gwen carefully pulled at the clip, bending it back into place before opening it to reveal photos. As promised, Gwen held the photos so Zoe could see.

Except she didn't want to see.

They were black and whites.

They were of her, not Gwen.

They were taken from the window in her bedroom, the afternoon of the winery, the day she'd—

Zoe couldn't finish that thought. Her entire face burned. Her stomach sank to the center of the earth and stayed there. Gwen's lips thinned, her face so impassive that Zoe couldn't figure out what she was thinking. Zoe had thought she was embarrassed before, but that had nothing on this. This was going to kill her.

"Gwen," Zoe's voice broke. But she had no idea what she was going to say. She had no clue what she could do to right this. "I'm so sorry."

"What are you apologizing for?" Gwen flicked her gaze up, meeting Zoe's gaze.

"This is..." Zoe couldn't even complete her sentence.

Gwen sighed, understanding coming over her. She bent down in front of Zoe, on her knees. She shoved the photos onto the desk and snagged Zoe's hand in her own. "I want to be outrageously clear when I say this, Zoe, do you understand me?"

Zoe nodded, her voice caught in her throat.

"This isn't about you. It's violating. You've been violated by this person, and there is nothing to be embarrassed about." Gwen looked so sincere, her gaze imploring.

With her heart in her throat, Zoe continued to stare.

"This isn't your fault. Nothing you did is wrong, ever."

"Ms. Fudala," her voice cracked.

"Nothing, Zoe. Do you understand me?"

"Yes," Zoe whispered. Staring into those pale blue eyes, Zoe could almost believe her. Almost. "No. No, it's all wrong. I shouldn't have—"

"Zoe," Gwen cut her off. "You've done nothing wrong."

She had nothing to do but to breathe through it and agree. She had to get out of there. She had to collect what was left of her dignity and hide away for the rest of her life because there was no way she would be able to survive to tomorrow.

"Do you understand?"

"Yes, Ms. Fudala."

"Good." Gwen stood up and was sitting on the desk again like nothing had gone wrong. She flicked through the pictures quickly and then handed over four. "You'll want to see these."

Zoe didn't want to look. But because Gwen had commanded, she reached for the photos and forced her eyes to see. They weren't photos of her masturbating, thank God. They were photos of the night Zoe had stayed late, when they had both stayed late.

"These are from the other night."

Gwen hummed her agreement. "I'm sorry to have dragged you into this."

"Dragged me into..." Zoe trailed off, her eyes glued to the photos in her hand. "These are from the other night."

"Yes, when we left after working late." Gwen snagged the photos back.

"I guess I should show you this." Zoe opened the desk again, slipping out the one photo she had stashed there. She handed it to Gwen. "That came with the others."

"Zoe," Gwen chastised. "You should have told me."

"I know," Zoe murmured.

Gwen stared at the picture in her fingers. Guilt mixed in with the utter shame Zoe was consumed with, and she tried to grasp onto it. It would be so much better than the shame. But she just couldn't move herself away from it. She couldn't believe Gwen had seen her naked. Not only had her boss heard her masturbate over the phone, but now she had seen her spread-eagle on her bed with fingers inside her. Zoe's cheeks heated again before the burning embarrassment moved throughout her entire body.

"Zoe," Gwen whispered.

She couldn't look up.

Gwen snagged her chin with her fingers, dragging Zoe's gaze to meet hers. "If we were in any other circumstance, I would tell you how stunning you are."

"What?" Zoe blinked. What had Gwen just said? Was she being for real right now?

"Don't be ashamed because of this. Be pissed off about it." Gwen moved in close, their noses almost touching. "Don't ever be ashamed about your body."

"Yes, Ms. Fudala."

Six

PROTECT, DON'T SERVE

What was she supposed to do now?

Zoe sat at her desk, completely dumbfounded. She couldn't work. She could barely manage to answer the phones. What was in the envelope was far worse than she expected it to be. She'd never thought it would be *that*. Tears formed in her eyes, and she brushed them away. She would *not* cry. She wouldn't allow herself to do that. Because she wasn't the target of this sick person's outcry.

Gwen was.

And Gwen was handling it like she'd done this a million times before. If she wasn't lying about how long she'd been stalked, and why would she? Zoe rubbed her cheeks. She should just quit while she was ahead. Not that she wanted to leave Gwen to her own problems, but how could they even work together again after what had just happened?

"Zoe?"

Jerking her chin up, Zoe made eye contact. Gwen had her jacket on, her briefcase in her hand, and her purse over her shoulder.

"Let's go."

"Go where?" Zoe gulped. Gwen couldn't possibly want to go anywhere with her. Not after—

"To the police station. We need to make a report."

Right. Of course they would. More people would be looking at those photos, studying them, staring at them. Those tears started right up again. She wasn't sure she could control them this time.

Gwen stepped forward, bent over the desk, and forced Zoe's gaze to hers. "It has to be done."

"I understand," Zoe squeaked.

She moved slowly, dragging her purse out of the drawer. Gwen turned off the lights, even though that was normally Zoe's job. They walked together in silence down the hall to the elevator. As they took the long elevator ride down to the main lobby, Zoe held herself together as much as she possibly could. But she was barely succeeding.

"You're stronger than this." Gwen's voice was strong but soft.

Zoe envied her ability to be so stoic in the face of all of this. Gwen reached forward and gripped Zoe's hand, lacing their fingers together as she squeezed.

"You are."

"How long have you done this?"

"Twelve years."

"What?" Zoe's eyes widened, and she turned on Gwen in shock. "Are you serious?"

"I don't know who it is, Zoe. If I did, we wouldn't be here." Gwen's sincerity seeped into Zoe's chest. "I'm so sorry."

"It's not your fault," Zoe countered. "Stop thinking it is."

"This has happened before."

Frowning, Zoe was about to speak, but the doors to the elevator opened up, and Gwen jumped back and broke contact. Zoe missed her touch. They walked side by side out the main doors of the building and onto the street.

"I'm parked across the street," Gwen said. "I'll drive us."

Zoe didn't argue. She wasn't sure she had it in her to manage it. Following Gwen, she sat in the passenger seat, remembering the last time this had happened. She'd been drunk. It had led to a night of masturbation and a regretful phone call, which had led right to where she was now—about to show a bunch of police officers photos of her touching herself.

"I can't do this," Zoe murmured to herself, realizing far too late that she'd said the words out loud.

"We don't have a choice. I wish there was another way." Gwen sent her a look filled to the brim with pity.

Zoe closed her eyes against it. Protect herself and maybe she would survive this.

When they got to the police station, they were escorted to a small room. Zoe sat next to Gwen at the small table, her foot bouncing off the floor because of her nerves. Gwen settled her hand on Zoe's knee to still her and shot her a glance full of control.

Right.

She could do this, especially if Gwen was with her. She had to. This was all for Gwen Fudala in the end anyway, wasn't it? And Zoe had vowed to do everything in her power to protect Gwen.

"All right, tell me what happened." A larger man came into the room, his head shaved, and his eyes beady.

Immediately, Zoe didn't like him.

"I have a file open already. Here's the case number." Gwen slid a piece of paper across the table when he sat down. "I'd like to speak to Detective Huxley."

"She's on leave."

Gwen wrinkled her nose. Zoe waited patiently for her turn to speak. She assumed she would be spoken to directly.

"I need to add information to the case file."

"Your file of stalking with no perpetrator."

Zoe felt Gwen tense instantly. She wanted to reach over, touch her arm, comfort her, but the energy in the room wasn't there. This detective, whatever his name was since he hadn't given it, was opposed to them the instant they had walked in there.

"I don't know who is stalking me, correct. Detective Huxley is well aware of my case."

He snorted.

Zoe stepped in. "I'm sorry. But what's your name?"

"Detective Frank Friendly."

"Really?" Zoe gave him a funny look.

"My parents had a sense of humor."

Frank clearly didn't. Zoe settled back next to Gwen.

"In the last two weeks, my stalker has contacted me twice with photos. These photos aren't only of me, but of my assistant, and they need to be added to the case file." Gwen put the two envelopes on the table, along with the packages they had come in.

Zoe hadn't even seen Gwen take the first package out of her wastebasket. She should have noticed that. She bristled at herself for not picking up such a small thing, especially when it was her job. She would do better next time.

"These photos contain some sensitive material. I believe my stalker is targeting my administrative assistant because of her relationship with me, but there's no reason so far to think that the obsession has shifted."

Frank gave Gwen a flat look.

Gwen sighed heavily. "Look, either listen to me or don't listen to me. It's your decision. I just want these filed with Detective Huxley and a request for a phone call when she returns from leave.

"Right. I'll do that." He snagged the envelopes and dumped the pictures onto the table.

Zoe's cheeks blazed, the heat of embarrassment completely obliterating any thoughts she had. Frank eyed her with a raised eyebrow as he riffled through the photos.

"Are you sure this isn't some sort of sexual game you two are playing?"

"Excuse me?" Gwen fired back.

"Get the detective to look at sex photos so you two can go back and bang to thoughts of being chained up."

"That's beyond unprofessional," Gwen stated. "File those, please."

Gwen stood up and sent Zoe a look. Zoe was on her feet in a second. She didn't want to be there to begin with. As soon as they were safe in the car, Gwen released a fit of fury and pounded her fist into the steering wheel.

"Fucking idiots!"

"Is it like that every time?"

Gwen shook her head. "No. Huxley isn't so bad, but there's very little they can do unless I have a name."

"And you don't know it yet."

"No matter how many people I hire, I can't find a name." Gwen covered her face with her hands. "I'm so sorry about that."

"You shouldn't be worried about his behavior."

Gwen frowned. "He's not the first. They don't take it seriously because I don't have a name and I strongly suspect it's a woman."

"And because you like women." It was an assumption, but Zoe was fairly certain she was right about it by this point.

"Yes." Gwen closed her eyes, a flush in her cheeks. "I'm so sorry."

"It's not your fault."

"You being in danger *is* my fault." Gwen rested back in her seat, looking Zoe over. "And for that I'm truly sorry. I understand if you want to quit."

"Quit?"

"Resign. Transfer to another department."

"Ms. Fudala..." Zoe couldn't believe what she was hearing. It was the out she'd been hoping for, but at the same time, she didn't want to take it now that it was within reach. "I'm not leaving you."

"You should."

"I'm not." Zoe puffed her chest out, realizing that the decision was the right one to make. There was no other choice for her.

"We can talk about that later. Would you prefer I take you home or back to your car?" Gwen put her seatbelt on and started the engine.

Zoe debated for a minute. She certainly didn't want to go home, not when she knew someone could be watching her. The one time she didn't close the damn blinds when she touched herself. Too much alcohol in her system to even be cognizant of it.

"Take me to my car, please."

"Of course."

Gwen drove back toward the office. Zoe watched the streetlights pass by. She hadn't realized they'd been at the police station that long.

"I need to file a report with Gruzska in the morning. I've kept him apprised of the situation since it started."

"No, please don't," Zoe whispered.

"I'll keep as much detail out of it as possible. And just so you're aware. I did make copies of the photos before I brought them to the station. Not because I wanted them but because I don't trust anyone."

Tears prickled at Zoe's eyes. "Anyone?"

"Well, I do trust you." The gentle uplift of Gwen's lips was a small victory, but Zoe would take it.

That at least made Zoe feel slightly better. But to think that she was one of the only people out there that Gwen trusted was gut wrenching. Gwen should have far more people in her circle than just one. She ran a business on making connections with people and making them feel like they were her deepest confidante.

"We'll work on figuring out the Amato situation in the morning," Gwen supplied, changing the topic. "We need that resolved by the end of this week."

"I'm already working on it, Ms. Fudala," Zoe mumbled. "I have a call scheduled with Katyana in the morning."

"Excellent." Gwen turned into the parking structure and pulled up behind Zoe's car.

Zoe hadn't even been entirely sure that Gwen would know which vehicle was hers. Did Gwen really pay that close attention to Zoe and who she was outside of the office?

"I understand if you're scared to go home."

Zoe's heart sank, the deep understanding in Gwen's words pure and simple.

"Why don't you get a room somewhere or go stay with a friend?"

"Not a bad idea, Ms. Fudala." Why had that little hope in the back of her mind that Gwen would offer to let her stay in the spare bedroom have to be so fucking loud? It would never happen, and Zoe had to stop living in fantasies that never stood a chance of becoming reality.

"I'll see you in the morning."

Zoe understood the dismissal for what it was. With the door cracked open, she stopped short and looked back at Gwen. "For the record, Ms. Fudala, it's not your fault either."

Gwen sucked in a sharp breath.

"Just wanted you to know that." Zoe got out of the car and walked to hers. She was inside with the doors locked before Gwen pulled away and left her.

Zoe's hands shook when she snagged her phone from her purse. She had to call Nikki. Who else was she supposed to call in a situation like this? But she really didn't want to tell Nikki what had happened either, that everything she'd said at lunch had come true and that Zoe was in way over her head. She'd never hear the end of it.

"Nikki?" Zoe pressed the phone to her ear. "Do you uh... mind if I crash at your place tonight?"

Zoe would have to go home in the morning for clothes anyway, but at least she'd have a little more distance between herself and the photos. Though she didn't relish the idea of Gwen having copies of those at all. Just what exactly was she going to do with them? And how many copies did the stalker have? Was the stalker going to send them out to other places?

"You sure? Okay. See you soon." Zoe hung up and closed her eyes. She needed a minute to gather herself before she went over there, before she talked about today. It was almost too much.

How had Gwen managed twelve years like this?

Zoe pulled out of the parking garage, gripping the steering wheel tightly. How could she continue on like this? She couldn't possibly be the new target in this obsession by a phantom stalker, could she? Or was she simply collateral damage because of Gwen?

If she was collateral damage, then Nikki might very well be right. Zoe could be in a whole lot more danger than she'd thought. Because if she wasn't the obsession, there was no reason she wouldn't be easily knocked out of the way. Sighing, Zoe drove toward Nikki's apartment. She would stay there one night while all of this settled, and then she would go back to her own apartment.

She couldn't let fear take over her life. She just couldn't. That must be how Gwen got through everything. Twelve years of fear hadn't knocked her down. Zoe would work to follow in Gwen's footsteps in that regard.

As she pulled into Nikki's apartment complex, Zoe shot off a text to Gwen. She had one job to do, and she would do it. Protect Gwen Fudala as best as she could.

Zoe: Text me when you get home. I just want to make sure you're safe.

When she was upstairs and Nikki opened the door, Zoe nearly collapsed into her arms. She felt safe for the first time all day, and relief flooded her. "Thank you so much."

"Anytime, you know that." Nikki looked so concerned. She'd pulled her hair back into a ponytail, the end of it curled onto her shoulder, and the yoga pants and tank top she wore were a soft blue. "I just want you to be safe."

"Right." Zoe forced a smile onto her lips. "You're right, of course. I just need to get my head on straight and then I'll go home."

"Take all the time that you need," Nikki said as she shut and locked the door behind Zoe.

Zoe took the extra pair of pajamas that Nikki handed her and went to the bathroom to change. Just doing that allowed her to relax and ease into a whole different mindset. She sat on the couch, curling up with her phone clutched in her hand.

"You want to talk about it?" Nikki was so sincere and strong.

But Gwen had told her she was just as strong, and Zoe would like to believe that. Finding that strength was a whole different problem, especially tonight. Zoe let out a wry chuckle. "I have so many thoughts running through my head right now. I don't even know where to start."

"Just list them off."

Sighing heavily, Zoe closed her eyes. "The justice system is a crock. Women should be allowed to walk around without fear. There shouldn't be a need for propriety when it comes to boss and employee relationships. We should all work together to make this world a better place. And people are assholes."

"That's it?" Nikki raised an eyebrow, her lips pulling into a smile. "No world domination or burning bras?"

"No." Zoe's cheeks heated, but this time it felt good. "No, not tonight. I'll save that for tomorrow."

Nikki chuckled, then rested her hand on Zoe's leg. "Whenever you're ready to talk about what happened, I'm here to listen."

"Yeah." Zoe yawned, exhaustion seeping into her pores. "Thanks, Nik."

"Anytime." Nikki handed over a blanket, which Zoe took.

She was curled up on the couch, staring at the television screen with re-runs of her favorite cooking show when Nikki went off to bed. She was only half paying attention because she kept checking her phone. Where was she?

It neared midnight, hours after Gwen should have gotten home, when she finally texted.

Gwen: I'm home. I'm safe. You are too.

Finally relieved of the last of her stress, Zoe closed her eyes and let sleep overtake her.

SEVEN

LATE NIGHT ESCORT

Gwen: I need the Granular file.

Zoe: Now?

Gwen: Yes.

Zoe frowned at her phone. The five days since filing the report with the police detectives felt like nothing, and they'd been thrown headfirst into detail planning for the event. Zoe hadn't been expecting a text to request the file. She wrinkled her nose at it. Why had Gwen forgotten it in the first place? Normally if she wanted to do work at home, she didn't forget a thing.

It must be the stress of being stalked while planning a major event.

Snagging the file from Gwen's office, Zoe shoved it into her bag before she locked the doors behind her and left. She usually wasn't there that late either, but since those photos had shown up on her desk, she'd been avoiding going home, especially when she was alone. But she couldn't keep imposing on Nikki either.

It didn't take long for Zoe to get to Gwen's condo. She pressed the key code into the main door and let herself in. She'd been there so many times over the last few years that she knew the way by heart and no longer felt awkward going through the halls. She texted when she was in the elevator to let Gwen know that she was almost there. That way Gwen wouldn't flip out when she knocked on the door.

Zoe made her way through the hallway, keeping her eyes peeled for anything that might be amiss or anyone who wasn't supposed to be there. But she didn't even know what she was looking for. That was the scariest part of this entire situation. She had no idea where the threat lurked.

Rolling her shoulders, she knocked four times on Gwen's door and said, "It's me."

Almost immediately, the door opened, and Zoe stepped inside. Gwen shut and locked the door behind her. "Thank you for bringing this. I didn't mean to leave it behind."

"It's fine. I was just leaving anyway." Zoe tried to slide in the half-truth and hoped that Gwen missed it, but of course, she didn't.

"You should have left the office hours ago."

Zoe hadn't wanted to. And since Gwen had a late dinner meeting, she'd gladly taken the excuse of having no one tell her to leave. She said nothing in response as she reached into her bag and pulled out the thick file.

"You should take a night off work." She couldn't believe she'd said that. Who was she and what had she done with Zoe the meek administrative assistant?

"It's a good distraction," Gwen murmured as she snagged the file and walked toward her couch. There was almost no reaction to Zoe's audacity. "Did you get confirmation from Amato yet?"

Zoe sighed and followed Gwen. She wasn't dressed in her typical skirt suit anymore. She'd changed into a pair of loose yoga pants and a tight shirt. The fabric looked smooth and soft. What would it be like to run her fingers over it?

"My face is about ten inches north of where your eyes are," Gwen stated, her tone not expressing any emotion.

Zoe's cheeks burned. She'd literally just been caught staring at Gwen's breasts, and she hadn't even meant to this time. This time? Fuck, she really had to get control of herself. Zoe twisted her hands tighter in front of her, trying to remember what Gwen had asked, but she'd been so damn distracted.

"Amato?"

"They confirmed they're not attending."

"Wonderful," Gwen muttered. She lowered herself onto the royal-blue couch, her gaze never leaving the file in her hands.

Zoe wished she could multitask like that, but she'd never quite mastered it.

"Sit down already."

"Yes, Ms. Fudala." Zoe did as she was told, her entire body stiff as she waited for the next reprimand. She couldn't believe Gwen had actually caught her staring this time. She'd done it so many times over the last few years, but something had changed in the last few weeks since the winery incident. And Zoe couldn't put her finger on what it was.

"I need you to resolve the issue with Amato."

"I'm working on it." Zoe's stomach sank. She had been struggling to concentrate all day every day. And the fact that Gwen hadn't brought anything up since that night they'd gone to the police station wasn't helping any. Zoe was a talker. She'd known for years that Gwen wasn't, but when it came to something like this, she needed the conversation to center herself. "Have you heard anything from Detective Dickwad?"

"Excuse me?" Gwen jerked her chin upward, locking her gaze on Zoe.

"Detective Friendly," Zoe corrected.

Gwen's lips pulled into a smile as she shook her head. "No, I haven't, and I don't expect to. The detective in charge of my case is still on leave, but I expect to hear from her when she returns."

"When will that be?"

Gwen sighed and slapped the file onto the coffee table with a loud thwack. "She's on maternity leave."

"Oh."

"So it'll be another month or two before she returns."

Zoe scratched the back of her head. "I guess it was too much to hope that it was just a sick day."

Gwen hummed her response. "Have you slept in the last week?"

"Excuse me?" Zoe's eyes widened, and when Gwen's gaze met hers, she found empathy. The silence intensified between them before Zoe broke it. "Not much."

Gwen rubbed her palms together. "I know it's unconventional, but do you want a drink?"

Zoe's instant response was to decline. Alcohol had only given her nightmares since that day. She would know, she'd tried to drink herself into a slumber one night and the others she'd just attempted to use it to relax. Gwen touched her knee lightly and stood up. When she returned, she had two wine glasses in her hands. She handed one over.

"When I first figured out that I was being stalked, I don't think I slept for months."

"Really?" Zoe spun the wine glass in her fingers.

Gwen took a sip and leaned back into the couch, trailing her arm along the back of it toward where Zoe sat. "It comes and goes in waves now."

"So have you slept?" Zoe leaned back into the couch, still spinning her wine glass. She wasn't sure she should drink it, not to mention that the last time she had wine brought back particular memories. Memories she would soon rather forget.

"No." Gwen eyed Zoe over, the scrutiny something far more akin to desire.

But that couldn't be right, could it? Zoe was Gwen's administrative assistant and had never been anything more than that. They'd never crossed any kind of boundary until Zoe had blown it up the afternoon after the winery. And even then, Gwen had kept those boundaries firmly in place. Except, Gwen had touched her—brushed the backs of her knuckles against Zoe's chest.

"I feel awful that this is happening to you now."

Zoe clenched her jaw. She raked her gaze over Gwen's body again, the curve of her breasts in the tight shirt she wore, the gentle slope of her waist to her hips, the strength in her thighs. She always wore tighter clothes, but this formed to her body perfectly, allowing Zoe the ability to see everything.

"Zoe," Gwen whispered.

Snapping her gaze up to Gwen's face, she realized once again she'd been caught in the act of ogling her boss. She really had to stop that and get her shit under control. She and Gwen weren't ever going to be something, and her fantasies needed to die yesterday. She should have never given in and touched herself. She'd done so well at stopping that over the last few years.

"I'm sorry," Zoe murmured, her cheeks heating again as she dropped her gaze to her lap. She couldn't bring herself to look Gwen in the eyes, not when she was being such a lunatic. How was she any better than Gwen's stalker at this point? She was giving Gwen unwanted attention. That thought sobered her. "I should go."

Zoe pushed herself up, setting the wine glass onto the coffee table. She hadn't even taken a sip yet. She was about to stand when Gwen's voice caught her attention.

"We need to discuss Amato Literary and the release event."

Why was she doing this? Zoe sat back down, keeping her gaze on her hands in her lap so she wouldn't be an idiot again. "I have a meeting with Katyana in the morning."

"Good." Gwen seemed so relaxed.

Zoe couldn't believe it because she wouldn't be relaxed at all. "Would you like to attend?"

"Only if you think I'll be of assistance." Gwen set her wine glass down, now empty. "You should try the wine."

"I don't really care for wine, Ms. Fudala." Zoe flicked her gaze to the table before bringing her eyes back up to meet Gwen's.

"You don't?" Gwen shifted on the couch, her thigh brushing Zoe's.

That wasn't on purpose, was it? Zoe had to keep her head on straight.

"You should try this one."

Zoe flicked her gaze back to the glass on the table. "Why?"

"It's the flavor you created. I bought a few bottles for myself." Gwen's lips curled up, and she snagged the glass, handing it over. "I thought you might like some."

For what? To remind herself what she'd done that afternoon? Zoe burned again with embarrassment. That day was going to haunt her forever, wasn't it? She should crawl in a hole and die. Maybe then she'd be rid of the memories of that one night.

"Ms. Fudala," Zoe started, not sure what to even say in response.

"We can talk about that day if you want, or we can ignore it ever happened. The choice is yours." Gwen kept the wine glass in her hand, offering it to Zoe.

Zoe stared at it, trying to figure out exactly what she wanted. To talk about it would put a lot of her nerves at ease, but would it only create more? "I'm not sure we'll get a chance to ignore it."

"Well, as much as we can." Gwen's voice lowered, a rough edge to it.

Zoe wished she knew what that meant, understood it. But she'd never heard Gwen talk like that to anyone. She shuddered, holding it in as much as she could. It seemed as though the wine was the key to her decision. Take it and the conversation or don't and they would leave everything alone. The question remained, however, what did Zoe want? She'd never once thought Gwen would know about her crush, but that had been blown out of the water in the last few weeks.

"I won't fire you because of it."

Snorting, Zoe shook her head. "I think that's honestly the least of my worries right now."

"Is it?" Gwen whispered. "What are you worried about?"

If Gwen could look into her eyes, she would know. To have that fantasy shattered would leave Zoe reeling for a long time, and with the stalking issues already in the way, she wasn't sure she could take another blow.

"It's embarrassing," Zoe barely made the word out.

"Because you're ashamed about sex?" Gwen set the wine glass on her knee, holding onto the stem lightly.

Zoe couldn't tear her gaze away from it. "I'm not ashamed about the fact that I masturbate or have sex." Though it had been some time since she'd had good sex. She'd think about that later.

"Then what are you ashamed about?" Gwen shifted, leaning in slightly. "Were you thinking about someone you shouldn't?"

Fuck.

They were doing this.

Zoe snagged the glass of wine and gripped it tightly before she brought it to her lips. She couldn't believe they were actually going to talk about this. But would she actually say the words she'd avoided for three damn years? It took her another second before she put the glass down and made eye contact with Gwen again.

"I was on the phone with you," Zoe said it so matter-of-factly, as though that was the real reason she was embarrassed.

"And thinking about me," Gwen finished the thought, the words Zoe would never have been able to say out loud and certainly not with that level of confidence.

"Yes," Zoe whispered, swallowing the leftover flavor from the wine she had barely tasted. Was it sour? She didn't remember it being this sour.

"Was that the first time you've thought about me while you touched yourself?"

How the hell was Gwen so calm? Zoe would be flipping out if she found out anyone was masturbating about her. Well, not really, but if she found out her boss was? Definitely.

"It's quite a compliment, you know," Gwen continued, as though Zoe had answered the question. "I find it attractive that you know what you want."

"I might know what I want, Ms. Fudala. But I also know what I can't have."

Gwen hummed, her gaze dancing all over Zoe's face, dropping to her lips, then her breasts. "I wouldn't be so certain about that."

"In three years, you've never indicated—"

"In the three years you've worked for me, I didn't know you were attracted to women. We've never discussed our personal lives." Gwen still had that seductive quality to her tone, her words precise.

"You don't discuss anything personal," Zoe countered.

"Not entirely true, but I have kept our relationship very professional until now."

"Until now?" Zoe tensed. What in the world was going on? Was that panic working its way up into her chest? Or was it fear wrapping around her heart? But everything was tinged with arousal. That was the worst part. This was exactly who Zoe had expected her boss to be with that intensity aimed toward her.

"Work is one kind of distraction, Zoe. But there are others."

Oh, Zoe was very familiar with the other kinds of distraction. She shivered when Gwen moved in closer, trailing her fingers along Zoe's shoulder, then her collar bone and across the front of her chest. Zoe's nipples hardened in her bra, the tightness nearly painful. Gwen's lips parted, and Zoe was close enough to feel her breath against her skin.

"Ms. Fudala..." Zoe trailed off, but it didn't sound like an objection. Instead, Gwen's name sounded like a cry of pleasure.

"Only if you want to." Gwen slid in, her cheek pressed to Zoe's, but her lips never touched Zoe's skin.

Zoe let out a shuddering breath. This had to be a dream, right? She'd had too much of that wine, and she'd wake up hornier than fuck with no Gwen next to her. "Did you call me over here for this?"

"No," Gwen whispered. "But I'm not opposed to anything physical happening between us. I trust that you can keep yourself together when we're in the office."

Trust.

There was that word again.

Gwen trusted Zoe to be exactly who Gwen thought she was. Someone who was meek and a go-getter. How many times had Gwen used those words to describe how Zoe did her work? But Zoe wasn't that person.

That was just who she presented at work, and it was very clear from their earlier conversation that she and Gwen knew nothing personal about each other. Hell, Zoe still couldn't call her Gwen to her face. Would she scream *Ms. Fudala* as she came against Gwen's mouth?

Zoe pressed her cheek into Gwen's, closing her eyes. She drew in her scent. Her mind whirled with thoughts and possibilities. The number of fantasies that could be proven and thrown out the window because the real thing would be so much better. But it all came back to one word.

Trust.

She couldn't break the small amount of trust that Gwen gave her. Pulling away, Zoe cringed.

"I need a minute." She stood up immediately and ran toward Gwen's bathroom. She shut the door, locked it, and leaned over the counter as she nearly collapsed.

What the hell was she doing?

Both of them.

It must be the stress of everything. Zoe was having a mental breakdown and nothing was right. When she opened her eyes, she realized the light was still off. Zoe reached out and flicked the switch on and was startled by what she saw. She narrowed her eyes at the mirror, her heart clogging up her throat as a cold sweat came over her.

Zoe reached over and turned the light off and then on again. She wasn't seeing things. Pressing her lips together hard, Zoe left the light on as she pulled at the mirror. There was nothing behind it, but surely she was making things up, wasn't she?

She had to tell Gwen. There's no way Gwen would do that

unless she was into some sort of kink that Zoe was unaware about. Which was entirely possible. But why did it have to be her? Zoe just wanted to leave the situation alone.

As soon as she stepped out of the bathroom, Gwen stood up. She canted her head to the side, her long hair pulling over her shoulder, and her face was riddled with concern. "What's wrong?"

"Um..." Zoe wrung her fingers together. "I just... you don't have any weird sex kinks do you?"

"Everyone's definition of weird is different, and I don't believe any kink is weird. It's all a matter of preference." Gwen walked closer, her bare feet silent on the wood floor.

"Right." Zoe was thoroughly chastised. She folded her hands together, her shoulders so tight her muscles pulsed as they protested. She was about to crash everything that was in Gwen's world. She had no doubt in her mind, and whatever their previous discussion had been, it was now over.

"You look like you've seen a ghost. Surely, I haven't scared you that much."

"You? No. Never." Zoe chuckled nervously. She didn't want to have to do this. But Gwen did trust her. She was trustworthy, and she wouldn't break that bond between them. "But um... well... there's no easy way to tell you this."

"What?" Gwen touched Zoe's elbow lightly, that connection calming.

Zoe could do this. She had to. Gwen needed to know what she'd seen, and they needed to handle it. Immediately. Raising her chin up, Zoe looked directly into Gwen's light blue eyes.

"Someone licked your mirror."

eight

LOOK IN THE MIRROR

"What?" Gwen's voice cracked through the tense air.

"Someone licked the mirror." Zoe's stomach rumbled, but not from hunger. The look in Gwen's eyes bordered on dangerous.

"Show me."

Zoe went back into the bathroom, this time with Gwen joining her in the small confined space. Her heart was in her throat when she pointed to the spot. From straight on, she couldn't see it, but if she angled herself to the side, it was clear as day.

Taking Gwen by the shoulders, Zoe moved her to the corner of the small counter and pointed. "See it?"

She was pretty sure it was a lick mark. There was a kiss imprint at the end of it in the center of the mirror ending right where the tongue mark left. Gwen was so tense, her arms bulging under Zoe's soft touch. Zoe wanted to move away and give her space, but at the same time, she wanted to stay close and give every ounce of support she could.

"She was here," Gwen whispered, the words coming from her lips in a prayer. "She was here."

"Are you okay?" Zoe had no idea what to say. She kept

holding on to Gwen's shoulders, making sure that she felt as safe as she possibly could. Intuitively, Zoe knew that was impossible. It was exactly what she had been feeling for the last few weeks. Gwen must have been living like this for years.

Gwen shivered. "We need to call the police."

"Detective Frank Friendly?"

"Unfortunately." Gwen walked out of the bathroom with fire in her step.

Zoe was hot on her heels, not wanting to give Gwen a moment without support. Gwen snagged her cell phone from the kitchen and had it pressed to her ear before Zoe caught up with her.

"I need to speak with Detective Friendly." She gave the case number and waited, eyeing Zoe carefully. Her look was all business now, that mask coming into place firmly and all signs of their conversation earlier about distractions was gone. Zoe blew out a breath of relief about that.

It took longer than Zoe would have liked, but Gwen finally got off the phone. Zoe had hot tea ready and handed it over, pressed against the counter in Gwen's kitchen. Gwen leaned next to her, arms crossed as she cupped the mug in one hand and stared at the floor.

"They'll be here soon."

"Never soon enough it seems with the police."

Gwen gave a wry smile at that.

"Was he upset?"

There was no response from Gwen. She continued to stare at a point off in the distance that Zoe couldn't make out. Zoe waited in the silence for longer than she cared to count. When she slid her hand along Gwen's arm to get her attention, Gwen finally turned those light blue eyes on her. Zoe saw all kinds of emotions swirling behind her gaze before the mask dropped back down.

"I'm so sorry this is happening to you."

"It's not your fault." Gwen locked her eyes on Zoe. She

reached out, wrapping her fingers around Zoe's wrist in a tight squeeze. "None of this is your fault."

"I know," Zoe whispered. "But I'm still sorry it's happening."

Gwen set her mug down, turning her entire body toward Zoe. She was so lean and fit. Gwen settled her hand on Zoe's upper arm, pulling slightly so that Zoe faced her and mirrored her position.

"No one should have to go through something like this." Zoe was entranced.

It was as if Gwen had taken control of her body and was gently tugging her closer. Gwen's hand was on her side, pressing into the curve of her waist. Her fingers were firm against Zoe's back, tightening as she controlled the move to bring Zoe in even closer.

"Ms. Fudala," Zoe said as an objection even as she moved closer. What was she thinking? Clearly, the answer was, she wasn't. Her body moved of its own accord. Gwen stepped in even closer, so they were nose to nose.

"Distraction, Zoe." Gwen dipped her head, her breath warm along Zoe's lips.

"Ms. Fudala..." Zoe trailed off.

The buzzer echoed through the room. Gwen winced at it, and Zoe instantly jerked with a start. She had to get out of there before they did anything stupid. Zoe bit her lip as Gwen looked her over purposely. "You're right."

Without another word, she stepped aside and walked toward the door. Zoe let out a sigh of relief as she was left alone in the kitchen. Gwen's voice was back to its usual cool tone as she let the police officers in and directed them toward the living area. She beckoned Zoe over with a single look. Bringing the tea with her, Zoe did as she was told.

She always did whatever Gwen told her to do.

But this time as she came when Gwen called, she could feel the shadow of Gwen's hand against her side, the pressure of her fingers, the firmness of her grasp. It would take Zoe years to get that sensation out of her head—if she ever wanted to.

Gwen took charge. She led the officers into the bathroom to the mirror. One of them came out looking disgusted. Zoe stood by, watching silently. Her role, as she saw it, was to support Gwen with whatever she needed. That was always her goal when Gwen was involved.

A second knock resounded, and the younger looking officer went to answer it. Detective Frank Friendly came in, a scowl on his face. Zoe's back immediately went up, and she could tell from Gwen's terseness that she felt the same.

"What is it now?" He huffed. The officers took him to the side to fill him in.

Zoe brought Gwen her tea after making sure it was still hot. Their fingers brushed when Gwen took it. She immediately sipped and closed her eyes, a moment of weakness and struggle overcoming her before it vanished as she sat down.

Eventually, Friendly came over and sat on the chair while Gwen stayed next to Zoe on the couch. She sat close, so she could be of assistance, but not too close. She didn't want to give off any hints that there was anything other than professionalism between them.

"You two again," Friendly started, his voice gruff with an edge of anger. "What makes you think this *stalker*"—he said it like a curse—"licked your mirror."

"You can see it," Gwen replied sternly. "And a full press of her mouth against it as well."

"Like a kiss?" Friendly sneered.

Zoe's back was immediately up. He didn't believe a single word Gwen was saying, did he? He was going to cause her death if he didn't pay attention or take her seriously. Gwen seemed to have hope in the other detective, but since Zoe hadn't been around to see her in action, she would have to trust that the entire police department wasn't full of shit.

"I guess," Gwen sighed. She reached for her tea, and Friendly's gaze followed her hand.

"Were you two having a date?"

The air stilled.

Zoe was about to set him right, but Gwen got there first. "No. My assistant brought by some papers I left at the office. *I* was having the wine."

Friendly snorted. "Let me get this right. Your assistant comes over to your condo late at night to bring you *papers,* and she happens to find someone licked your mirror after you've split a bottle of wine."

He didn't believe anything they said.

"My stalker broke into my condo." Gwen stared at him flatly. "I don't know how. No one has a key but me. I don't know why since all I've found amiss is the mirror in the bathroom. I don't know when other than it was after last Thursday."

"Why Thursday?" Friendly asked.

"That's when my cleaning service was in." Gwen leaned over to Zoe. "Will you get my phone?"

"Sure." Zoe stood up and went to the kitchen to retrieve the requested item. When she got back, Friendly still wasn't very friendly.

"So you have no idea who your stalker is or why this person is stalking you." He wasn't even looking at Gwen.

"No. I don't, and I've told Detective Huxley that. I do know it's a woman."

Friendly snorted. "Do you know the percentage of stalking cases that are perpetrated by women?"

"Less than fifteen percent," Gwen fired back. "But that's not zero percent."

Friendly didn't look happy with her response. "You sure this isn't some rogue lesbian lover you had who didn't want to break up?"

"That's out of line," Zoe fired, the words out of her mouth

before she could stop them. "I'm sick and tired of you not listening to her. She's scared, can't you see that? Fuck, I'm scared. And you're ignoring everything. Get the stick out of your ass or find someone else who doesn't have one shoved up so far he can't see straight."

Gwen's hand was on her knee immediately, squeezing tightly. It hurt. Zoe instantly bit back her next comment and clenched her molars together tight. It was clear Gwen didn't want her to talk, but Zoe wouldn't be able to resist standing up for her again.

Friendly glared at her before focusing on Gwen. "If you can't get your girlfriend under control, I'm going to ask her to leave."

"She's not going anywhere," Gwen countered. "I don't know who my stalker is, Detective Friendly. I do know she's a woman based on the letters she has written to me."

Letters?

That was a first for Zoe. She hadn't heard anything about that, but she did have twelve years of stalking history to catch up on. And it wasn't like Gwen had exactly been open about everything that had happened so far. Which was another reason them not kissing was a good thing.

Also, what was up with that?

Distraction was one thing, but Gwen seemed to be more into it than that. She was at least pushing for it more. Or was that all in Zoe's head, too? Gwen's fingers still wrapped around her knee moved upward on her thigh.

"What did the letters say?"

"They're in the case file."

That was Gwen's answer to everything, wasn't it?

Gwen's grip tightened.

"What's in the letters?" Friendly replied firmly.

"She wants to become me. So no, there's no history of a romantic relationship." Gwen's voice was tight, though Zoe doubted Detective Dufus noticed.

"Are you sure you didn't imply your interest in her? Assuming it is a her?"

Gwen sighed heavily. Zoe was ready to come to her defense

again, but that hand heavy on her leg was a reminder of exactly what Gwen wanted her to do, which was nothing.

"The information is in the case file," Gwen repeated. "I would like samples taken from the mirror."

"We'll be taking the whole mirror," Friendly answered.

"Perfect," Gwen mumbled. "I'll be staying at a hotel until I can get the locks changed."

That wasn't a bad idea. Zoe was annoyed she hadn't thought of it first. She should have. Her job was to anticipate everything that Gwen might possibly need and provide it before she knew that was what she needed. And she had failed at even that tonight.

Zoe lost track of what the asshole said, and before she knew it, he was leaving. He hadn't even done that much investigating from her point of view, but then again, she thought the world should be turned over to figure out who this person was. Gwen relaxed as soon as she shut the door on him. She leaned against it, her hands behind her as she looked Zoe over.

"You should probably go home."

"I'll wait until you leave," Zoe replied, never more sure of her decision.

Gwen didn't argue. She walked directly into her bedroom. Zoe followed. It wasn't the first time she'd been in here. She'd had to snag Gwen an outfit on more than one occasion or pack a quick bag for her when there was an emergency trip that came up, but it was so different being in there *with* her.

Now especially.

Since the tension.

Since the almost kiss.

Zoe stayed by the door, leaning against the frame much like Gwen liked to do at the office. Gwen snagged her clothes and threw them into a suitcase. The thought rolling around in Zoe's head needed to be unleashed, but she was worried about what it would mean and exactly how Gwen would take it. Still, it needed to be said.

"I think we should cancel the party."

Gwen froze.

"Or at the very least, you shouldn't attend."

"Nonsense," Gwen muttered as she angrily snagged another outfit from her closet and put it into the suitcase. "I'm not going to stop living my life because *she* can't get one."

"It's for your safety," Zoe tried again. Though she should probably add in that it was for her own. That would at least make Gwen stop and think about things twice, but Zoe didn't want to guilt trip her into it either. Gwen had to make her own conclusion.

"No. I won't do it." Gwen zipped up her bag and stalked into the bathroom to get her things. "I won't stand down in fear."

Zoe admired that. She really did. But she also thought it was fucking stupid. "How do you think she got in here? Huh?"

"I don't know." Gwen shoved her toiletry bag into her suitcase. "I'll work on that."

"You'll work on it? You've hired a private investigator. You're working with a lawyer. You're twelve years into this, and no one knows who this lady is. Don't you think it's time to take some extra precautions?"

Gwen shot her a glare. "You're out of bounds, Zoe."

"No. I'm not." Zoe planted her feet. This was a battle she was going to fight. "You kept this a secret from everyone. I've worked for you for three years, and I didn't even know about it. You don't have to do this alone."

"I do!" Gwen's voice rose. "Because of this very reason. I'm not some fragile, breakable person who is going to cower in the face of danger."

"I'm not saying you are," Zoe countered. Why was she fighting this so hard? Right. To save Gwen's life. "I'm saying you need to be smart about what decisions you're making."

"I really don't need this from you of all people." Gwen glared, zipping her suitcase with a jerk.

"Maybe you do." Zoe snagged Gwen's wrist as she walked by, stopping her in her tracks. For the first time ever, Zoe was going to stand up to her boss and make her voice heard. "Don't take unnecessary risks."

Gwen stayed put, dropping her gaze to Zoe's mouth before slowly making eye contact again. "What's life without risks?"

Was Gwen still talking about the party? Zoe's heart raced, and she let go of Gwen's wrist, stupefied back into her role as the assistant. They weren't in a relationship. It wasn't her place to protect Gwen like this or to force her opinion to be heard.

Gwen stepped forward. Zoe pushed her shoulders back into the door frame. She shook her head slowly. "What hotel?"

"The Plaza."

Right where the party was going to be. It was ideal, honestly. Gwen could be on the ground to finish up any last-minute details or issues with the party. Zoe gritted her teeth before she shifted and slid away. Angrily, she grabbed her cell phone and her bag. She was out of there. When she reached the front door, she tossed a look at Gwen over her shoulder.

"I'll have your reservation made by the time you get there."

nine

THE BOSSLADY IS LATE

"Gwen Fudala's office. This is Zoe speaking. How may I help you?" Zoe snagged the phone as soon as she stepped into the office. She moved around her desk, holding the corded phone to her ear as she listened to the caller.

It didn't take her long to take the message for Gwen and end the call. Zoe turned on her work computer and set up for the day, glancing toward Gwen's office door, which was shut with the light off. She frowned at it briefly before focusing on work. Gwen had made it very clear the night before that she didn't want Zoe's help.

They wouldn't work out—ever. Zoe should have figured that out sooner.

Still, when ten in the morning rolled around and there was still no sign of Gwen, Zoe started to worry. This was so unlike her, and the calls and texts Zoe had made had gone unanswered. When Gruzska, the main executive that Gwen dealt with, called to make an appointment for that day, Zoe's radar went off.

Something wasn't right.

She managed to schedule the meeting for the next morning and grabbed her purse. The Plaza wasn't that far from the office building. Something in Zoe's gut told her that she needed to find Gwen immediately.

With the office door locked, Zoe booked it as quickly as possible to the elevator. Instead of taking her car, she grabbed a ride share and made her way to The Plaza. Within twenty minutes, she stood at the front desk and eyed the young woman over.

"I need a key to my room. I locked myself out."

"What's your room number?"

"Twenty-one-twenty, and my name is Gwendolyn Fudala." Zoe laid her hand flat on the counter. The woman didn't even ask for her ID. She'd have to yell at them for that later. Right now her priority was finding Gwen.

Zoe got into the elevator and hit the button for the twenty-first floor. What was she walking into? She could find Gwen dead. Worse yet, the stalker could be in there doing awful things to her. Zoe worked her best to calm herself down. Panicking before she knew what she was facing wouldn't do anyone any good.

When she got to the door, Zoe knocked. If there was any chance Gwen was going to answer, then she wanted to take it. But silence was all she was greeted with. Zoe knocked again, louder this time. "Ms. Fudala, it's me. Zoe."

Like Gwen wouldn't be able to tell who she was from the sound of her voice. Her cheeks burned. She was such an idiot sometimes. And if the stalker was in there, then all Zoe was doing was alerting whoever it was to the fact that she was about to be discovered. She could be slashing Gwen's throat right this minute.

Zoe knocked again, but this time she didn't wait. The nerves were too much. She pressed the keycard against the handle and waited for it to click green. She could do this. She needed to know if Gwen was okay or not, even with the way they had left things last night. Holding her breath, Zoe stepped into the dark hotel room.

Her heart thumped with each step she took. She reached for the light switch and flicked it on in the small hallway. She wasn't violating Gwen's safe space, was she? But she wasn't there, and no matter how many times Zoe had called and texted, Gwen hadn't answered. She was worried, and she felt as though she had a responsibility to make sure that Gwen was okay.

"Ms. Fudala?" Zoe said as she stepped closer to the bed.

The lump under the covers was definitely a person. The only problem was she couldn't tell if Gwen was dead or alive. Zoe fisted her hands as she walked closer to the window curtain and pulled it open slightly. Gwen's eyes were closed, her cheeks rosy from sleep, and her back rose and fell gently with slumber.

She was alive.

Zoe opened the curtain more, letting the full light of the day into the hotel room. She moved toward the edge of the bed and shook Gwen's shoulder lightly. She softened her tone to wake Gwen slowly because no matter which way she looked at it, Zoe was going to get yelled at for intruding.

Gwen rustled. She brushed her fist over her cheek, but she didn't pry her eyes open. Zoe moved her shoulder harder.

"Ms. Fudala, you need to wake up."

Groaning, Gwen turned onto her back. There were imprints of the wrinkles in the sheets on her cheek. It was adorable. If they were in a completely different scenario, Zoe would be climbing over her and kissing the lines.

"What time is it?" Gwen slurred as she talked.

The pill bottle on the nightstand was still open. Zoe frowned at it before murmuring, "Almost eleven."

"In the morning?" Gwen still had that slur in her words.

"Yeah." Zoe snagged the bottle and read the label. "How many of these did you take?"

Gwen turned onto her side and squinted at the bottle. "I don't know."

Sighing, Zoe put the lid back on and set the bottle down. "You're three hours late to work."

Groaning, Gwen buried her head back into the pillow.

"Oh, no, you don't." Zoe pulled the blanket down Gwen's

ADRIAN J. SMITH

body, revealing smooth skin littered with freckles all along Gwen's shoulders, arms, and upper back.

Zoe had to bite back her groan and the desire to press kisses to every single one of those freckles. It wouldn't do either of them any good right now. Gwen rolled onto her back and nearly dragged Zoe on top of her by accidentally catching her arm under her body. Zoe had to pry herself away, and the heat from Gwen's body was damn tempting.

"It's not eleven."

"Ms. Fudala, it is. Otherwise I wouldn't be in your hotel room, trying to wake you up."

Gwen reached down and snagged Zoe's wrist, wrapping her fingers around tightly and holding on. Her breathing was slow, but her gaze was steady and locked on Zoe's face. "How did you get in here?"

That sounded more like the Gwen she knew. Zoe pulled her lip between her teeth and shook her head. "That's a short and stupid story, but we'll fix that so no one else can."

Gwen jerked with a start, sitting up and then lolling. Zoe reached forward quickly and pulled Gwen upright, holding onto her back with arms wrapped around her to keep her in place. Gwen pressed her forehead to Zoe's shoulder and evened out her breathing again.

"I'm so dizzy," Gwen whispered.

"Probably a side effect from those pills you took."

Gwen hummed. She skimmed her fingers down Zoe's arms and then up, circling them around her neck as if they were embracing. "I needed sleep."

"So this is how you do it?"

"Normally on a weekend when you won't find me."

"It's Thursday."

Again, Gwen hummed her answer. It had taken years, but Zoe had gotten used to that sound and to deciphering exactly what it meant. This one meant that Gwen agreed, but she wasn't happy about it.

"Eleven?"

"Gruzska's called for you twice now."

"Fuck," Gwen mumbled. She dragged in a deep breath and slowly straightened up, taking the weight off Zoe so she was sitting on her own. "How did you get in here?"

"I told the front desk that I lost my card and needed a new one. I gave your room number and name. They never questioned it."

Gwen instantly paled. Zoe understood why. If she could get the key then anyone else could just as easily, which meant that Gwen might be more susceptible to the stalker now than she was before.

"I'll talk to them before we leave."

"Thank you." Gwen pulled her legs together, sitting cross-legged on the bed. She ran her fingers through her tangled mess of hair and rubbed her eyes. Her nipples were hard, poking against the thin fabric of the T-shirt that she wore. "I can't seem to make my brain work."

"Again, probably the drugs still in your system. When did you take them?"

"Around three, I think. I don't really remember."

Zoe bit her lip. The sleeping pills and the wine Gwen had before probably weren't the best combination to try. "Why don't you take a shower, and I'll make you some coffee."

"You're an angel." Gwen still wasn't moving to stand up.

Zoe pulled the blankets off the rest of the way and pulled on Gwen's arm to get her to stand up. Then she walked her into the bathroom, trying not to look at her body any more than she already had. She'd never seen her boss this vulnerable or bare before. She was completely stripped of all her power, but it was still underneath her skin instead of the outward mask she wore every day.

Starting the shower, Zoe left her alone in the bathroom and went back into the room. She made two coffees and started to pick up because she didn't know what else to do. She pulled an outfit for Gwen to wear and made the call down to the front desk to yell at them.

Zoe sat on the edge of the bed, having nowhere else to sit when Gwen came out of the bathroom with the small white towel wrapped tightly around her chest and another one twisted in her hair. Her skin was pink from the hot water, which brought out those freckles even more.

Gulping, Zoe squeezed her legs together as she cupped the coffee mug in her hands. "Your coffee is on the nightstand."

"Thank you," Gwen murmured as she moved to sit next to Zoe on the bed with her own mug.

"Did the shower help?" Zoe asked, struggling to tear her gaze away from every inch of skin she was finally seeing. She'd dreamed of it, that was for sure, but she'd never thought this was how she'd finally be able to see it.

"Some," Gwen answered, sipping her coffee. "Did you call the front desk?"

"Yes. And I need to speak with Katyana in twenty minutes."

Gwen sighed and closed her eyes. "Do it from here. We don't have time to make it back before then."

"Are you sure you want to be around for the call?" Zoe raised an eyebrow. Before Gwen hadn't wanted to be involved at all, so this was quite the change from earlier.

"Might as well." Gwen didn't even start to get dressed. She simply sat on the edge of the bed and drank her coffee.

Zoe pulled out her phone and checked emails and messages at the offices before asking Gwen the only thing she could. "Can I use your computer for it?"

"Why?"

"Because it's a video call. It's not a simple phone call."

"Oh." Gwen looked around the room. "Yes."

Zoe didn't wait for more. She stepped over to the desk and opened Gwen's computer, turning it on, inputting the password, and getting the programs running. "This shouldn't take too long."

"Good." Gwen did finally start to get dressed then, snagging the outfit that Zoe had laid out and walking back into the bathroom.

She was stunning bare, her skin still flushed, her hair damp tendrils against her shoulders, and her face bare of any makeup. Zoe had to force herself to turn to the computer. She could do this. She could convince Katyana to go back to Amato and fix all their problems for the upcoming party. She cringed. She couldn't guarantee that, but at the very least she could try.

"Hello," Zoe said into the camera, smiling at the older woman.

Katyana nodded. "Hello."

"I'll make this quick since I know you're busy. We're in the process of the final touches for the launch event, and were informed that you'd left Amato." Zoe's nerves worked in overdrive. She glanced around the room, catching movement out of the corner of her eye. Narrowing her gaze, she realized it was Gwen. Getting dressed. Her reflection caught in the mirror in the hall. Zoe cringed and forced her gaze back to the computer screen in front of her. She wouldn't do that to Gwen. Ever.

Katyana frowned. "I haven't left Amato officially."

"Oh?" Well that was certainly different information than what Zoe had been informed. "In the interest of making this conversation quick, Amato has pulled out of the launch because of the drama going on in the company."

"I'm well aware of the conflict."

"Right," Zoe mumbled. "Well, I'm not here to convince you of anything. I'm just curious if there's anything we might be able to help with."

Katyana glanced at something off screen. Zoe wished she knew what it was, but she didn't. "Did they say why they pulled out?"

"Lack of clients who might be interested in joining them."

"Not surprising." Katyana bowed her head slightly. "I'll speak with them."

"You will?"

"It's in everyone's best interest for them to attend." Katyana pressed her lips into a thin line. "Thank you for letting me know they'd pulled out. Having that information at my fingertips helps me to make more informed decisions going forward."

"Are you leaving them completely?" Zoe worried she'd just caused even more drama, backfiring her plan to begin with.

"That remains to be seen." Katyana nodded again. "Was there anything else you wanted to discuss?"

"No."

"Then I'll see you at the launch." Katyana ended the call swiftly.

Gwen came over, her hand on Zoe's shoulder and finally dressed. "Seems that conversation went well."

"Oddly, it went better than I expected it to." Zoe's heart was back in her throat. She'd nearly seen Gwen fully naked, though not intentionally. If she'd been more of a pervert, she would have just leaned over to catch a sneak peek.

"We'll see what happens. If Amato doesn't show up, then we'll find a way to still make this party worthwhile." Gwen squeezed Zoe's shoulder and picked up her coffee mug again. "As for Gruzska..."

"He didn't tell me why he wanted to speak with you," Zoe quickly stated, wanting to make sure that everything was out in the open with Gwen. She didn't want to keep anything hidden from her if she could avoid it.

"I'm pretty sure I know why."

Zoe spun in the chair and looked up at Gwen.

She must have taken pity on Zoe, because she canted her head and shook it slowly. "I need to talk to him about the escalation with my stalker."

"Escalation." Zoe said it like a statement, but she meant it more like a question. There was still so much she didn't know about Gwen and her stalker.

Gwen raised her eyebrows and dropped them. "Thank you for waking me up. I promise you won't have to do it again."

But Zoe wanted to do it again. That was part of the problem. If she could find Gwen in that state again, she'd absolutely love to...minus the sleeping pills. But waking Gwen up? Yes. Zoe was on board for that. Especially if it involved trailing kisses—

Fuck.

She had to stop that.

Her cheeks burned again as she closed Gwen's computer and squared her shoulders. "We should get to the office. You have a meeting at one that you can't miss."

"Yes, ma'am," Gwen teased, her fingers trailing over Zoe's shoulder as she slipped into her heels.

Zoe was doomed.

ten

SOMEONE'S WATCHING

The day had been hell.

Gwen had at least shown up on time and Zoe hadn't had to go find her passed out at The Plaza, but they were finally in crunch time for the event. Zoe had spent most of her day in email and on the phone, tying up all the loose ends she possibly could for the party on Saturday.

Most of the day Gwen had been locked in her office, except when she hadn't needed to be. Zoe stared at the door, losing herself in her thoughts. Everything had been awkward between them since she'd woken Gwen up. The shadow of Gwen's attraction toward her had vanished. Rightly so. Zoe had been nothing more than a distraction—Gwen had made that obvious.

"Ms. Fudala," Zoe said as she knocked on the door to Gwen's office. "I'm going to head home for the night."

"All right." Gwen didn't even look up from her computer on her desk. She had a deadline to meet with the Granular file that was taking up most of her time. She'd tried to pawn it off on another marketer, but Gruzska would have nothing of it. She'd been nose deep in it all day.

"I think we just have to do the run-through to make sure everything is where it should be tomorrow." Tomorrow being

Saturday. The weekend had snuck up on Zoe faster than she'd thought possible, but with the major event of the year and with the stalker, it was no doubt that she'd lost track of time.

"I'll be there." Gwen still didn't look up.

Zoe frowned. "See you tomorrow then."

She didn't wait as she went back into her office and sat down at her desk. Zoe did one last check of her email, stopping short when she saw a new one pop in. She hesitated before opening it. But the subject did say for immediate action, although Zoe didn't recognize the sender information. It was probably something for the event.

I'm watching you.

Zoe looked around the office before reading it again, as if she could see whoever had sent the email and would immediately know what it meant. The hairs on her arms raised as it sunk in.

This was the stalker.

This was a threat to Gwen.

Zoe slid her gaze to Gwen's closed office door, biting her lip. She really should tell Gwen about it, but it had taken days for her to show any signs of calming down after the last incident, and it wasn't like Detective Dimwit was going to help the situation anyway.

Closing the email but keeping it in her inbox, Zoe shut down her computer. She scratched her scalp as she once again looked at the door. She should wait Gwen out and see if she wanted an escort back to the hotel. She hadn't made any comments about going back to her condo, but who would? Zoe wouldn't want to go home either.

She'd be too damn scared.

Gwen was so much stronger than she was. Zoe wouldn't be able to handle this situation if she was in the center of it. Before she left, Zoe walked back to Gwen's door and knocked. She opened it and leaned in, eyeing Gwen over.

She was stunning still. The green tank top she wore fit to her form, her blazer hanging off the back of the chair. Zoe dragged her gaze over Gwen's body before she realized belatedly that Gwen was staring directly at her.

"Um...would you do me a favor?" Zoe hesitated.

"What?" Gwen stated firmly, as if she couldn't be bothered with whatever favor it was.

"Will you call me when you leave?"

Gwen jerked her chin up at that, locking her gaze on Zoe. "For?"

"It'll put my mind at ease." Zoe wasn't sure if that would be reason enough, but she hoped Gwen would give in and let it be without poking any deeper.

"Zoe..." Gwen trailed off.

Shaking her head, Zoe put her hand up to stop Gwen from saying anything else. "Call it a gut feeling that I'd love to be proven wrong on. Please."

Gwen pursed her lips but nodded her agreement.

"Thank you."

Without another word, Zoe snagged her stuff and left the office. Just as she was arriving home to her small apartment on the other side of town, her cell phone rang. She smiled at it when she saw Gwen's name on the screen.

"I didn't think you'd leave this early," Zoe said as she slid her key into the lock.

Gwen sighed. "You leaving put the thought in my mind that I probably should as well."

Zoe's lips curled up. "Well, that does make me feel a bit better. I just got home."

Shutting the door, Zoe immediately locked it before she threw her keys onto the small kitchen table and dropped her butt into one of the chairs. She was ready for a drink and to relax for the rest of the night—at least as much as she could because that email was still working through her brain.

Someone was watching Gwen.

Well, that wasn't new information by any means. Someone had been watching Gwen for the better part of twelve years.

"Zoe?"

"What?" Zoe tensed.

"You didn't answer my question." Gwen sounded somewhat amused.

"Sorry, I was distracted. What was the question?"

"Distracted?" Gwen teased. "That doesn't sound like you."

Little did Gwen know that Zoe had been distracted since she'd been hired three years ago. Not that Zoe would ever admit that, and definitely *not* to Gwen, the distraction herself. "What was the question, Ms. Fudala?"

Gwen hummed, and Zoe could hear the engine roaring to life through the phone. She reached into her fridge and stopped. She thought she'd had two cans of beer left, but there was only one in the door. She frowned at it before snagging it and popping the lid. She would have to add that to her grocery list in the next few weeks. With as much stress as was going on right now, she wanted to make sure she had it around to take the edge off.

"Have you heard anything from Amato?"

"No." Zoe frowned. "I tried to call them again, but they haven't returned any of my calls."

"I suppose I should just give up hope that they'll be coming."

"I'm not one who gives up easily." Zoe flopped onto her couch and stared at the blanket. Was that folded when she left that morning? She often only folded it when she was rage cleaning, which she'd done a lot of that lately, but she had snuggled up in the comfortable soft blanket the night before, hadn't she? Fuck, she was too stressed to even remember what had happened the night before.

"Don't I know it." Gwen's tone was lighter than Zoe had expected. "But you seemed to give up on distractions easily the other night."

"I'm sorry?" Zoe wrinkled her brow. Was Gwen referring to their almost kiss? Surely not. That had been a bad idea from the beginning, and there was no way Gwen would be talking about that again.

"The party, Zoe. I'm not referring to anything else."

"Oh." Her cheeks burned. How did Gwen keep managing to do that. On the one hand, Zoe hated it, but on the other, she loved it. Only Gwen could manage to keep her on her toes like this. "What about the party?"

"When everything seemed to go wrong, you didn't give in to distractions, and you managed to straighten it all out."

"Well, not all of it," Zoe countered. She sipped her beer and wrinkled her nose. She'd almost forgotten just how bitter the flavor was. It had been such a long time since she'd had a can. Zoe relaxed into the couch, pulling the blanket over her legs and looking out the window at the city lights.

She'd been keeping the blinds closed in every single room since she'd seen those photos, but that had become suffocating. She had to see the sky at some point. "How do you do it?" Zoe asked unexpectedly.

"Do what?" Gwen answered, her voice having that echoing quality to it as the sound went through her car speakers and microphone.

Closing her eyes, Zoe relaxed. "How do you keep moving forward with your life when this stalker keeps tugging you right back?"

Gwen sighed heavily. "Hold on."

Zoe did as she was told. She stared at her television that she hadn't even bothered to turn on, loving just being on the phone with Gwen in a less formal environment than the office. They'd started down that road several times, but every single time, Zoe had pulled back. Talking on the phone was a safe bet.

She was surprised when Gwen came over the line, her voice clear as day. She must be at the hotel already. "You're stronger than you think you are."

Gwen had told her that once before. Still the words didn't

seem to make a dent in her thick skull. "I wasn't asking about me."

"Sure you were," Gwen replied. "I'm stepping into the elevator. I might lose you."

"Then call me back." Zoe cringed. What was she doing? She shouldn't be talking to her boss like this at all.

"Are you trying to distract me?"

Before Zoe could answer, the line went dead. She smirked at her phone before setting it down. She really should get up and make herself some dinner, but the energy that was left in her was fading fast. Getting up to cook was the farthest thing from her mind.

Zoe went to the bathroom and then stared at the fridge longingly before giving up and going back to her couch. She'd eat later. She gripped her phone and was just about to turn the television on when her phone vibrated. Again, Gwen's name lit up the screen.

"I take it you're in your room," Zoe said as she answered.

"And where are you?"

"Plastered on my couch. Pretending I have enough energy to eat dinner." Zoe wrinkled her nose. She shouldn't have said that. It was far too much like flirting.

"Watching anything entertaining?"

"Nope." Zoe gnawed on her lip. "I haven't had a minute to turn the television on yet."

"And what do you normally watch when you want down time?" Gwen's sudden curiosity in her life was intriguing. Zoe wanted to know what the change was about.

Zoe was about to answer honestly and say true crime shows, but she bit her tongue. That probably wouldn't be the best answer to give at the moment. Instead, she replied with her second go-to. "Just cooking shows."

"Do you like to cook?" Gwen asked, and Zoe could hear rustling through the phone, as if Gwen was changing or maybe snuggling under the covers in her bed.

"No. Do you?"

"I used to," Gwen murmured. "I enjoy taking care of those I'm with."

Why did that sound like she meant more than simply food? Zoe bypassed that comment. "When will you go home?"

"After the event tomorrow. I've had my condo rekeyed and everything checked. Nothing was put into my condo that shouldn't be there."

"You mean no cameras."

Gwen sighed lightly. "Yes. Or microphones."

"I guess that's a good thing."

"I still want to know how she managed to get in there."

That was the ultimate question, wasn't it? Gwen hadn't found out, but with getting new locks on everything, Gwen would hopefully have a bit more protection. "If only Detective Jerkface was more helpful."

Gwen laughed, her giggle filling Zoe's soul with hope. "Yes, if only he was helpful. I'll see you tomorrow, silly girl."

"See you tomorrow," Zoe answered.

Hanging up was hard, but she managed it. However, it did take her longer than it should have to drag her ass back into the kitchen to find some kind of food. If she didn't, the can of beer would go straight to her head, which would make waking up in the morning to get work done harder than it should be.

Zoe ate on her couch. When she was done, she went to her bathroom and took a shower before crashing in her bed. It was going to be a long weekend. But everything would be better once it was done.

eleven

THE PARTY

Everything was perfect, though Zoe expected nothing less. Amato had shown up and Gwen had wooed them with her talents. The ballroom was filled to the brim with people mingling, the food was set about at different tables where people could grab small plates to eat as they mingled. Music played softly, and there was even a dance floor near the large windows that looked out on the city below.

This had been everything she and Gwen had worked months for.

And this was Zoe's favorite part.

Seeing the dreams come to fruition, the full-fledged concept in the world. Zoe stepped out into the main room again after dealing with a minor issue in the back. Her job was to deal with those while Gwen dealt with the people issues. The wine, however, was the highlight of the party so far. At least from what Zoe had seen.

Zoe stared at a waitress with a tray of wine glasses as she moved around the vast room and distributed it. Zoe's stomach clenched at the memory of what that wine held, not just her first stupid mistake of getting drunk, but her second one of masturbating while thinking of her boss and not double-checking that the phone call was ended. It had been the beginning leading to where they'd ended up the night before, a beautiful conversation, one that was simple in form but vulnerable in undertones.

"Are you going to have some?" Gwen's voice reverberated in her ear, sending shivers down Zoe's spine.

Zoe tensed, turning slowly to find Gwen right over her shoulder with a wine glass in hand. Thankfully, only one. "I think I've had enough of that wine to last me a lifetime."

Gwen chuckled lightly. Her mood was different than it had been the past few weeks. She seemed lighter in a way Zoe couldn't describe. Maybe it was just being in a room full of people or perhaps it was the fact that she had something massive to distract her.

"Perhaps sticking to water would be best." Gwen brought the glass to her lips and took a small sip as she stepped in closer to Zoe, right behind her shoulder.

Zoe swore Gwen placed feather light touches against her back, but she had to be making it up. It was her fantasies playing out. Not real. Gwen had never touched her like that. "Yes, I think that would be wise. At least while I'm working."

Gwen's gaze became amused before she immediately masked it again. "It's a party, Zoe. At least learn to enjoy yourself a little."

Zoe wasn't sure how to respond to that. While yes, she wanted to enjoy herself, she was at work, and she was there for a purpose. If she wasn't Gwen's personal assistant, she was pretty sure she would never have been invited to something this rich. Turning so they were facing each other, Zoe had to hold back her groan. She should have stayed put because Gwen's fingers had definitely been on the small of her back, and when she moved, they slid around her side to her hip.

Gwen was dressed impeccably—classically. The black material smoothed over her pale skin as it draped around her curves. A lump formed in Zoe's throat as she lost the ability to form all words. Her mouth was dry. One of Gwen's shoulders was bare while the other covered, but skin was revealed just below. Zoe would love to trace her tongue right along that line, across the top of her breasts, under the hem of the material.

She clenched her jaw shut tightly, dropping her gaze to the slit, high on Gwen's thigh, high enough that she could easily reach in and—fuck, she had to stop that train of thought. Licking her lips from her suddenly parched mouth, Zoe deliberately raised her eyes to see exactly what Gwen was thinking.

"Wine?" Gwen looked...amused?

Surely, she didn't find this entertaining. Zoe took the proffered glass and put it to her lips, sipping the wine she had spent hours creating so that it was the perfect flavor for the night. It hit the back of her throat, and she nearly sputtered at the intense stare Gwen gave her.

"We never did have that chat, did we?" Gwen's voice was so quiet, Zoe wasn't sure she'd heard correctly.

"What chat?" Zoe asked, holding the glass tightly between her fingers until Gwen took it from her grasp, their fingers brushing and inciting arousal.

"The one about the winery and what happened...after."

Zoe's stomach clenched hard. They had started to talk about it, been interrupted, and she'd thought it was dropped. Especially after the conversation at Gwen's condo. Gwen stepped in closer, lowering her tone so it was just above a whisper as she leaned in and put her lips right next to Zoe's ear.

"I want to talk, and I get the feeling you can't stop thinking about it."

Oh fuck.

She was done for.

Zoe listed forward, and Gwen put a hand on her arm to steady her. Her fingers were so warm, so firm. Zoe whimpered at just the thought of what she could use them for. She closed her eyes, breathing in deeply and regretting it instantly because all her senses focused on Gwen's subtle perfume.

"Don't be afraid," Gwen dropped her voice even lower. Zoe

had to lean in to hear her, pressing against Gwen's side as they stood together.

The way she said the words sent a shiver down Zoe's spine, ending right between her legs. Zoe had to press her thighs together at the intrusive thoughts that hit her brain. Again, Gwen's fingers were at her back, pressing firmly into the bare skin where her dress didn't touch.

"I promise you, this is what I want." Without another word, Gwen stepped away with her wine glass in her hand. She moved to talk to one of the board members, as if nothing had been exchanged between them.

Zoe tried to shake the thought from her head. Damn it. Embarrassment flooded into her again, her cheeks heating as a waiter walked by her. Zoe requested water, and when the waiter returned, she was glad for the cold liquid flowing through her body.

She couldn't take her eyes off Gwen the entire night. For some reason, Zoe felt safe here. As if the world outside of them and the stalker couldn't touch them or find them here. Gwen seemed to flirt with everyone, her eyes lighting up as she moved from person to person, the conversation flowing from her as she found an ease she hadn't seemed to have in weeks. Zoe had seen her in this environment before, but she'd never paid close enough attention to see the underlying emotions flashing through Gwen's gaze—the annoyance, the temper, the true genuine friendship.

Gwen was stunning when she relaxed.

Zoe took in every aspect, stilling when Gwen looked across at her, their gazes locking. Gwen raised an eyebrow, lips curling upward into a seductive smile. It lasted only a brief second before Gwen's attention was pulled back to the two people in front of her. Zoe breathed out a sigh of relief and stepped away from the ballroom.

She needed some fresh air. Zoe set her glass on a table as she stepped out into the hallway and made her way toward one of the balconies. They were on the fifth floor, and the city ran circles around them outside. Everything inside had stopped for fun, for celebration, for a moment to be together. But outside, reality touched her.

There was a stalker on the loose.

She probably shouldn't be out there by herself, but Zoe needed the cold air to make her think straight. She had to stop reading so much into what happened between her and Gwen. It was all in her head. Gwen wanted a distraction, but Zoe wanted more than that. She'd spent too many nights fantasizing about what they might do together, but that's all it was, fantasy. Gwen would never be interested in her for anything beyond a quick fling.

"I hope you're not thinking of jumping."

Zoe stiffened, straightening her back as she spun around to find Gwen eyeing her up and down. That dress was still gorgeous on her, nothing that would ever suit Zoe and her tastes. Gwen's hair was done up, twisted into a simple bun near the top of her head, her makeup painted beautifully so her eyes seemed bigger, her features more exotic.

"No, not planning on jumping."

"Couldn't have that." Gwen stepped in close, her fingers flitting over Zoe's arm.

They had never really touched before, or if they did, it was extremely rare and never quite with this intention minus that one night. Zoe had taken great pains to maintain a professional distance between the two of them. She also had no idea what to say.

"I hope..." Gwen stopped, moving her gaze from Zoe to the city below them. "Is this where you'd like to talk?"

"Talk about what, exactly?" Zoe looked Gwen over carefully, trying to read every intonation in her voice, her gaze, her stance.

Gwen hummed, but instead of a noncommittal answer like it normally was, this held something in it. Zoe stepped in closer, taking a firm risk in reaching out and covering Gwen's fingers with her own.

"Are you firing me?"

"What? No." Gwen raised her gaze. "I told you I wouldn't. Why would you think that?"

"Because you've been acting odd for weeks now, and we've..." How did she say this? Zoe clenched her jaw, searching for words. "We've pushed boundaries. And with your stalker coming in full force—"

"Silly girl," Gwen whispered this time as if it was a term of endearment instead of a simple tease. "I'm not firing you. And certainly not because of something someone else is doing, something out of your control."

"Oh good." Relief flooded through Zoe, and she let go of Gwen's hands, only to have Gwen grip her fingers.

"What's wrong?"

"Don't ask me that," Zoe muttered. Because she was awful at lying, and if Gwen pushed, she'd have to tell her everything.

Confusion clouded Gwen's eyes, and Zoe had to step away from her, putting space between them. Her heart thundered as she leaned over the railing, trying to push Gwen from her mind, but it was so hard with her standing right there, right next to her, the heat from her body warming the chill that had taken over.

"Talk to me, Zoe."

Zoe lifted her chin up, defiantly. "I love my job, Ms. Fudala. I love working for you and the work that we do, and I don't want to lose my job."

Gwen frowned but stayed stoically still. "Why do you think you'll be fired?"

That was a question she hadn't been expecting. "Because of the winery." That wasn't really it, but it was the easiest truth to grab onto.

"Because you drank while on the job?" Gwen pressed her hand to Zoe's back, encouraging Zoe to stand up straight and turn so they could look at each other. "We're drinking on the job tonight."

"Not because of that." Zoe's voice was so quiet she wasn't

even sure Gwen had heard her. In fact, she would be happier if she hadn't. With no alcohol in her system as an excuse, she couldn't easily get out of this confession if she were to make it.

Gwen's eyes lit up, and her lips curled seductively. Leaning in, she pressed her mouth to Zoe's ear and squeezed her fingers tightly. "Do you know how many women and men are attracted to me?"

Zoe's stomach plummeted. She hadn't wanted the conversation to turn this direction, and with what Gwen had just said, she knew exactly where it was going. She was no one. She was a personal assistant to a high-powered woman, and she couldn't compare to anyone Gwen could have if she so much as said the word. All she would be was a distraction, thrown away when Gwen was done with her. And that wasn't what Zoe wanted.

"But all of them want something from me." Gwen wrapped her arm around Zoe's side, holding them close together. "You have never once asked for anything from me. You're unique in that, silly girl."

Zoe's heart fluttered, but again, she was at a loss for words.

"I thought your crush would go away quickly after that night. But I was wrong. It's deepened."

Her heart sank. Gwen's words were so pointed. Zoe had thought she'd hidden it well for all these years, but she hadn't. And the phone call, the masturbation, the photos Gwen had seen, they all told Gwen exactly what she needed to know. Zoe wasn't just in lust with Gwen—she was in love with her. But it was too close to what a stalker might do, wasn't it? Zoe wasn't any better than the woman in the shadows.

"I don't know what you mean," Zoe protested.

Gwen chuckled, all knowing. "Don't start denying it now."

"I'm not." Zoe tilted into Gwen. Where was this conversation going? "We probably shouldn't be out here."

"Probably not," Gwen answered. "Have you changed your mind?"

"Changed my mind on what?" Zoe looked into Gwen's pale blue eyes, wondering where the conversation was going now.

"About my offer."

"What offer is that?" Zoe pulled her lower lip between her teeth.

"Distraction, Zoe. This will be the last time I offer." Gwen ran her fingers down Zoe's arm to her wrist, moving them off with a flick.

Did she want this?

Yes.

Was she willing to risk her job and what measly friendship they had for it?

Zoe wasn't sure.

"How about this..." Gwen trailed off, but she turned, pressing her front into Zoe's. She skimmed fingers up Zoe's arms to her collar bones, trailing them across before diving her hands into Zoe's hair. "...we try once. If it's too much, we stop."

"Why would you even want me?" Zoe breathed the question, not sure that she'd truly spoken aloud until Gwen's eyebrow raised. The curl of her lips was all-encompassing, and Zoe was consumed by it.

"You don't give yourself enough credit," Gwen whispered. Her fingers never stopped moving against Zoe's skin. "You're brilliant. Stunning. One of the most supportive people I've ever met. You've never wavered in your ability to stand by me or protect me."

"That's not a reason for this to happen." Zoe lifted her chin, looking directly into Gwen's eyes. "None of that makes me anything beyond your assistant."

"It makes you so much more." Gwen's fingers moved across Zoe's lips, the pads of her fingers rough. "It makes you my best ally."

"Ally against what?"

"The world," Gwen whispered, her gaze dropping to Zoe's mouth. "Will you let me this time?"

Zoe's heart raced. This was more intense than the last time. She had no escape. She had to answer. But what was it that she really wanted? She had to take the initiative. Holding her breath, Zoe leaned in and pressed their lips together in a hesitant touch.

Every emotion, every feeling, every sensation rushed through her in an instant. Zoe parted her lips, closed her eyes, and moved in. If this was going to be the only chance she got, she was taking it. Enough with the fantasies, the dreams, the desires. Reaching up, Zoe curled her fingers around the back of Gwen's neck and pulled their bodies closer.

Gwen pushed her into the railing, smooshing their bodies together. Their breasts touched, Gwen's chest rising and falling as her tongue tangled with Zoe's. Zoe was at a complete loss. She did everything she could by instinct. She moaned, dropping her hand to Gwen's waist and holding on tightly. Tingles raced through her and pooled between her legs.

"Don't stop," Gwen whispered briefly before diving back in for another long kiss.

Zoe held on tight, digging her dull nails into Gwen's side and the back of her neck. She smoothed her hand up over Gwen's back, pushing between her shoulder blades. She nipped Gwen's lower lip, their embrace intensifying. This was so much better than she had dreamed of. Gwen was hot in her hands, a fire that Zoe hadn't even known existed.

Gwen tweaked Zoe's nipple, and it instantly hardened through the fabric of her bra and dress. Zoe grunted and clenched her eyes tight. Gwen pulled away with a cocky smile on her lips. She looked into Zoe's eyes deeply, tightening her grasp.

"Will you come with me?" Gwen asked, hardly able to catch her breath long enough to speak.

Zoe swallowed hard. She knew exactly what she was agreeing to, and she wanted nothing else.

"Yes."

twelve

THE SEDUCTION

What was she doing?

Zoe's hand was clasped in Gwen's as they moved swiftly through the hallways until they reached the elevator. Zoe's heart was in her throat as soon as they were inside and Gwen pressed a button for the twenty-first floor. Zoe stood still, Gwen's fingers curled around hers as they stood at the door in absolute silence. She knew her boss wasn't someone who spoke in abundance. For as much as she read, she was rather quiet. But when she did say something, everyone in the room listened.

"Where are we going?" Zoe asked.

Gwen glanced at Zoe. "To my room."

Zoe looked at the buttons as they moved from one floor to the next. She'd known that. Why had she even asked? She wasn't going to back out now, was she? She trusted that Gwen would stop if she said the word, but that wasn't what she wanted. What she wanted was Gwen.

Bringing Zoe's hand up to her lips, Gwen pressed a delicate kiss against Zoe's knuckles. Staring forward, she was surprised when Gwen lifted her chin with one finger and pressed their lips together in a tender kiss.

Heat seared through Zoe's body. Every place they had

touched outside on the balcony, screaming for more. This was better than anything Zoe could have imagined. She moved her free hand up, curling it around the back of Gwen's neck and holding her in place as she deepened the kiss.

Gwen pushed her against the door to the elevator, skimming her hand down Zoe's chest, over her breasts, and back up again to curl delicately around the front of her neck. Zoe let loose. She'd been dreaming of this moment for years, and it was everything she had imagined and more. Gwen was fire underneath pure control.

Smashed between her hot boss and the cold elevator doors, Zoe focused on every touch, every brush of their bodies, every slide of Gwen's tongue. Their bodies were pressed tightly together, her hand at the back of Gwen's neck tightening to keep her right where Zoe wanted her. Zoe bucked her hips, needing Gwen to touch her everywhere.

"Oh God," Zoe muttered, tossing her head back into the door as Gwen trailed kisses down her neck. She had never imagined this night would move in this direction, but every thought of the stalker had flown from her mind in an instant. She hadn't realized how much she had needed this distraction, this release from the pent-up tension of the last month.

Gwen chuckled low, her voice reverberating through Zoe's chest and causing her nipples to harden. Zoe would do anything for this woman. She'd never had any doubt of that.

The elevator stopped, and Zoe waited for Gwen to move away, but she didn't. She nipped at Zoe's collarbone, brushed fingers over her breasts again, and pecked her lips quickly. "My room."

Zoe whined. Gwen led the way as they moved swiftly from the elevator to the door. She pressed the card to the sensor and opened it as soon as the lock beeped. In seconds they were inside, and Zoe found herself plastered between the door and Gwen again, this time their kisses furious. She was surrounded by Gwen —her scent and her touch.

She wanted to speak. She wanted to say what she was feeling

and thinking, but she worried that to utter even one word would ruin the moment and pull them out of it—that it wasn't what Gwen wanted beyond distraction. Zoe held Gwen close, her hands on each side of her face. In an instant, Zoe pushed off the door and flipped them around.

Gwen grinned, that saucy smile intimidating. Zoe filed this moment away to remember the next time she needed to use her hand because surely this was only going to happen once. She did what she had wanted to do all night, and she found the slit in Gwen's dress, high up on her thigh and wove her hand under it.

"Touch me," Gwen murmured, her eyes half-lidded as she rested her shoulders against the door and let Zoe have access to every part of her body. "I'm yours, silly girl."

Zoe's heart shattered. This was more than a quick fuck for her, but she would take everything Gwen offered. Like she did every day, she would do anything Gwen asked of her. She nipped down Gwen's neck, sliding her tongue under the fabric of her dress and across the tops of her breasts. She tasted just as good as Zoe had imagined.

"Take me already." Gwen looked down at her, cool blue eyes boring directly into Zoe's soul.

"Yeah," Zoe whispered, sliding her hand up Gwen's thigh. She didn't need to be told three times. She fumbled at first, trying to find the best way to slide her fingers, to rub and move.

Gwen groaned, her voice echoing into the room beyond them. Zoe drew in a deep breath to steady her hand and pressed her lips to Gwen's neck again. She needed to distract not only Gwen but herself from her own trepidation.

"Fuck me," Gwen commanded. "I need you to touch me."

She'd been told enough, and Zoe loved when Gwen told her exactly what she wanted. That was no different now than when they were in the office. Zoe pushed aside the thong and slid two fingers inside, using Gwen's own moisture against her clit as she rubbed circles. Fuck, she was soaked. The inside of the thong was wet against the back of her hand as she began a slow thrust.

Gwen rocked her hips, no doubt increasing the friction between them.

Zoe matched her rhythm. This woman was a goddess in human form. Gwen's cheeks flushed as pleasure poured into her. Zoe loved seeing every change in her, the relaxed jaw, the half-lidded eyes, the red spreading over her chest and neck. Leaning in, Zoe nipped at Gwen's neck and bit hard enough to leave a mark. All boundaries between them vanished.

Gwen whined. The noise sent shivers through Zoe. She could come just from listening to Gwen's noises. She bit again, changing the angle of her wrist and the pressure of her thumb to make it slightly harder than before.

"That's it," Gwen said through clenched teeth, digging her fingers into Zoe's hair and holding her tightly. "Don't stop. It feels so good."

Zoe dashed her tongue against Gwen's salty neck then scraped her teeth down until she ran into the damn dress again. It might have been fun to play with for a brief second, but Zoe would much rather have her naked.

"Just a little bit longer," Gwen's voice was breathy, and she struggled to form the words.

Zoe did exactly as she asked. She kept the pace, she kept the pressure, and she made sure Gwen came first.

Gwen clenched hard against Zoe's fingers, her entire body tightening as she gripped Zoe and held her in her arms. She grunted lightly, her breathing uneven. Satisfied Zoe had done what was asked, she removed her hand and licked her fingers. Gwen's flavor burst on her tongue, and she was determined it would be something she would never forget. If this was all she got, it was well worth it. She would make this satisfy her soul and curiosity no matter what happened moving forward.

Without another moment, Gwen gripped Zoe by the back of the head and pressed their mouths together. In seconds, she had the back of Zoe's dress undone and slid it down her body to land in a pool of fabric on the floor. Gwen stepped forward, making Zoe step backward. Her bra was next.

Her back collided with the wall, and Gwen's mouth was on her breasts, circling her nipple with her tongue before flicking it hard. Zoe dug her fingers into Gwen's dark luscious hair, pulling it out of the damnable bun she'd had it in all night. Gwen moved down her body to her belly before trailing her way back up and kissing Zoe so hard she lost all sense of time and space.

"Touch yourself. I need a minute," Gwen whispered into Zoe's ear, stepping away. She eyed Zoe pointedly until Zoe moved her panties down to her thighs and plunged the fingers she'd just used in Gwen into her own body. "Absolutely perfect. Watch yourself in the mirror."

Zoe turned her chin toward the large floor-to-ceiling mirror across from her. This was the mirror she'd watched Gwen in all those days ago, the form of her shoulders, the slide of the towel against her skin. Zoe had never masturbated for someone before, not like this, but it was the most erotic thing she had experienced to date. Gwen disappeared into the bathroom, and when she came out, she was completely bare. Her lips curled at the sight of Zoe still fingering herself.

"I think we should take these off." She stepped in front of Zoe and pulled her panties the rest of the way off.

Instead of standing up like Zoe had thought she would, Gwen stayed on the floor, her knees pressing into the carpet as she spread Zoe's legs a little wider. Her mouth was on Zoe instantly. Crying out in surprise, Zoe pushed against the wall to hold herself up and couldn't stop staring at Gwen's back in the mirror, her head between Zoe's legs as she took deep breaths and put all that concentration she had into one thing.

Zoe.

Biting her tongue to hold back her groan, Zoe pressed her palms flat against the wall until she had to hold onto Gwen to keep herself upright. She clenched her eyes tightly, trying to rid her brain of the powerful woman between her legs. It made her weak in her knees. Zoe took in shallow breaths, her hips jerking as she got even closer to the precipice of her orgasm.

She tried to speak, tried to say anything that would tell Gwen exactly what she was feeling or needed, but she couldn't form a single word. Gwen's fingers dug into her hips to hold her steady, and she was pretty sure she was going to fall over without the added stability. It felt amazing, so good, so far beyond what any stupid imagination and her own hand could do.

Sweat riddled her skin, her chest covered in red splotches. Zoe opened her eyes and stared down at Gwen, crashing through her orgasm unexpectedly. She jerked, she clenched her fingers tightly, she held on for dear life as Gwen continued to suck and tease without showing any sign of slowing down. Her brain couldn't compete, her body making her lose complete control.

"Enough," Zoe breathed out, unable to form any other word.

Gwen kissed the inside of Zoe's thigh, nipping her tender flesh. "Talk to me, Zoe."

She shook her head, unable to speak. No matter what she tried, she couldn't even come up with one single damn word. Her thoughts were so scattered, as if her brain had short circuited in the process.

"Zoe," Gwen cooed, standing right next to her and running soothing hands over her arms and fingers over her cheeks. The pattern was the same, fast at first and then slow, as if Gwen was trying to calm her down. "Talk to me. Trust me like I trust you."

Shaking her head again, Zoe pried her eyes open and stared directly into those blue eyes, ones she had dreamed about for years. This couldn't be real, could it? Pulling Gwen in closer, Zoe took her mouth in a gentle kiss. She tried to make it all physical, but she couldn't. She wanted more than just that even if she knew it wasn't going to be more. Gwen didn't have relationships. The closest thing Zoe had seen in three years was a repeated fling.

Zoe took a step, pushing away from the wall and steering Gwen toward the bed. They walked like that, hands teasing, mouths connected until Gwen fell back. Zoe kept her mouth closed as she climbed onto the mattress and kissed her way down Gwen's chest and stomach.

"Zoe, please."

She had no idea what Gwen was asking for. It could be so many things. She fingered Gwen's clit again while her tongue was occupied with drawing designs on her smooth skin, on the hard point of her nipple, on the fullness of her breast.

"Talk to me," Gwen begged, but her hips moved upward in an invitation for Zoe to go further, deeper. What did Gwen want? The signals were mixed. Conversation or fucking? Zoe was lost to her.

Listening to the physical call, Zoe covered Gwen with her mouth. The flavor she'd only gotten a taste of before blossomed on her tongue. She drew in deep breaths as she pulled Gwen up for a second orgasm of the night. If they could stay in that position all night, giving each other pleasure, taking what they wanted, Zoe would be a happy woman, but she would make sure she was gone by morning.

She swirled her tongue, the tip teasing Gwen's clit in a tight little circle before she covered her and sucked. Gwen cried out, her back arching off the bed as she reached above her. Zoe closed her eyes, remembering the feel of her own fingers between her legs, the pressure, the tease, the arousal. Her pussy clenched hard.

Fuck, she was ready for a second orgasm already.

They could go like this all night and Zoe would never complain about not sleeping. She would do anything for Gwen Fudala including fucking her into oblivion and back again. And she would give her the best ride of her life.

Zoe's body reacted in ways she never expected, the tingles and pleasure pooling again without the delicate touch of a hand or toy. Never before in her life had she come just from giving someone else pleasure. Then again, she had wanted this for years, and that had never happened before either. Her long-unrequited crush was blooming into reality.

Rocking her hips against the mattress, Zoe reached between

her legs to touch herself as she continued to pleasure Gwen. She matched the rhythms, not that Gwen would know, and closed her eyes as she put her entire focus into the one reason they were there that night.

Distraction.

Good fucking distraction.

Gwen gripped her hair tightly, tugging hard as her muscles clamped down. Zoe continued to lick until Gwen gasped for air and turned on her side to stop it. Wiping her face with the back of her hand, Zoe sat on the edge of the bed and looked Gwen over. She was even more beautiful now than before if that was even possible. Her hair was a mess, falling across the sheets, her eyelids half-closed from sleep, and her skin riddled with goosebumps from the aftermath of sex. Zoe trailed her fingers in delicate patterns along the side of Gwen's thigh, waiting until she had enough brain power to speak or move again. Zoe could wait.

"Come here," Gwen said, her voice rough.

Zoe complied but still said nothing. She climbed into Gwen's arms, turning so her back was against Gwen's front. Zoe couldn't look at her. She would be too embarrassed to think this would never happen again, to realize how Gwen would look at her from now on when they were in the office. To question whether there was an underlying meaning to her words.

For years, Zoe had managed to avoid that because she hadn't given in. She hadn't pushed or let Gwen in on the fact that she very much had a secret crush on her boss. Now that glass wall was shattered into a million pieces. Zoe's heart ached, but she didn't regret it for one moment. Gwen traced fingers down her side, over her hip, and to her thigh.

"Talk to me, Zoe. I need to know what you're thinking."

What was she supposed to say? Fears raced through her. Why had Gwen even wanted her? She'd said the prettiest of words, but Zoe had such a hard time believing them. What if someone had caught them kissing outside? What if the stalker had? Or making out in the elevator? What would the stalker do next? Come after Zoe more than she had before?

"Zoe," Gwen whispered as she pressed delicate kisses to the back of Zoe's neck. "Silly girl, stop thinking the worst."

She almost whimpered. Gwen's hands enticed her body, bringing her back to the moment between them, to the sexual tension running between them, to the soft touches in the after-sex glow. Gwen's kisses increased, moving down her shoulder and across the top of her back. Zoe reached for Gwen's hand, dragging it over her side and sliding Gwen's fingers between her legs. If they were going to do this, they weren't going to stop until they had to.

thirteen

WHAT HAPPENS NEXT?

Light warmed Zoe's cheeks. She brushed her hand over her face, moving her hair away from her nose as she sucked in a deep breath. What time was it? She wanted to pry open her eyes to see, but she couldn't make herself do it. To wake up would be to spoil everything.

"Don't move," Gwen whispered.

Her hair tickled Zoe's bare back and down toward her ass. Gwen's breath was hot against her skin as she moved. Zoe's heart was in her throat, the stickiness between her legs increasing in an instant.

"What time is it?" Zoe mumbled, her voice muffled by the pillow she turned into.

"Almost lunch time." Gwen pressed a kiss to Zoe's spine, right in between her shoulder blades. "I didn't want to wake you."

"What?" Zoe's brain struggled to keep up. She'd had sex with her boss, that was for sure. The ache between her legs told her that she had come so many times last night she'd lost track.

"You blacked out around four in the morning." Gwen scraped her teeth down Zoe's back. "I didn't want to continue until you woke up."

"Continue?" What was going on?

"Mmhmm." Gwen dashed her tongue out.

Zoe wiggled, her hips pushing into the mattress as she clenched her eyes. Gwen surrounded her. Mouth, tongue, teeth, the brush of her hair, her hard nipples. Zoe would give anything to turn over and look at Gwen, make sure this was really happening and not just some sort of fantastic dream she was having again.

"We didn't talk about sex while the other person slept, so I held off."

What the hell was Gwen even talking about?

"But I want to finish what we started." Gwen's voice was raspy, her mouth against Zoe's ass cheek. She parted her lips and nipped Zoe.

Zoe grunted. "What we started?"

"Yes," Gwen replied. "Will you let me?"

"Ms. Fudala..."

Gwen clicked her tongue before biting the round curve of Zoe's bottom just at the top of her thigh. "Spread your legs a little."

Zoe complied before she could even think straight. She'd always done exactly what she was told by Gwen. Every single thing. "What time is it?"

"Nearly lunch."

Why couldn't Zoe think straight?

"I want to be inside you again."

"Yes," Zoe hissed as heat rushed between her legs. With her eyes closed, she could remember those touches, her own fingers between her legs, Gwen's fingers pumping inside her.

"Are you ready?"

Zoe moaned, the sound leaving her lips as she raised her hips up, her ass in the air as she pushed toward Gwen. She would take any kind of touch that Gwen was willing to give her. Anything and everything.

"I need an answer, Zoe." Gwen's voice was so commanding,

but the bite to the back of Zoe's upper thigh was such a damn tease.

"Mouth," Zoe breathed. She wanted Gwen's mouth to cover her completely. "I need your mouth."

"Are you going to pass out on me again?"

"No." Though Zoe knew she couldn't guarantee that. She'd been struggling just to come back to reality since she'd woken up, some eight hours after she'd apparently blacked out. Sex had never made her pass out before.

"I don't believe you." Gwen pressed her nails into the backs of Zoe's thighs and dragged her fingers downward. "And until I believe you, I'm not going to let you come."

"Fuck," Zoe muttered. She pulled her knees up under her chest so that her ass truly was in the air now.

Gwen moved behind her. Zoe still hadn't seen her face, seen what she looked like with that fresh fucked look. Hell, what did Zoe look like? Probably hell warmed over, but she was no beauty compared to Gwen. She dressed nicely because she had to, but she'd barely managed to keep up her appearance throughout the last few years.

"Zoe," Gwen chastised, her full palm landing against Zoe's raised ass.

Cringing, Zoe sucked in a sharp breath. That had felt amazing. She'd never liked it before when someone had spanked her, but Gwen's hand against her was something else entirely. Everything with this woman was so much more erotic than it had been with anyone else.

Gwen chuckled, her voice low. She moved up, leaning over Zoe's form and pressing her down into the mattress. "You know I can smell your arousal? The scent is intoxicating."

What was she doing? Zoe buried her face deeper into the pillow and clenched her eyes tight.

"I can see your slick pussy, so I know you liked that. Want me to do it again?"

"Yes," Zoe whispered.

"I didn't hear you." Gwen reached under Zoe's form and cupped her breast, rolling her nipple between her fingers.

Zoe gasped and rocked back, her butt moving precisely into Gwen's hips. She groaned. "Yes."

"Excellent." Gwen didn't do it right away. She took her sweet time moving back down Zoe's body with kisses and scrapes of her teeth. The anticipation was going to kill Zoe. When would Gwen spank her again? When would she use her fingers? Her mouth?

"Ms. Fudala," Zoe murmured. "Your mouth."

"Are you going to black out?"

"I don't want to."

"What do you want me to do if you can't control yourself?" Gwen's teeth pushed into Zoe's butt again.

Her pussy clenched hard against nothing. Zoe needed Gwen's fingers in her. Maybe her tongue. Anything. "Inside me."

"What was that?" Gwen lavished her tongue along the curve of Zoe's ass.

"Inside me. Now."

"And when you pass out?"

"Fuck me," Zoe commanded. She wanted Gwen to never stop again. She wanted this to last for as long as she could make it.

"Perfect." Gwen shifted onto her knees, pushing apart Zoe's legs before she bent down.

This time, Gwen moved with precision and dedication. She kissed Zoe's skin, she bit her, nipped at the tender flesh that was so rarely touched. Zoe had to work hard to stop her hips from moving, from seeking any kind of physical touch that she could get from Gwen. She held as still as possible until

Crack!

Gwen's palm against her ass rocked her forward with a loud grunt. Tingles pulsed sharply between her legs. What if she could come just from that? Zoe wanted to test those waters, but not tonight—no, today. It was the next day. Today she wanted Gwen's mouth against her. She wanted a swift and hard orgasm to shock her fully into the waking world.

"Mouth," Zoe reiterated the command from before.

Chortling, Gwen did exactly as she had been told. Her mouth covered Zoe completely. She laid her tongue flat against Zoe's clit, licking and then sucking. Fuck, the suction. Zoe nearly lost her balance, falling to her side, but she caught herself just before she collapsed.

"I said, 'Don't pass out.'"

"Wasn't doing that," Zoe ground out the words. "Mouth."

"You demanding is sexy as hell." Gwen didn't wait for a response. She went straight back to sucking Zoe's clit before thrusting her tongue inside.

Zoe groaned, not even bothering to bite it back and try to hold it in. She'd done that several times the night before, but Gwen seemed to thrive on those noises, the lack of control that Zoe had with her. Huffing, Zoe dug her fingers into the blanket and gripped it hard to hold herself in place. She wouldn't move. She finally had Gwen's mouth right where she wanted it, and she wasn't going to let her move again.

Gwen moved her hand around, using her fingers against Zoe's clit while she continued to fuck with her tongue. Zoe hadn't expected to wake up like this. She'd thought it had been a dream and she'd wake up hungover in her bed at home. She didn't think Gwen would—

"Ahh," Zoe cried out. Her entire body tightened, her head spinning, her ears ringing.

Damn it, she was close to passing out again. Gwen was right. Taking slow and steadying breaths, Zoe tried to get control of herself. She mentally pulled out of the pleasure that Gwen was giving her to calm her racing heart. But Gwen didn't stop. She kept pleasuring. She kept pushing. She kept moving her tongue in and out and swiping her fingers back and forth. Zoe pushed back into her, unable to stop herself from moving now.

A scream ripped through her chest as she came, darkness moving over her vision while the ringing in her ears intensified.

She couldn't breathe. It was so stifling. Zoe grasped onto anything she could, but everything slipped away from her.

The next thing she knew, she was on her back, her head flat on the mattress, and Gwen lay next to her, propped up on her elbow as she trailed her fingertips over Zoe's breast and belly. When had that happened?

"Did I pass out?" Zoe asked, heat kissing her cheeks with embarrassment. The one thing Gwen had told her not to do, and she couldn't even manage that.

"No," Gwen replied, tweaking Zoe's nipple. "But you were close."

Zoe blew out a breath. She turned her head to lock her eyes on Gwen's pale blue ones. "What are we doing?"

"Distraction." Gwen winked. "One of the best distractions I've ever found."

But even in her statement, Zoe could see the shadows fall over her face. She wished she hadn't brought it up. She should have held herself together better, held back on the reality of the world outside these four walls. "Ms. Fudala…"

"Don't think about it, Zoe." Gwen shifted so she laid against Zoe's side, curling into her body.

Gwen's skin was so cold compared to Zoe's. How long had she really been lying there? She must have passed out. Gwen was lying to her. Zoe skimmed her hand down Gwen's shoulder to her elbow, tugging her in closer. Gwen threw a leg over Zoe's and snuggled into her side.

"It's Sunday, right?" Zoe asked.

Chuckling lightly, Gwen nodded. "Yeah."

"And the party is done?"

"All over."

"So we can stay here a bit longer?"

"We can stay here all day." Gwen covered Zoe's breast with her hand, her nipple between two fingers as she pinched it. Zoe gasped.

"I feel like I haven't given you enough attention." Zoe twisted her hips, moving to straddle Gwen. She stared down into her eyes, her dark hair haloing her.

Gwen's lips pulled tight to one side, a half-cocky smirk on her lips. It was sexy as hell. "I will never say no to more attention, Zoe, but you have feasted on me plenty."

Zoe hummed, bending down and melding their mouths together. The kiss was tentative at first, like they were just starting out, but they weren't. They had spent hours naked in bed together, naked against the wall together. Zoe was never going to forget this. She wouldn't allow it.

Clasping her thighs tightly around Zoe's thigh, Gwen gripped onto her arms and raised a daring eyebrow. Zoe knew exactly what she wanted. Rocking her entire body and undulating her hips, Zoe allowed Gwen to grind against her thigh as hard or as soft as she wanted. Gwen's cheeks pinked, the red flowing down her chest and onto the tops of her breasts.

Zoe bent down as often as she could, pressing kisses to any skin that she could touch. She nipped Gwen's neck, biting hard enough to leave mark after mark. She'd discovered early on the night before that Gwen loved Zoe marking her, and if the opportunity arose, Zoe took it. She sucked hard, tightening her teeth to pull at the tenuous line between pain and pleasure.

Gwen rode her leg. She writhed against Zoe's body, humping her over and over. Pushing at Zoe's arms, Gwen tilted her head back, pleasure cascading over her face. Zoe bent down and kissed her, leaning into the pleasure that would no doubt help Gwen to find her own orgasm. Zoe couldn't believe they were actually fucking, that it wasn't just a quick elevator fling either. They had spent all night and all morning tangled together in each other's arms.

They'd forgotten the party and the event, and they'd abandoned everything they both held dear for each other. She pulled Gwen's nipple between her lips, teasing her tongue over the hardened tip. Zoe concentrated on Gwen's body, wanting to give Gwen exactly what Gwen had given her. This night and this day were all about pleasure. Pure and simple. Pleasure and distraction from the world, and Zoe was going to get as much of that as she could.

"Are you close?" Zoe whispered as Gwen rode her leg harder.

"Yes," Gwen murmured through her pleasure.

Zoe kissed her, staring down into her eyes. "Look at me when you come."

"I'll never stop looking at you."

While the words were beautiful, Zoe wasn't sure how much truth was in them. They certainly were true in sentiment, but in reality? Zoe had to question it. She was Gwen's administrative assistant and nothing more. They were using each other for exactly what they both needed.

Distraction.

From a stalker, from stress, from the shit show that was both their lives. But they knew it going in. This was one brief period of time, one night that had turned into one weekend. Zoe would never expect more from that.

"Come," Zoe commanded.

Gwen pushed her pussy harder against Zoe's thigh. She closed her eyes, pinching her face as she concentrated. She really was taking Zoe's command as law. When did Zoe start to have that kind of power? She watched, completely enraptured by Gwen's body, by her breaths, by the changes in her face. Her lips parted. Her fingers tightened. Gwen bore down on Zoe's leg, crying out as her orgasm consumed her.

Zoe took over the motion, dragging out Gwen's orgasm for as long as she could. She kept up the motion until Gwen flipped them over, covering Zoe's form with her own. Then she collapsed onto Zoe's chest, her body sweat-riddled, her chest rising and falling sharply from her pleasure, and her eyes closed. Zoe dragged her fingers up and down Gwen's back, trying to soothe her as best as she could.

"We should probably eat something."

Gwen snorted loudly, burying her face in Zoe's neck. "Yes, if you're talking about food, then yes. If we're going to make it through the rest of today, we need some sort of nutrients to keep us going."

"The rest of the day?" Zoe asked. She tightened her grasp on Gwen's hips.

"Yes, Zoe. You're mine until Monday morning." Gwen licked the shell of Zoe's ear.

Groaning, Zoe's eyes fluttered shut. "I'm pretty sure I'm always yours, Ms. Fudala, no matter the day."

fourteen

YEA OR NAY...SEXUAL HARASSMENT?

"Please, sit down," Gruzska motioned to the empty chair in the small conference room.

Zoe hesitated as she moved toward the seat and slid into it. She'd never been called down for a meeting like this in her life, and she had no idea what it was for other than the fact that she was about to be fired. The only reason she could think of had to do with everything that happened during the party and after it. Her entire weekend spent in Gwen's room.

Pressing her lips together tightly, Zoe kept silent. She waited for some kind of direction from the people who sat in the room with her. They were all executives. Zoe had really only dealt with Gruzska before, but she recognized their faces from corporate memos.

"This is Sandra Emmett, she's in charge of human resources. Frankie Cohen who is in charge of personnel." Gruzska didn't give any more introductions. He simply stared at her like she knew what to do, but Zoe had no clue why she'd even been called in there, and hell if she'd give them a reason to come down on her.

"It's good to meet you," Zoe squeaked out, though she wasn't sure it was true.

Gwen would tell her to keep her shoulders squared and go

into this meeting like she had all the power in it, even if she didn't. It's exactly what Gwen would do herself. Zoe dragged in a raw breath and played confident. She only hoped that she could pull it off. She eyed each of them down.

"Why have I been called down here?" Zoe asked.

Sandra started, "We're inquiring into the complaint filed against Gwen Fudala."

Zoe pursed her lips. What complaint? Gwen hadn't mentioned anything, and if there was something like that going on, surely Zoe would know about it. Wouldn't she? Except Gwen rarely shared anything that wasn't pertinent.

"All right," Zoe replied. "How can I help?"

The tension in the room tightened instantly. With no clue why, Zoe leaned into it. She had so many questions, and yet nothing was being answered. She would have to pull those answers from everyone around her, a mystery in and of itself.

"We need you to share with us what happened," Sandra said, her voice lowering.

Zoe blinked, canting her head to the side. Was it just her or were they all speaking a different language? She looked at each person sitting across from her, but their faces were stoic and impassible. "What do you mean what happened?"

"With the harassment," Sandra supplied.

Flicking her gaze to Gruzska, Zoe frowned. Gwen had told her that she'd spoken to the executives about what was happening with her stalker, so shouldn't they already know everything? Surely Gwen hadn't lied about that. It would be stupid not to report something like that to her supervisors, especially if it did affect her job on occasion.

"The letters and emails are increasing," Zoe finally said, dipping her toe into the waters of explaining.

Sandra immediately started writing something down on her yellow legal pad.

"I got one the other week that said *I'm watching you.*"

"And what did you do with it? Did you confront Ms. Fudala?" Frankie chimed in.

Zoe's brow drew together as she shook her head. "No, I didn't mention it to her. I didn't want her to worry about anything." Her stomach tightened with anxiety. She should have said something. It might have changed everything they had done, but it would have kept Gwen safer in the long run, wouldn't it? "I'm sorry, but has something more happened with Ms. Fudala?"

"No," Gruzska stepped in. "Nothing has happened with her so far. We wanted to investigate first."

"Investigate," Zoe murmured. Why did this conversation feel more like an attack than an investigation? Zoe had to do some footwork of her own to figure out what was going on, that was for sure. And she wasn't going to hold back on that anymore. Gwen would tell her not to, to use every opportunity to her advantage. "So she hasn't reported anything about this?"

"She hasn't." Sandra this time. "And before any recommendations are made as to a plan of action, we need all the details."

Zoe bit her lip. Again she flicked her gaze between all three of them. She was the center of their attention. Zoe smoothed her sweaty palms over her thighs and bit back her fear. "There really aren't many details that I can fill in, Ms. Emmett. Especially without knowing what's been shared."

Sandra squinted at her. "I need to know the details of the report that was filed. We take sexual harassment very seriously, and if Ms. Fudala has been a perpetrator, then we need to protect you."

"Me?" Zoe squeaked.

Gruzska nodded grimly. "I don't want to believe any of this has happened, but I won't stand for my employees being harassed in the workplace."

As much as Zoe appreciated the sentiment, she still had no idea what they were talking about. "What report?"

"You filed a report last week after the launch event." Sandra eyed her.

Zoe shook her head slowly. "No, I didn't."

"It's right here." Sandra dug into a folder she had underneath the legal pad and pulled out a stapled paper. She slid it across the table.

Zoe stared at it. She wasn't sure she wanted to touch it, to read it. But the words sexual harassment were across the top. The email seemed to come from her account, but she didn't send it. She never would have. Gritting her teeth, Zoe reached forward and pulled the paper closer so she could read.

Zoe's heart was in her throat, clogging it and making it hard to breathe. It detailed and outlined what happened at the party, up to a point. She bit the inside of her cheek to shock her back into reality. The kiss on the balcony. Anyone could have seen that honestly. The hand holding toward the elevator. The disappearing into Gwen's room until the morning. But the other details were wrong.

Gwen hadn't forced her to do anything.

Gwen hadn't threatened her job for sexual favors.

Gwen hadn't ever implied that this was sex for hire.

Zoe's hands shook as she flipped the page and read more. It included a timeline, them leaving the event before it was finished, and exactly what time Zoe had left the next evening. Had she really spent that much time naked and tangled with Gwen? Cold washed through her, and she dropped her hands into her lap. She had to dare herself to look up into Sandra's eyes.

"I didn't write this email."

"It came from your internal account," Frankie stated firmly, like he was talking to an idiot. "No one else could have sent it."

"I understand that, sir." Zoe eyed him, finding her voice. She wouldn't let Gwen hang for something she didn't do. Well, they did do that, but it wasn't in the circumstances that were being presented at all. "But I didn't send that email. I never made a report of sexual harassment."

"False reports also have repercussions," Gruzska replied.

"I understand." Zoe clenched her jaw. They weren't going to

believe her, were they? She had to find some way to convince them, to make them see what had happened. Someone else sent that email, and Zoe had a pretty good idea of who the hell it was.

The stalker.

All of them stared at her, as if they expected her to retract her statement again. How was she even going to navigate this? She had to do something, that much was for certain. Zoe shifted in her seat as she gathered her strength. She could do this.

"I didn't send that email, Ms. Emmett. Ms. Fudala has never been anything but an exemplary supervisor, and she's never indicated that in order to keep my job I had to have sex with her. None of what's in this email is true. Ms. Fudala simply wouldn't coerce me." Zoe looked each of them in the eye. "I know that Ms. Fudala has a stalker. She told me that she's informed you about some incidents that have occurred recently."

"We can't discuss other ongoing HR issues." Sandra paled.

"I get that." Zoe was finally finding her voice. "I didn't write this report, and I don't want my name anywhere on it. Ms. Fudala isn't this person." Zoe jabbed her finger into the paper. "And I won't stand for anyone calling her that."

Gruzska at least looked eased by that fact.

"Ms. Fudala shared with me recently about her stalker. I suspect that's who sent this, trying to get her in trouble and trying to diminish what little support Ms. Fudala has." Indignation rose in Zoe's chest now. This wasn't something she was going to keep down. The injustice of everything surrounding Gwen's stalker was beyond anything Zoe had witnessed before.

Sandra, however, seemed more pissed now than before. "This is a false report."

"It *is* a false report," Zoe retorted. "And it was likely made with the intention to get Ms. Fudala in trouble with you."

"What proof do you have of that?" Frankie put his hand flat on the tabletop, like he was trying to calm the raging storm that was about to break loose on the world.

"I don't have any. I didn't even know about the report until this meeting." Zoe still glared down at the paper in front of her. She wanted to pick it up and rip it into a million and one pieces. She wanted to burn it in the pits of hell where this stalker surely belonged.

Delivering pictures was one thing. But this? This was actively trying to get Gwen fired for something she never did. Rage burned within her. Zoe clenched her jaw tightly and straightened her body. She wouldn't stand for this.

"I didn't make this report. It's a false report. You want to hold me accountable for it, fine. But I won't sit here and tell you lies. Ms. Fudala did none of the things on this piece of paper. She never coerced me or threatened my job for sexual favors. She never once brought up something as inappropriate as that." Zoe had to be so careful with what she said because they had crossed boundary lines. But these people didn't know that. They had absolutely no proof of it unless they pulled security footage from the hotel, and she doubted they'd have the power or the tenacity to do that.

"Did she threaten you again? Is that why you're rescinding?"

"No!" All the anger she had carefully contained burst from her in that one word. Zoe clenched her fists, her nails biting into her palms. "No, I'm not rescinding because I never filed this report. I wouldn't do it because it's not true."

Gruzska put his hand out to calm her down, but Zoe wasn't sure she could. This wasn't the time to be calm. This was the time to stand up and fight. It didn't matter if she didn't know what the enemy looked like. Someone had to do something already.

"Ms. Fudala has been nothing but an amazing supervisor, and I won't stand behind this letter."

"Zoe, I need you to calm down," Sandra started in.

Zoe shook her head. "No. You need to look into Ms. Fudala's stalker and the situation surrounding that, not this. I didn't file that report. I wouldn't." Zoe had worked too hard for her relationship with Gwen, not just the sexual one they'd had but the trust they had built between them. Gwen trusted her, and Zoe wasn't going to break that trust no matter what happened. She would defend her boss with every breath she had.

"We can talk about this later."

"Not unless you're going to actually look into the root of the problem." Zoe glared at each of them. "If you're not, then this conversation is done."

They remained silent. Disappointed, Zoe stood.

"I guess that answers my question." She turned on her toes and walked out of the room.

Anger continued to surge through her, wave after wave. This was absolute bullshit. Injustice. Gwen was being stalked, and whoever this stalker was would take it to the extreme. Why couldn't anyone else see that? Zoe walked into the office and stared at Gwen's closed office door.

She'd left hours ago, for some meeting. Had it been a ploy to get her out of there so that they could come down on Zoe? She wouldn't put it past them. Playing the politics of the office wasn't something Zoe was ever good at doing, and she didn't want to. She was an administrative assistant, nothing more than that.

What the hell were they thinking?

She should have grabbed that piece of paper.

Wait!

Zoe swung around her desk and turned the computer back on. She went into her email and searched for the report. But she couldn't find it. It was nowhere in her inbox or her sent folder, but it had clearly been an internal communication and sent from her account. Cursing, Zoe flopped back into her chair.

She stared at the phone on her desk. She needed to talk to Gwen, but it wasn't going to be a good conversation, and she really didn't want to set her off when she'd finally gone back to her condo that week, feeling safe enough to return. Pulling her lower lip between her teeth, Zoe did the only thing she could think of.

"Nikki!"

Nikki answered the phone on the second ring.

"I don't know what to do. There's a sexual harassment report, and I didn't file it, I swear, but they think I did."

"Whoa, whoa, whoa. Slow down." Nikki's voice was soothing and calm.

Zoe just wanted her to match her damn energy already. "I can't. I'm so pissed off."

"What happened?"

"I was called into a meeting. They think that Gwen's been sexually harassing me. Apparently I filed a complaint, but I didn't. I swear to God, I didn't."

"Calm down. I believe you."

Thank fuck for that because Zoe wasn't sure what she would do if Nikki didn't believe her. She relaxed slightly, just having the validation easing her stress. "I don't know what to do. They're going to come after me for filing a false report, but I didn't file it, Nikki."

"So who did?"

"I don't know. It came from my work email. The only person who might have access to it is Gwen if I left it open while going to do something." Zoe gnawed on her lip again, staring at her email and seeing nothing in it.

"You don't think she'd do that, do you? She's not making up this whole stalker thing, is she?"

Zoe clenched her jaw. She hadn't thought so, but then again, Gwen had been pretty reckless in the last week or so with everything they'd done. For a woman being stalked, she didn't seem that perturbed by it either. A little bit, but not much.

"What if she's lying?" Nikki asked.

Zoe gulped. "I don't think she is."

"Have you actually seen any evidence that it's someone else? What if she's the stalker and you're her new victim?" Nikki sounded worried. "Zoe, I don't know about this. I've got a bad feeling."

"Me too." But it was for an entirely different reason. Zoe

wasn't afraid. She was enraged. "What can I do about this false report?"

"Ride it out, probably. If it's really false, they'll figure it out quick enough, won't they?"

Zoe pressed her lips together hard. Because she and Gwen had done things. It wasn't under duress of any kind, but they had fucked so many times over that weekend. She could still feel the ache between her legs if she thought about it. Rubbing her hands over her face, Zoe groaned. "What if they don't believe me?"

"Then they'll try to push you out. Maybe it's time to start looking for a new job."

"I love my job," Zoe whined. She really did. It was the first job she'd truly enjoyed in years. It was rough at times, but she was happy doing what she did. Closing her eyes, Zoe dragged in a deep breath. "I don't know what to do."

"Sit on it tonight and think about it tomorrow. You don't have to make any decisions right now."

That was true. Zoe leaned into that comment and held onto it like a lifeline.

"Do you want me to come over so we can talk?"

"No. I think I'm just going to go home and pass out. This was exhausting." Normally Zoe would have gladly asked for Nikki to come over, but her accusation toward Gwen had irked her. She didn't want Nikki to talk down about Gwen any more than she already had, but Zoe also needed to process through the accusations. Was there truth in them?

"Okay, well if you change your mind, let me know. I'll be there in a heartbeat."

"Thanks." Zoe glanced at the clock. "I'm going to head home."

"You do that."

After hanging up, Zoe packed up her bag for the weekend and left the building. She went to her car, sitting behind the wheel and blowing out a relieved breath. She wasn't sure what to do, honestly. It seemed as though Gwen was being attacked from every side, and Zoe couldn't let Gwen think that she was one of those people.

Putting her car into reverse, Zoe pulled out of her parking spot and left the garage. But how would Zoe convince her? Because just saying that she hadn't filed a report wasn't working. No one believed her. When Zoe reached the street, she glanced left and right. She had to talk to Gwen. She had to prove her loyalty. Turning the opposite way of her apartment, Zoe drove toward the hornet's nest.

fifteen

SAY MY NAME

"What are you doing here?" Gwen's eyes widened as Zoe stood in her doorway.

Nerves ran wild in her belly. Now that she stood in front of Gwen, she had no idea what to say. Anything she said would shatter the illusion they had managed to find in the last week, and Zoe sincerely didn't want to do that.

"Zoe?" Gwen prodded.

"We need to talk." That was the worst line ever. She closed her eyes, rolling them so Gwen couldn't see, and her shoulders sagged.

"If this is about last weekend—"

"It is, but probably not in the way you think it is. I promise you. We need to talk, and we need to do it inside." Zoe knew she was probably flipping Gwen out, not that she would ever show her anxiety on the outside, but she had to get her attention somehow.

Gwen said nothing as she opened the door wider and allowed Zoe inside. Standing awkwardly, Zoe waited until the door was shut and immediately started in on the reason they were there. "They know."

"Who knows what?" Gwen trailed back toward her couch, wine glass on the table.

Zoe wanted to follow her, but with what happened the last time they were on the couch, she wasn't so sure that was a good idea. "Gruzska called me into a meeting while you were gone, with Sandra Emmett and Frankie Cohen."

Gwen faltered at that, her steps no longer smooth. She sat down stiffly. Were her hands shaking? "What did they want?"

"There's a report that's been filed against you for sexual harassment. They think I filed it."

"And did you?" Gwen wasn't looking her in the eye.

Zoe's heart leapt into her throat. She couldn't let Gwen think that. Racing over to the couch, she sat down next to Gwen and took her hands. They were shaking, and they were cold. Zoe curled their fingers together and shook her head. "No, I didn't."

"You could if you wanted to."

"I don't want to. We had sex, Ms. Fudala. That was it. You didn't threaten me to have sex with you nor did you imply that it would change my job ever. This week has proven that to me."

Gwen's cheeks had a rosy tinge to them.

"That's all you wanted it to be, right? A distraction?"

"Yes." Gwen's jaw clenched, the muscles bulging at the sides. She finally raised her gaze up to meet Zoe's. "Yes, that's all because anything else will only bring you into the line of fire."

"I think I'm already in it." Zoe's lips parted. "Look, I didn't file that report. I promise you I didn't. I wanted last weekend as much as you did, and I don't regret it for an instant."

Gwen frowned. "What do you mean you're already in it?"

"Ms. Fudala, you can't be blind. Your stalker took pictures of me in my home. She has repeatedly targeted me in the last few weeks. I fully believe this is another one of those attacks. I think she hacked into our system and used my email to file this report. It separates us if anyone believes it."

"You think she's trying to separate us?"

"Why wouldn't she? Ms. Fudala, in all the years you've been stalked, how many people have truly believed you?"

Gwen sucked in a breath. "Not many."

"Exactly, and I do. And not only that, but with what happened last weekend, she probably sees that there's more between us than there actually is." Zoe was on a roll now, everything clicking into place. "She was accurate with the timing of everything, with anything we did in public, but once we were in your hotel room, she knew nothing. Ms. Fudala, this is escalating."

"I know," Gwen whispered. "She's done this before."

"When?" Zoe implored her.

"When I was engaged." Gwen dropped her head, as if ashamed by her reply. "My fiancée couldn't handle it. I don't blame her. I've been with people before and since then, but my stalker never seemed to care about them."

"Then why does she care about me?" Zoe squeezed Gwen's hands. "Because it was only one weekend." *Right?* Zoe didn't take on the question because she had to believe it was never more than that.

But Gwen didn't answer. Her shoulders were drawn, her lips pressed tightly together. Zoe needed to know what she was thinking. Reaching forward on instinct, Zoe cupped Gwen's cheek and lifted her chin so she could look into those eyes. That would tell her what she needed to know, wouldn't it?

"Zoe," Gwen's voice broke.

"It was only one weekend," Zoe repeated, as if trying to reassure herself that there was never anything more between them than that.

"Is that what you want?" Gwen's lips remained parted, her eyes locked on Zoe's face.

Before Zoe knew what was happening, she was shaking her head. "It was only one weekend."

"Stop saying that," Gwen whispered. "You don't mean it."

"I want to," Zoe whispered back. Why? She had no clue. She dropped her hand into her lap, but Gwen didn't look away from her. Instead, her stare intensified.

"You want to mean it?"

Zoe nodded slowly, heat rushing to her cheeks. "Ms. Fudala, you are so out of my league. And I'm nothing compared to you."

Gwen clicked her tongue with a scoff. "Who made up those stupid rules? We're in the book business, Zoe. We sell and market whatever we want, but books are fiction, not reality. You're gorgeous in your own right. Not just in looks but in your heart, in the fact that you're the only person in three years that I have trusted."

Zoe jerked at that. "No one?"

"No." Gwen stood up suddenly, striding to the window and back. "How can you think that about yourself?"

"Because it's true." Zoe watched her pace. "It's absolutely true."

"Enough." Gwen cut her hand through the air. "If you want to believe that you're not good enough for me, then believe it. But know that I don't see the world that way, and I never will."

"What are you saying?" Zoe stood up slowly, her heart in her throat and those damn nerves right back in the pit of her belly.

"I'm saying it wasn't one weekend."

"But that's what you said it was." Zoe held her breath, not sure what to do next. This entire conversation was about to blow up in her lap, and she couldn't make it stop. The train wreck was coming and there was no emergency exit.

"I lied." Gwen flexed her fingers at her sides. The tension between them increased, deepened. "I lied, and you know how I know that I did?"

Zoe shook her head. She really didn't want to hear it because she already knew the answer. She'd known all along despite telling herself repeatedly it wasn't true. But with the pictures, the first set with that last image at the winery and her apartment, the photo she'd stashed in her desk, with the photos of her masturbating, with the sexual harassment claim. She knew. "Because she's coming after me."

"Yes. Because you're a target, and this is escalating again."

"Gwen," Zoe's voice cracked, and she froze. It was the first time she'd ever said that name out loud to her face.

Gwen's lips pulled upward in a half smile. "Say it again."

"Say what?" Zoe stayed still, not sure what to do. She wasn't able to keep up anymore.

"Say my name."

Zoe shook her head. "I don't know if I can do this."

"Then you need to tell me if you can't. Because I'm not going to do this if you don't want to."

But did she? Before all of this, Zoe would have still hesitated. The fantasy was nice, but when it became reality? That shifted everything. It was no longer a question of what if. It was all about did she want to? Zoe stayed put. She couldn't make her feet move toward Gwen or away from her.

"What do you want me to do about the harassment claim?" Zoe whispered.

"I'm not sure there's anything you can do."

"They threatened me because of a false report."

"They would do that to anyone who falsely reported." Gwen stayed where she was, near the window but watching Zoe. Her back rigid, expecting a rejection. How many of these rejections had Gwen experienced throughout the last twelve years?

But more importantly, would Zoe be the next one?

Taking a step forward, Zoe walked. She was sure each time her foot planted onto the floor that this was the right decision. She almost didn't even have to make it. She'd never thought fantasy could potentially become reality, and since it had, she wasn't about to give it up. Gwen was everything she had dreamed of.

She stopped right in front of Gwen, snagging her fingers and wrapping their hands together. Zoe moved into her, claiming Gwen's lips. Gwen hummed, her eyes fluttering shut as she leaned into the embrace. Zoe reached up, wrapping her fingers around the back of Gwen's neck and digging into her hair.

Gwen hummed, running a hand across Zoe's back and pulling her in tighter. Zoe allowed it. She moved into Gwen. She pressed their fronts together and held on with everything she had. Something about this moment was so pure, vulnerable and holy. She stayed put, sliding her tongue across Gwen's lips and silently asking for permission.

"Zoe," Gwen breathed out her name.

But was it a protest or a caress? Zoe had no idea, so she did it again. This time, Gwen parted her lips and slid her tongue across Zoe's. The bitter flavor of the wine was strong, and it blended with the scent of Gwen's perfume. Zoe couldn't give this up. She didn't want to. She pulled Gwen's head down to hers and continued the kiss.

Groaning, Zoe moved her fingers down Gwen's front to her blouse, finding her way underneath the fabric so she could touch hot, smooth skin. Gwen was a goddess in her form, so unlike Zoe. If anyone were to see the two of them together, there would be no doubt who had settled and who had risen above her station. But did that really concern Zoe? She'd never thought about that before in a relationship, not until now.

Were they even in a relationship?

"Will you fuck me?" Zoe asked, letting her brain turn off and her body take over. This was what they both wanted, so why not give in to it? She didn't think that they would regret it, neither of them.

"Zoe," Gwen said again. She pulled back and pressed their foreheads together, her eyes closed. "Are you sure that's what you want?"

"I've wanted that for years, Ms. Fudala. And you've proven you want it too."

Gwen sucked in a deep breath. She reached up, putting her hands on Zoe's cheeks and pulling her in to kiss her hard and fast. "Go get naked, get on my bed, and start touching yourself."

They were doing that again? Did Gwen take pleasure in watching Zoe touch herself? In having Zoe orgasm with or without her?

"Why aren't you moving?" Gwen demanded. "The bedroom is that way."

Zoe opened her mouth to protest, but she stopped herself. This was exactly what she had asked for, and Gwen was giving it to her, even without an answer to her question, even without Zoe saying her name again. With a bolstering breath, Zoe stepped backward. She pulled off her blouse, letting her hair fall around her shoulders and dropping the shirt to the floor. She had no doubt that leaving the condo messy would annoy the crap out of Gwen, and she wanted Gwen to be a bit distracted.

Reaching behind her, Zoe flicked the clasp on her bra and let it fall away. Gwen's gaze dropped to her chest, her cheeks flushed with arousal. That was exactly what Zoe wanted to see. She covered her breasts with her hands, teasing them and pinching her nipples.

"You do know how to turn me on," Gwen murmured under her breath, not tearing her gaze away from Zoe.

"If you like what you see, then come and take what you want."

"Oh, I plan to, silly girl."

A wave of heat pooled between Zoe's legs, dampening her underwear. If she wasn't careful, then it was going to soak right through her pants. "Why do you call me that?"

Gwen followed her slowly, her bare feet silent on the floor as Zoe walked backward toward the bedroom. Gwen raised an eyebrow at her. "Don't you know?"

"No." Zoe reached down and pulled at her belt. She hadn't come here for sex, but she definitely wasn't going to say no either. She relaxed her shoulders as she pulled her belt loose, and then the button and zipper on her slacks.

"Three years is a long time to have a crush and do nothing about it." Gwen pulled Zoe's pants and tugged her back. Their hips rubbed together. Zoe dragged her gaze up to meet Gwen's eyes. "We could have been doing this for years."

"I already told you why."

"Did you?" Gwen sounded so full of herself. She pressed her mouth to Zoe's neck, scraping her teeth against the soft skin. "Because I don't think that's a very good reason."

"I do." Zoe moaned.

"I still have bite marks from last week."

Zoe laughed, so damn pleased with herself.

Gwen cracked a grin, shoving Zoe backward until her back hit the wall. "I'm pretty sure I told you to touch yourself."

"You did. And I expect the same."

Humming, Gwen pressed their mouths together. "Fine. But you better be naked on my bed in the next five seconds."

"Yes, ma'am." Zoe winked, heat rushing through her body. Her nipples hardened when Gwen dipped her head and covered one with her lips and the other with her hands. Zoe tossed her head back into the wall, her eyes fluttering shut. "Do you know it's impossible to get to the bed with you doing that?"

"Then you'll be punished for not listening."

Why did that send another wave of wetness between her legs? Gwen was a demanding boss, but it was never anything quite like this. This was hands down the sexiest thing Zoe had ever experienced. "And what will that punishment involve?"

"Are you willing to find out?" Gwen flicked the tip of her tongue over Zoe's wet nipple.

Her heart raced. This was at least one answer to the question that remained between them, and it was one that Zoe was willing to give. "Yes."

"You always were a quick learner. Perhaps today will be the same, silly girl."

"Fuck," Zoe ground out, arching her back, her shoulders pressing into the wall.

"That is the entire point." Gwen covered her, and Zoe did everything she asked—eventually.

sixteen

INVESTIGATORS...START YOUR ENGINES...

"I have a meeting this afternoon," Gwen stated from the doorway to her office.

Zoe's cheeks heated. She had spent so much of her time watching Gwen from that doorway, admiring her, and now she knew exactly what was underneath those clothes. A few more hickey marks than she'd had the week before and curves that begged to be touched.

"It's not in the calendar," Zoe answered, skimming through the shared schedule on her computer. She would have remembered if Gwen had needed to take the entire afternoon off, because it involved a lot of rearranging. She scratched the back of her head as she squinted at the screen. "How long will the meeting last?"

"I don't know, but I probably won't be back today."

Zoe blew out a breath. "I'll need to reschedule your call with Amato Literary, then."

"I think everything else should be fine though."

Pinching her face, Zoe wasn't so sure about that. Amato had a lot of issues with Gwen lately, and rescheduling a call with them could be more detrimental to the relationship than anything else.

"About Amato...I don't know if they'll take kindly to rescheduling."

"This isn't something that can be avoided." Gwen pushed off the doorframe and moved closer to Zoe's desk. She sat on the edge of it on the same side as Zoe. Her skirt rode up, revealing skin and a few bite marks along her inner thigh.

Zoe was pleased with that, but she struggled to tear her gaze away from Gwen's legs, from the pull of the fabric over her skin, the tight way it moved as she shifted.

"Zoe," Gwen chastised.

"Right, scheduling." Zoe flicked her gaze back to her computer screen.

Gwen skimmed her hand down Zoe's shoulder, her fingers leaving a trail of goosebumps along her arm. Warmth flooded after the touch, followed closely by the tingles of arousal. They couldn't here, right? Gwen wouldn't allow that. Add in the fact that Gruzska and the others were after them for sexual harassment. Gwen shouldn't even be touching her now, but it felt amazing. It was a reminder of what they both seemed to desperately want.

"I can move them to tomorrow morning."

"I have another meeting then." Gwen's voice was soft.

Zoe gave her a hard, almost disbelieving look. "You do realize that I'm supposed to be in charge of your schedule, right?"

Gwen gave a half smile, but it turned into a frown. "I have personal meetings."

"All right. Don't give me details." Zoe winked before she went into the system to change things around.

"I'm meeting with a new private investigator this afternoon. Tomorrow, I'm meeting with my lawyer."

The words sent a chill down Zoe's spine. She stopped working. "A new private investigator."

Gwen nodded firmly, but she closed her eyes, and Zoe swore she saw water filling them. "I need a resolution."

"It's been twelve years of nothing."

"Yes." Gwen looked Zoe directly in the eye. "And twelve years is too much."

"What changed?" Zoe regretted the question as soon as it was out of her mouth. She bit her lip. "I mean, it's been twelve years. And I realize she's escalating, but why now?"

"Because it's time for change." Gwen reached forward and tugged on one of Zoe's curls. "It's time for me to do something more than sit around and wait."

"But you haven't done nothing for years."

"I know. But it's time for more." Gwen dropped her hands back into her lap, folding them together. "Don't think this is only because of you, because it's not."

"Wouldn't dare to think that." Zoe's lips quirked slightly, but she had wondered. Gwen wasn't someone who liked change. In three years, Zoe knew that well enough.

Gwen dragged in a deep breath, flicking her gaze to the open door and then down at Zoe. "Wait here."

Where would she go, anyway? Gwen stood up and walked precisely to the open door and shut it, locked it, and then moved straight back to Zoe. She put her hands on the arm of the chair and spun Zoe so they faced each other before pressing their mouths together firmly.

Zoe squeaked in surprise. Her eyes fluttered shut, and she cupped Gwen's cheeks. This had been what was missing the last few days. The comfort—the physical comfort—that they felt with each other when they were at Gwen's condo. It had been an amazing night, the two of them together, hearts bared—mostly. Zoe had held back, but not when it came to sex.

"I'm doing this for me, because I deserve it," Gwen whispered before kissing her again quickly. "Private investigator today. Lawyers tomorrow. They might be contacting you."

"I figured." Hopefully they would get more done than the detectives. Even if Gwen seemed to like the one who was on leave, Zoe wasn't impressed with her.

"I'll see you Thursday."

"See you."

One last quick kiss that left a wake of longing, and Gwen was gone for the day. Zoe finished up what she needed, somehow wrangled a reschedule out of Amato Literary, and then clocked out to go to lunch with Nikki. Her best friend had been harping on her all week for the outcome of the harassment claim, but honestly, Zoe didn't have much to add. Nothing had come of it so far.

Nikki was already sitting at the table when Zoe slipped into her seat. She let out a sigh and dropped her purse to the floor. "I'm starving."

"Did you skip breakfast?" Nikki responded, skimming the menu at the same time.

"Yeah." She most definitely had, because she'd fallen asleep and dreamed of nothing but Gwen's body against hers and had woken late. The coffee she'd managed to guzzle was her saving grace. "I can't stay late today. Boss is out of the office."

"That sucks." Nikki still didn't bother to look up. "Getting the usual?"

"Yeah." Zoe didn't even bother to look at the menu. What she needed was comfort to keep her sanity going for the next few days. Whatever the private investigators found for Gwen was going to make a huge difference. She had to believe that. Maybe they would even have a name for her soon. A name for the stalker would mean a face Zoe could finally picture in her head. That would be amazing.

Nikki curled her fingers around a strand of hair, pushing it behind her ear. The brown color she'd dyed it didn't suit her well. It made her skin look ashen. Zoe wasn't about to comment on that though. The last time she'd said something about Nikki's changes to her looks, Nikki had blown up at her and not talked to her for a couple days.

"Whatever happened with the harassment claim?" Nikki put her menu down in front of her, signaling that she was ready to order.

Zoe's lips parted. "Nothing."

"Really?" Nikki frowned. "I would have thought they'd take that seriously."

"They did. They called me into a meeting with the bigwigs to grill me about it." Zoe's hand shook as she reached for her water glass. The cold liquid didn't calm her quite like she'd hoped it would.

"But if they haven't followed up..." Nikki lowered her voice. "I just worry that they're not listening to you."

Zoe furrowed her brow and eyed Nikki over. Her makeup was done up that day, in ways it hadn't been before, with dark liner around her eyes to make them pop and seem bigger. Zoe had never managed to master that technique even though she'd tried on and off for years. She would stick with her simple look instead of the double wing like Gwen wore.

"I didn't make the report for sexual harassment, Nikki. I told you that." Zoe smiled as the waiter brought their food order over. "I told them that as well, but I don't think they believed me."

"Well, at least they're taking you seriously."

"Nikki," Zoe whined. She pinned her best friend with a hard look. "Why aren't you listening to me? I didn't file that report."

"Then how else would it have gotten to them?"

"I have no idea." Zoe had been mulling that one over for days now and hadn't managed to get anywhere with it. They had a secure system when it came to emails, but that didn't mean it wasn't hackable.

"Well, who has access to your email?"

"No one," Zoe mumbled, staring down at her food. She wasn't sure she wanted to eat any more, her appetite vanishing. "I mean, Gwen probably has the most access since I don't always log out of my email or computer when I leave the office to grab something."

"Do you think she did it?" Nikki lowered her voice, conspiratorially.

"Oh my god. No! Why would she?" Zoe ran her fingers along

the napkin in her lap. The paper was rough against the pads of her thumb and forefinger, but it was a good distraction. Nikki never seemed to like Gwen much, or how she treated Zoe, but this was taking it a bit to an extreme, wasn't it? "Why would she try to get herself fired?"

"Unemployment."

Zoe snorted. "That's ridiculous."

Nikki shrugged. "Not unheard of."

"She'd effectively be unemployable if she was fired for sexual harassment." Zoe wrapped the napkin in her fist and tightened her grip. "Why would she make up a lie like that about herself?"

"Maybe she wanted to get you in trouble." Nikki sipped her soup, her gaze pinning Zoe.

"I don't think so." Zoe cut into her food, deciding she needed to start eating, otherwise Nikki would seriously think something was wrong. It seemed Nikki always wanted to up the ante on making Gwen the enemy. She'd been doing that a lot more lately, as if she was jealous.

"But you do still like her, don't you?"

Zoe's cheeks heated. She wasn't about to tell her best friend that they'd had sex. Twice. That it had been amazing and something Zoe didn't want to avoid if there was another chance for it. The memory of Gwen's mouth against hers when she'd left the office that day came back full force. Her lips tingled. She nearly moaned out loud, but she caught herself and grabbed her drink to take a long cooling sip.

"It's just a crush, Nikki. Gwen is so out of my league that she'd never give me a second thought."

Nikki pursed her lips, lines forming in her bright red lipstick. "If you say so."

"I do." Zoe put her drink down and went back to eating. "Let's talk about you. How's work going?"

Nikki lifted a shoulder and dropped it. "Same old as always. Input data. Get more data. Input data. Round and round in a circle."

"I do wish you'd look for a job that was a little more interesting."

Snorting, Nikki shook her head. "It's exactly the kind of job that I want. Easy and it pays the bills."

Zoe clenched her jaw. She'd said that about her own job before. But she honestly loved working with Gwen. Her mother thought she was an idiot for staying in an administrative role for so long, never moving up or trying to find *a career*. But Zoe honestly didn't feel the need to leave. She liked her work, and she liked her boss. In more ways than one, she had to remind herself.

"Same here. It's why I keep my job. It'll be doubly easy today since Gwen is out of the office until late tomorrow afternoon."

"Oh? What's she doing?"

"She's meeting with a private investigator."

"Over the stalking stuff?" Nikki flicked her gaze up and then dropped it to the plate in front of her.

"Yeah." Zoe rubbed her lips together. She probably shouldn't have told Nikki that. It had just slipped out. But Nikki was her best friend and someone she could trust. She'd been there through some of the roughest parts of Zoe's transition to living in the city. "I think she just wants to find out who it is."

Nikki frowned, leaving her fork on the edge of her plate. "You do realize that she's basically stalking her stalker at this rate, right? She's using her money and her power to find someone who obviously doesn't want to be found. Are you sure she isn't the stalker?"

"I'm sure," Zoe mumbled, not able to raise her gaze to meet Nikki's. She'd wanted to get off this topic and yet somehow they had swung full circle back around to it.

"I'm not so sure."

"Well, that's your opinion." Her words were biting, and she knew that, but frustration burned in her chest over it. She was exhausted from holding the line between the two of them. "I've got to get back. With the boss out, I've got to hold down the fort."

Zoe waved the waiter over so she could pay for their meal. She wasn't even going to fight it today. She just wanted to get out of there and get back to work. More than anything, she wanted to get out from under Nikki's scrutiny.

"Zoe," Nikki started, seemingly surprised. "I didn't mean to upset you."

"I'm just exhausted and stressed." Zoe frowned. "I'll catch you next week. Okay? Same time and place?"

"Yeah."

"Good." Zoe snagged her card and shoved it back into her wallet and purse. She couldn't put her finger on why she was so upset. But the constant poking and prodding from Nikki had done her in that afternoon. Her patience was gone. "See you next week."

"Zoe," Nikki started and stopped. She looked pitiful.

Zoe really should give her a break, but at the moment she couldn't. Every nerve in her wanted to jump up and defend Gwen. Just like she always did.

"I'm sorry I offended you."

"You didn't offend me." Or had she? Zoe would sort that one out later. "I'm just tired and need to get back."

"Let's do brunch this weekend."

"I'll look at my calendar." Zoe gave in, sighing. "I'll send you a text."

"Sure."

Zoe left without another word. She made her way back to her office and sat down in her chair with a huff. She was beat. Lunches with Nikki used to brighten her day, but lately, they were more of a stress than anything. She took another minute to center herself before logging into her computer. Then again, Nikki did have a point. Zoe had to get better about logging out when she wasn't near her computer.

Her cell phone buzzed with a text. Zoe wrinkled her nose, hoping it wasn't Nikki. She didn't have time to placate her nerves.

Gwen: I think this new investigator is going to work out.

Zoe smiled. She hadn't asked for or expected an update. But Gwen had given them more openly lately. Maybe Gwen was finally trusting her. That'd be a feat. Through it all, Zoe knew she'd do whatever she could to protect her. That's all the conversation with Nikki had been about. Zoe wanted to make sure that her boss's business wasn't splattered everywhere.

Typing furiously on her phone, Zoe smiled when she hit send.

Zoe: Finally some good news.

Seventeen

THE DESK

Zoe had to bite the inside of her cheek when she walked into the office Monday morning. She hadn't seen Gwen in four days since she'd had a quick flight for some work at the beginning of the week. Zoe slipped her bag into her bottom drawer and headed for the open door to Gwen's interior office. She stopped short.

Gwen was leaning over her desk, deep in work, glasses perched on her nose and tendrils of hair falling across her face to obscure her gaze. Zoe wet her suddenly parched lips before silently turning on her toes and going back to her desk. She turned on her computer and got to work.

It was hours before Gwen stepped out of her office, crossing her arms as she leaned against the door frame, and staring directly at Zoe as if she had all the time in the world to stand there and wait. Zoe was at a complete loss for words as she raised her gaze to meet Gwen's.

"I knew I was right about you," Gwen stated, her voice firm with an edge to it that Zoe couldn't quite place.

Zoe's stomach dropped. "Right about what, Ms. Fudala?"

Gwen stayed still one moment too long, her gaze roving all over Zoe's body before flicking back up to her eyes. In silence,

Gwen stood up straight and strode to the main door, shutting it before facing Zoe down with a stern look.

"I'm in need of a distraction."

Zoe's heart thumped wildly as Gwen stepped closer, the lines of her legs shifting the tight pencil skirt as she moved, and Zoe had to work too damn hard to lift her gaze back to those all-seeing blue eyes.

"That's it right there, isn't it?" Gwen sounded as though she'd figured it out.

Whatever it was, Zoe had no idea. She was going to keep silent for as long as possible. She was going to let Gwen tell her exactly what was happening.

"Did you know I spent all weekend thinking about it?"

Gwen slid onto the edge of Zoe's desk, crossing her legs so her skirt hiked up high, revealing small circular bruises on the inside of one of her thighs, bruises that were nearly gone. A thrill ran through Zoe at the thought that she'd caused those. She dragged her gaze along them, trying to make out the one peeking from just under the royal blue fabric.

A throat clearing caught her attention.

Immediately, she looked to Gwen's neck to see if there were bite marks there, but she didn't find any. Gwen bent down, the open line of her button up shirt revealing the edge of her beige bra as she moved.

"Oh yes, they're still there," Gwen accused quietly. "I had to spend quite a bit of time putting concealer on them every day since."

Zoe drew in a sharp breath, her lips parting as if she was going to say something, but words still failed her. Tentatively, Zoe reached out and ran her fingers along Gwen's smooth skin, across the bruises she had left. They looked beautiful, covering Gwen's leg as though Gwen really was hers. Except Zoe didn't own her. It had been a few nights together and nothing more.

Pulling her hand away, Zoe squared her shoulders and sat up straight in her chair. "I have work to do, Ms. Fudala."

Gwen grinned, satisfaction settling into her look as she leaned in even closer, putting her hand on top of Zoe's. "I do believe I'm your boss."

"Y-yes," Zoe stuttered, not moving.

"Which means I get to decide what you do when."

Zoe clenched her jaw and shook her head. "No, Ms. Fudala. I do what needs done for you, to make your job easier and smoother."

"Yes, I would like for that to happen." Gwen moved in closer, nipping Zoe's earlobe and pulling. "And I would like it if you would talk to me."

"There's nothing to talk about," Zoe whispered, turning her cheek so her face brushed against Gwen's.

Confusion riddled Gwen's eyes as she pulled away. "I thought this was something you wanted."

"It was."

Gwen jerked her head sharply to the side. "It was or it is?"

Zoe's lips parted, but again, it seemed as if she had no answer. Whatever they were doing couldn't go anywhere, could it? "I don't know."

Gwen hummed, leaning in again and flicking the tip of her tongue over Zoe's earlobe. Heat rushed through Zoe's body, moving straight between her legs. What she would give to have Gwen touch her again, anything. Distraction yes, but touches would be pure heaven.

Taking Zoe's hand, Gwen pressed it to her warm thigh. "I want a distraction from all this chaos going on around me."

Zoe couldn't deny that it sounded like a pleasant idea, and she was even more distracted than before. Gwen reached up and pulled the button on her shirt, revealing even more of the lacy beige bra she wore. Zoe flicked her gaze up to Gwen's eyes. "What are you doing?"

"Exactly what I've wanted for years."

"Years?" Zoe choked out.

"Mmhmm." Gwen pulled another button. "Unless of course you want me to stop."

"No," Zoe murmured, completely entranced by the woman in front of her. Raising her hand, she reached into Gwen's shirt and cupped her breast, flicking her thumb over the hard nub of her nipple.

"Silly girl," Gwen whispered as she bent down again, parting her legs so Zoe could slide right between them in her rolling chair. "Why would you think after these last few weeks that I wouldn't be completely addicted to your touch?"

"Oh God," Zoe muttered just before Gwen took her mouth. She couldn't say no. She could never say no to this woman. She held so much power, so much control, that everything she said was exactly what the world needed to do in order to be graced with her presence.

"Perfect," Gwen mumbled as she kissed along Zoe's jawline and slid off the edge of the desk. Once again, Gwen was on her knees, her back to the desk as their mouths connected. Zoe whined, needing more of this woman, needing more touches.

Gwen pressed her palms to Zoe's knees and pushed her skirt up. Zoe lifted her butt off the chair so that Gwen would have more access. She was already wet, dripping. One look from her boss could do that to her, and it hadn't been something she ever wanted to give up. It had been three years of unrequited touches, and after getting a taste of the real thing, she didn't want to give it up.

Pressing kisses over Zoe's clothes, Gwen bent her head to tease the supple flesh at Zoe's legs, much the way she had done for Gwen that night at her condo. Whimpering, Zoe shifted in her chair, unable to stay still. She was about to cry out when Gwen bit particularly hard, but the door to the offices opened, and she jerked with a start, pushing her chair into her desk to cover the fact that Gwen was still seated between her legs. And to cover her exposed skin.

"Mr. Gruzska." Surprise reverberated through the room and

there was no way she could cover it up. Thankfully, Gwen stilled. Zoe's heart raced as she stared at the middle-aged man with salt-and-pepper hair. "What can I do for you?"

"I need to speak with Gwen."

"She's...uh...not in her office right now." It wasn't a complete lie, but it was the best she could do at the moment.

Mr. Gruzska frowned and glanced at Gwen's open office door with the light still on. "I can wait."

"She's out at a meeting. I'm sorry, but it's going to be a bit before she gets back." Zoe clenched her jaw, her knee slamming into the top of her desk when Gwen's thin fingers worked straight between her legs. The gentle press of fingertips on her clit made her squirm even more.

He eyed Zoe suspiciously. "She didn't have anything on her calendar."

"I must have forgotten to put it in. It was a last-minute meeting." Zoe tried to give him a smile to assuage any ruffled feathers, but she worried it came out more as a grimace when Gwen pressed one finger deep inside her, curling it up.

She had to swallow back a moan when Gwen pushed her knees apart, the heat from her mouth covering Zoe's clit. Zoe's cheeks flushed hot, and Mr. Gruzska leaned over her desk and pointed at the calendar she had lying out on the top. "I need to speak with her as soon as possible. When is she back?"

"Oh...um..." Zoe dragged the calendar closer and stared at it, having to refocus her eyes twice in order to read her own handwriting on it. "She should have some time around three this afternoon."

"I'll see her then." He raised an eyebrow at her in scrutiny. "Are you all right? Not sick?"

"No," Zoe squeaked when Gwen hit a particularly pleasurable rhythm. "I think I'm still recovering from this weekend. It was busy catching up on everything I neglected while we were organizing the launch. But I think the party went really well, don't you?"

"It did." He pursed his lips at her. "It was an excellent party. I hope Gwen let you enjoy it."

"She did." Zoe dragged in a deep breath. "Trust me, she did."

He nodded at the calendar. "Pencil me in."

"Will do." She gasped on the last word, Gwen pushing hard into her clit. Zoe held herself as still as possible until he got to the office door, giving him the best smile she could under the circumstances, she asked, "Will you shut it, please?"

Mr. Gruzska gave her an odd look but complied with her request. Zoe wished she had a moment to get up and lock it, but she was pretty sure Gwen wasn't going to give her a chance. She didn't even have a moment to pull her chair away as Gwen flicked her tongue hard against her clit.

Zoe groaned, gripping the edge of her desk to hold herself steady while Gwen fucked her harder than she had ever dreamed. Her entire body heated, tingles running through every fucking nerve she had, and in seconds, she crashed through an orgasm that left her head reeling.

As she came back to herself, she eased the chair away only to find Gwen grinning like an idiot under the desk. She climbed out, but when Zoe went to drag her skirt down, Gwen stopped her by leaning in and capturing her lips in a passionate kiss. Their tongues tangled fiercely, as if battling for control, but Zoe knew Gwen would win any battle they had. She moaned again when Gwen bit her lower lip, sucking it hard enough that Zoe was sure it would be red and swollen.

"You are such a good pet. I think I'll keep you," Gwen murmured, kissing her hard again.

Zoe forgot all about the unlocked door, about the fact she was at work in the middle of the day with her boss between her legs, about the fact that this wasn't supposed to happen again. She couldn't have asked for it any other way. As soon as Gwen released her, Zoe looked deep into those pale blue eyes.

"What now?" Zoe whispered.

The wicked grin on Gwen's mouth was enough to scare her if

it wouldn't result in so much pleasure she might combust, but if this past week was any indication, Zoe was pretty sure they would both get off so many times they would lose count. Gwen stood up and headed for the door, locking it this time.

Tossing a look over her shoulder, she moved between Zoe and the desk, bending over and pulling her skirt up to reveal a black lace thong. Zoe's heart thundered, and she reached forward, unable to resist touching.

"Fuck me hard," Gwen ordered, her command soft.

Standing to comply, Zoe ran her fingers over the curve of Gwen's ass in gentle patterns before she slapped her, the sound sharp. Gwen grunted but smiled when she looked over her shoulder.

"Do it again."

Zoe spanked her several times before she slid three fingers inside Gwen's hot pussy and began a brutal rhythm. The fear of being interrupted again didn't leave the back of her mind, only this time they wouldn't be able to hide it. While Gwen might say she wouldn't fire Zoe, that didn't mean the board wouldn't if they found out what the two of them were doing, in the office even. Or that the sexual harassment claims wouldn't immediately be proven.

Gwen was soaking as Zoe plunged her fingers in and out. Zoe bent over her, kissing the line of her neck. She dashed her tongue out for a taste of salty skin. Zoe breathed heavily, sliding another finger in as she nipped Gwen's shoulder. "How hard?"

"Harder," Gwen muttered, scrunching her face up.

Writhing, Gwen clutched her fingers at the edge of the desk to hold on. Zoe slid down Gwen's body and used her mouth. She pressed into Gwen from behind, her tongue fully enveloped within her as she abandoned her fingers. Gwen gasped, sending a shiver through Zoe, and she pushed into her harder to give Gwen as much friction as possible.

Gwen's voice filled the room as she came, Zoe lapping up as much as she could. She smoothed her hands over Gwen's soft flesh and held her there for a minute before helping her to stand. Zoe straightened her skirt and fixed her hair when Gwen captured her chin and raised her face to meet their mouths in a tender kiss.

"I always knew there was something different about you," Gwen said, wiping the rest of her juices from Zoe's mouth. "I'm glad I finally found out what it was."

"Ms. Fudala—"

"I really think you should call me Gwen."

Zoe's heart thudded hard, and she repeated the name, "Gwen." It felt so weird rolling off her tongue, but at the same time it felt good. Biting her lip, she stared into those light blue eyes as she desperately searched for an answer. "What are we doing?"

Gwen's cheeks pulled tight as she smiled, a blush rising to her cheeks. She fixed her skirt and leaned against the desk, sitting like she had when she came out, but her blouse still unbuttoned too far. Instinctively, Zoe reached forward to put the buttons back into place. When she finished, Gwen cupped her cheek.

"What do you want to do? And before you say nothing, Zoe, I need an actual answer this time."

Zoe's lips parted in surprise at being called out, but she knew Gwen was right. They had to come to some sort of resolution and boundaries.

"I'll state for the record that what we have right now, I'm very comfortable with. I would love to continue it." Gwen had never sounded more confident than she did in this moment.

Nodding, Zoe ran gentle fingers over Gwen's neck and collarbone before dropping her hands to her sides. "I've only ever fantasized about this."

Gwen's lips twitched as she whispered, "Me too."

Zoe locked their gazes together, not quite believing what she heard. "I don't know what to say."

"What do you want?" Gwen ran her thumb down Zoe's cheek.

A pounding knock reverberated through the office. They

jerked with a start. Zoe's lips parted in surprise and she stepped back from Gwen.

"Open the door." It was a man's voice, one Zoe didn't recognize.

She tossed a look at Gwen, one of curiosity and confusion.

"Answer it, Zoe." Gwen straightened her shoulders and smoothed her blouse before stepping around the desk. "And then you need to call my lawyer."

"What?" Zoe furrowed her brow. "Your lawyer?"

"His number is on a card on my desk."

"Ms. Fudala—"

The pounding echoed again.

"Open the door, Zoe. I expected this might happen."

The doorknob was cold against Zoe's fingers when she clasped it. Three policemen were on the other side. Mr. Gruzska behind them. Everything was a whirlwind of emotion. Gruzska stood by silently while handcuffs slapped around Gwen's wrists. She was read her rights. Gwen made eye contact, never wavering in that connection between them.

"Um...what is she being arrested for?" Zoe sounded more timid than she wanted to. But hell, she was scared.

"Stalking."

Gwen was led out of the office, one officer behind her. Zoe froze on the spot. Nikki was right. How had she been right? How had she known?

Saying nothing, Gwen locked her eyes on Zoe right before the elevator doors closed. "What do we do now, Mr. Gruzska?"

"We put her on unpaid leave."

Zoe blew out a breath. "And me?"

"You'll stay in her office until there's no more work for you. Then we'll temporarily move you somewhere else."

"Right." Zoe squared her shoulders. "I assume there will be a meeting?"

"Keep that three o'clock slot open."

"Yes, sir." Zoe crossed her arms and went back into the office.

She shut the door behind her and closed her eyes, blowing out a breath.

What the hell?

Doing exactly as she had been told, Zoe walked into Gwen's office and found a sticky note on her desk with *Silly Girl* written on it in Gwen's scrawl. On the other side of it was a lawyer's contact card. She took it to her desk and typed in the number.

"I'm so fucked."

eighteen

BONDS THAT CAN'T BE BROKEN

Waiting outside the jail wasn't what Zoe had expected. Three. Days. It had taken her three days to get everything done to bond Gwen out. Between getting the office in order, her meetings with Gruzska, and the panic weaving masterpieces in her belly, Zoe managed to call the lawyer, the private investigator, and then do exactly what she was told to do.

And here she was. Waiting.

Waiting.

Waiting.

They'd told her to wait outside after she'd presented everything she needed. Still, seeing Gwen coming out of that building wasn't anything Zoe could anticipate. Her heart was in her throat, her eyes peeled. Was the stalker watching her now? Waiting to see if Gwen was going to get out of jail?

Or was Gwen really the stalker?

Nikki's words reverberated through Zoe's mind. She didn't want to think that. Really, she didn't. Gwen had been her boss for nearly three years. They had worked closely together, relied on each other, shared intimate moments of their lives.

But what did she really know of Gwendolyn Fudala?

The answer was not much. Gwen kept to herself. She shared

moments, yes, but it was never more than that. The professional persona she had while in the office never left when Zoe was around. Not until...not until the winery and that damned phone call afterward.

Zoe held her breath when the doors opened to the jail.

Gwen walked out, hair around her shoulders, blowing in the wind. Her gait wasn't strong like it normally was, her shoulders were drawn, and her chin was tilted down. Stepping out of the car, Zoe wrapped her arms around her middle. The air was chilled. Or was that just her countenance?

Sound of Gwen's heels clicking on the sidewalk reached her ears far before Gwen did. Zoe's lips parted. She reached out, about to touch Gwen's arm when Gwen jerked back slightly. Gwen raised her gaze, her eyes so dark in the streetlights.

"Take me home, Zoe."

"Yes, Ms. Fudala." Zoe's heart was in her throat.

She rounded the car and got in as Gwen slid into the passenger seat. Did Gwen really have no one else to call for help? Zoe was her personal assistant, that was it. Well, and her fuck-buddy? Three times in the span of a few short weeks didn't mean she was in any kind of relationship with Gwen, did it? Zoe snorted quietly as she pushed the car into drive and stepped on the gas.

The drive was quiet and long. She had so many questions she wanted to ask, but Gwen's eyes were closed, her breathing deep and slow. Perhaps she had fallen asleep. Holding her questions at bay, Zoe drove in silence.

She pulled up outside of Gwen's condo, parking by the front doors. She put the car into park and took her foot off the brake. Reaching over, she touched Gwen's arm lightly, surprised when Gwen turned to look at her with wide eyes.

"Come in with me." Gwen's voice was filled with sadness, each word dripping with exhaustion and a tinge of fear.

"Sure." Zoe bit her lip and moved her car to park in one of the designated visitor spots.

With the engine off, she was about to get out when she realized that Gwen wasn't moving. Settling back into her seat, Zoe briefly touched Gwen's arm again to get her attention. Gwen flicked her gaze up to Zoe's eyes, locking them together in a deep search for each other.

"I'm not going to ask if you're okay, Ms. Fudala. I know that you're not."

Gwen drew in a shuddering breath.

"So let's go upstairs, and I'll make some tea. Okay?"

"Yes." But still, Gwen didn't move to leave the vehicle.

"Unless you want to sit here for a minute." Zoe ran her fingers over Gwen's arm, down to her hand. Was Gwen trembling? Zoe wanted nothing more than to care for her. That was all she'd ever wanted, wasn't it? All her fantasies boiled down to one thing— taking care of Gwen.

"No. Let's go home." Gwen moved out of Zoe's grasp.

Zoe bit her lip as she got out of the car and walked side by side with Gwen toward the elevator. The ride up and the walk down the hall to Gwen's condo was also in silence. Worry filled every crevice of Zoe's body. She'd never seen Gwen like this. Then again, knowing at least an outsider's view of what Gwen had just been through did explain this odd mood switch.

"I don't have my keys," Gwen said as they reached the door.

"Oh." Zoe bit the inside of her cheek. She did remember that. Riffling through her purse, she found the spare set that Gwen had given her and handed them over. "I'll get the rest of your things from the office tomorrow and bring them to you."

Gwen raked her gaze over Zoe's body and up to her face. "Is it safe to assume they put me on leave?"

Zoe frowned. "They'll formally tell you that as soon as you can set a meeting with them."

"Perfect," Gwen murmured. She closed her eyes before reaching forward and opening the door.

As soon as they were inside, Zoe locked everything up. They didn't need an intruder into this calm moment. Or at least a moment that needed to be calm. Zoe immediately started toward the kitchen.

"I'll get the water going for tea."

"Zoe?"

She stopped.

Gwen stood stoically in the center of the entryway, her shoulders finally back in their usual position, although her head was still tilted down. Seeing Gwen in the full light of the condo was terrifying. The rings under her eyes were dark, her hair dirty and unwashed, unkempt. Zoe stuttered in a step toward her, finally stopping herself from any more forward motion.

"I'll do anything you need," Zoe whispered.

Swallowing hard, Gwen tilted her chin up and put her hand out in front of her. "I'm going to take a shower."

"Right." Zoe nodded.

Gwen walked swiftly toward the bathroom, the door closing with a resounding *click* that Zoe would never forget.

The water boiled for the tea, catching Zoe's attention. She turned off the burner and started to steep the leaves. Gwen was taking her time in the shower, not that Zoe could blame her. She'd been in jail for three days. Zoe would probably want the same. She leaned against the counter in the kitchen and played on her phone. Did she dare tell Nikki what had happened? That Gwen was out?

Zoe bit her lip and closed her eyes. What was she thinking? She was in the home of someone arrested for stalking. Obviously the police had enough proof to arrest her, which would mean that she very well was feet away from a stalker. She shook her head slowly.

"I can see the thoughts running through your head." Gwen's voice shattered her reverie.

"Ms. Fudala," Zoe answered nervously, straightening up at the intrusion. "I'm sorry. I..."

Gwen canted her head to the side, running the towel over her wet hair. She was wrapped tightly in a fuzzy cotton robe, one that

Zoe had seen hanging from the back of the bathroom door several times. Seeing it on Gwen now sent shivers through her.

"You think the charges might be real." Gwen's lips pulled tight, not quite a smile, but not a frown either.

"Ms. Fudala—"

Gwen cut her off, waving a hand in front of her. "You may leave if you want. Thank you for all you've done."

Zoe's heart broke. She'd never seen Gwen look so defeated. Everything they had gone through over the years, and this was what shattered her. Zoe had to do something. Stepping right into Gwen's space, Zoe wrapped her arms around her and tugged Gwen into her chest.

Gwen's sob tore through the room unexpectedly. Zoe pulled her in tighter, raking her fingers up and down Gwen's back as she held on. She had no plans of leaving now. Not when this was what she was presented with.

"I'm not abandoning you," Zoe whispered. She had no idea what else to say, nothing that might help.

Gwen shook her head and pulled away slightly, but her hands came up and circled Zoe's back, gripping her desperately.

"I can't imagine what the last few days have been like for you, but I'm not going to leave you to deal with this by yourself." Zoe tilted her cheek into Gwen's wet hair. The scent of Gwen's shampoo filled her senses, enrapturing her. "You'll be okay."

"I don't know, Zoe. I just don't know if I will be." Gwen dug her fingers into Zoe's back, clutching her.

This was raw.

"Tell me what I can do," Zoe whispered. "I'll do anything."

And she would. No matter what doubts her brain had, those thoughts Nikki had put into her mind, Zoe knew Gwen. It was impossible that she'd been stalking someone for years, that she'd taken the time and energy to have that obsession with someone. And all for what? Turning her cheek, Zoe pressed a delicate kiss into Gwen's skin, just under her ear.

"We thought this might happen. But I didn't think…" Gwen

trailed off. She turned her face into Zoe's neck, sucking in a breath as hot tears spilled down her cheeks and onto Zoe's skin. "...I didn't know how bad it would be."

"Your lawyers are already working on it."

"I know," Gwen whispered. "I know they are, but I feel so stuck. My hands are tied."

"They've been tied for years." Zoe squeezed her tighter. "But I think this might be the first time you're really free of them. At least as free as you can be."

She had to trust this, right? She had to trust that Gwen was telling her the truth. What would be the fallout if she didn't? Gwen would start stalking her? That she would be Gwen's next victim?

"I'm not free." Gwen pulled back, brushing her fingers over her cheeks. Her eyes were red, the dark purple rings prominent against her pale skin. "I'm not."

"Not yet. But eventually, you will be. You have to believe that."

"It's hard some days." Gwen closed her eyes and shook her head. "I'm sorry. This isn't a burden you should have to deal with."

"Ms. Fudala," Zoe stated firmly, catching Gwen's eye. "This isn't a burden."

"I know when you're lying." Gwen snagged the tea pot and poured herself a mug. She wrapped her fingers around it and sipped, humming at the flavor.

Zoe's body vibrated as Gwen parted her lips. She was bare of any makeup, her hair still wet and down her back, her skin still pink from the heat of the water, damp from it. What would she taste like now? Now that she was clean and wet and vulnerable. This wasn't the Gwen Fudala that Zoe was used to seeing. This woman was bare, stripped of all her defenses.

"I don't know what to do," Gwen murmured. "For the first time in my entire life, I don't know what to do."

"You'll figure it out." Zoe couldn't drag her eyes away. "You just got out of jail. Give it a night of rest before you run full force into whatever is coming."

Gwen snorted lightly. The sound was adorable. Zoe wasn't sure what to do with this side of Gwen.

"I should eat," Gwen started. "But I can't summon the energy for it."

"Then eat in the morning." Zoe slid in closer, leaning against the countertop, right next to where Gwen pressed into it. "I think your soul needs more care than your stomach tonight."

"My soul?" Gwen raised an eyebrow in Zoe's direction.

"Yes." Zoe had never felt more certain about something in her life. "Seeing you taken out in handcuffs..." She pressed her hand along the back of the counter, making sure that Gwen would know she was there no matter what. "I can't imagine what you went through in the last few days. Hell, I can't imagine what you've gone through in the last twelve years."

Gwen stilled. She looked Zoe over carefully, her gaze flitting from here to there. Finally, she took another sip of her tea. "Stay with me tonight."

"All night?" Did that mean Gwen wanted more? Did she want sex?

Nodding, Gwen stared into her cup, as if the tea leaves held all the answers. "I haven't felt safe in a very long time."

"And you'll feel safe with me here?" God, Zoe wanted an answer. Her entire life seemed to hinge on what Gwen would say next. But that couldn't be right, could it? Gwen was her boss and a distraction, nothing more.

"I don't know." Gwen's voice dropped so quiet that Zoe had to strain to hear her. "But I'd like to find out."

"Come on."

Zoe gripped Gwen's hand. She put the tea onto the counter, knowing that she'd clean it up in the morning. Gwen allowed Zoe to lead her toward the bedroom. She settled Gwen under the blankets before drawing the curtains and closing the door. Her heart was in her throat as she slid onto the bed and slipped under the covers. She pressed her front to Gwen's back, tugging Gwen tightly against her.

Dragging in a deep breath, Zoe let it out slowly. She rested her head on the pillow and allowed her eyelids to flutter shut. She might fall asleep first, only because she had no idea if Gwen would actually sleep. But at least this way Gwen would get what she needed. Zoe pressed her lips to the back of Gwen's neck and said the only thing that came to her mind.

"I'd like to find out, too."

nineteen

SEXUAL HARASSMENT TAKE TWO

"Uh...hello?"

Zoe walked into the office to find Gruzska waiting for her. He leaned against her desk, the door to the office open, and Zoe had no way to get to the side of her desk to put her things away. She pressed her lips together tightly and stared at him.

"We have a meeting at eight."

Zoe knew damn well it was five minutes until eight, when she was actually due in the office. She'd spent the night at Gwen's, and when they'd woken up in the morning, she'd made coffee, cleaned up the unused tea from the night before, and left to get ready for work. She hadn't been certain about leaving Gwen by herself all day but Gwen had seemed better at least. More back to her normal self.

So finding Gruzska in the office waiting for her this morning was not what she had expected. "I didn't realize one had been scheduled."

"It's scheduled now." He still didn't move.

Zoe was lost on what to do. She wanted to be at her desk, her safe space, and the tone of his voice was putting her on edge. "What's the meeting about?"

"You know exactly what it's about." He pursed his lips.

A shiver ran through her. Did he know about the desk the other week? Had she not managed to hide Gwen under it swiftly enough? Her heart pattered away relentlessly, and Zoe had to bolster herself. "How long will this take?"

"As long as it takes."

"Okay." Zoe pulled her lip tightly into her mouth. She bit down on it hard enough to bring her senses back around. He clearly wasn't going to leave her in the office by herself, and that was the main issue she was just now coming to grips with. He was going to escort her to the meeting, insist that she be there. She was getting fired. "Can I put my stuff away?"

"No."

"Okay," Zoe repeated. She hitched her purse and bag higher up on her shoulder. The straps in her hand were the only lifeline she had. She couldn't even text Gwen to tell her what was going on, not that she should do that. Gwen had enough on her plate to deal with.

"Now, Zoe."

"Right." Turning on her toes, Zoe left the office.

Mr. Gruzska followed closely behind, and he shut and locked the door behind her. Again that resounding *click*. It was the end of the world as she had known it, and whatever chaos she was about to be thrown into. Who knew one day at a winery, one rogue email, and one phone call would flip her life like this.

A stalker had never even been on her radar until then. Zoe stopped by the elevator, not sure which direction Mr. Gruzska was going to lead her. To her immediate termination and straight to the lobby or down to the conference room to give her a proper send-off?

"Conference room," Gruzska said firmly.

Zoe let out a sigh of relief, although she wasn't sure why. This was only prolonging the inevitable. She shivered as she turned down the hallway and walked toward the same room she'd been dragged into the last time he'd called her in for a meeting. Clenching her jaw, Zoe held her breath as she stepped inside, finding Frankie and Sandra sitting in the same chairs they'd been in before.

Sliding into her seat, Zoe dropped her bags next to her feet and tried to hold her shaking hands still. What was she supposed to do now? Because she couldn't defend herself. If they asked her outright what she and Gwen had been doing at the desk that day, she couldn't lie. She was a horrible liar.

The door shut, and again, Zoe couldn't help but think she was going to be flat on her ass in the next five minutes.

Fired.

Destitute.

Broke.

Unhireable.

Her future hinged on how she managed to walk through this conversation, on finding a way to salvage her work history enough that she could get another job in the future. She bit the inside of her cheek to center herself. *Think, Zoe. Think.*

"We received your second complaint," Sandra started, disappointment in her tone. "I don't know why you insisted the first was false and then submitted a second."

Second? Zoe's ears perked up. She'd never filed the first complaint, and now there was a second? She swallowed an overwhelming lump in her throat. Her entire body burned as if she would be consumed in the pits of hell for the sins she'd committed.

"We're concerned that you tried to pull back on your first complaint because Gwen Fudala was still working here," Sandra continued.

Still working here? Did that mean they'd fired her? Zoe couldn't be the one to break that news to Gwen, but considering their conversation last night, no one from the office had talked to her yet. About anything.

"We wanted to use this time, with Gwen not in the building, to truly sit down and discuss these claims with you."

Zoe still hadn't said a word. What was she supposed to say? It was all false? It was all a bunch of lies? That Gwen's stalker was doing this? That Gwen was being stalked even though she was arrested for stalking only a few days ago? Zoe's chest was so tight that it was hard to breathe. It hurt to draw air into her lungs. But she couldn't relax, not now.

"Tell us, in your own words, what happened." Sandra locked her gaze on Zoe.

What was she supposed to say? She had no idea what the complaint was even for. Panic swelled in Zoe's chest. She wanted to call Gwen, tell her what was happening. She wanted to text Nikki and get advice. She needed to ease her mind. She needed to breathe.

"Relax, Zoe. You're not in trouble," Frankie commented, his voice so much softer than Sandra's.

Why wasn't he the HR person? He'd do a much better job at it.

"I'm sorry," Zoe murmured. "I didn't..." She trailed off. She was so fucked. "I didn't file a report, so I don't know what you're talking about."

"This again?" Gruzska muttered sharply. "Gwen Fudala is on leave from the company, Zoe. She can't retaliate against you."

"I'm not afraid of retaliation." Zoe's words had a bite to them, one she hadn't expected. She needed to make sure that she could use Gruzska as a reference, especially because Gwen's reference would be complicated by their relationship and the fact that Zoe had just bailed her out of jail. "I'm not. I don't know what complaint has been filed."

"Sexual harassment." Sandra's tone was cool.

Zoe locked their gazes and shook her head. "Again, I don't know what's in the complaint since I didn't file it."

"Sexual advancements in the office. Unwanted touching. Late night house calls."

"I will cop to late night house calls," Zoe said. "But never for sexual reasons. Ms. Fudala works hard, and sometimes she needs something at home. So yes, I bring it to her. But she's never coerced me to her condo for the purposes of sex."

If anything, it had been the opposite.

Zoe had seduced Gwen. Tightening her lips together so she wouldn't say that—that would be the complete wrong thing to say—Zoe looked each of the executives over. "Are you firing me?"

"No," Frankie answered.

"That isn't the intent of this meeting," Sandra corrected. "But if we find you've done something, or if these claims are false, then this situation may come to termination."

"The claims are false." Zoe dropped her gaze to the papers in front of Sandra. "Because I didn't make them. I promise you I don't know what's in those files. I didn't file any complaints against Ms. Fudala. She's the best boss that I've worked for."

"Two complaints in a few short weeks." Sandra canted her head to the side, studying Zoe. "You're saying that someone hacked into your computer to do this not once but twice?"

Zoe nodded, her mouth suddenly very dry. "Y-yes. I don't know how else they would have done it." She wasn't a computer wiz. She understood the programs that she needed to get her job done, she could mess around with a few others, but when it came to hacking, Zoe was clueless. "Is Ms. Fudala fired?"

"Ms. Fudala is on leave," Mr. Gruzska jumped in. He and Sandra made eye contact, an unstated communication flying between them.

"Then I need to rearrange her schedule. She has a list of appointments this week that need to be handled."

"They will be," Mr. Gruzska said. "Mr. Cohen here will be taking over part of her workload. The rest will be divided among some junior staff."

Perfect. Zoe was glad she had managed to keep that word in her head and not out loud. She hated working with the junior team. She guessed it was a good thing that the party was done with and the next one wasn't for a few months. It gave her time to sort out what was happening in between.

"And these sexual harassment claims?" Zoe prodded. She needed to know exactly what was going to happen.

"They will be investigated."

"You won't find anything."

"And if we find you made false claims, you are liable to be terminated."

"Fire me for it then." Zoe jerked her chin up. She wasn't good at playing these games. She never had been. Zoe dragged in a deep breath. "If that's everything, can I please get back to work?"

Sandra opened her mouth like she was going to speak, but Frankie was the one who spoke first.

"We're only trying to help you, Zoe."

"I don't think you are." Zoe glared. "If you were trying to help me, then you'd listen to what I had to say. You'd listen to what Ms. Fudala is facing. You'd see the connections between everything, that this person, whoever is stalking Ms. Fudala, has gone to extremes to make her life a living hell, and you would be able to see that this is only one more extreme."

Sandra shook her head. "You mean the person that Ms. Fudala is stalking."

"I..." Zoe stopped talking. Did they really believe that Gwen was capable of that? She'd worked for them for years, they *knew* her, so if they believed it, shouldn't Zoe?

"I can see that you're very protective of Ms. Fudala," Frankie said, his voice a placating tenor again. "Don't let your desire to protect her or your loyalties to her because she hired you get in the way of what's really happening."

Is that what this is?

Zoe had no idea, but she didn't like the way they were talking to her. Like she was incompetent. She wasn't. "I didn't file those complaints."

"We'll be investigating them deeply."

"Good. May I leave now?" Zoe had already reached down to grab her purse and her bag. Even if they told her no, she was going to be leaving. She'd had enough of this. When they nodded her dismissal, Zoe raced from the room.

She locked herself in her office and pressed her forehead to the cold door, her hand still on the doorknob. She wouldn't cry. Her fingers trembled as she reached into her pocket and pulled out her phone. There was a text from Gwen, asking if she'd gotten to work okay. Instead of answering it, Zoe called her.

"Hey, I didn't think you'd call."

"Gwen?" Zoe's voice wavered.

"What's wrong? Did she do something?"

Zoe shook her head, forgetting that Gwen couldn't see her. She had to get her shit together so that she could say something, because freaking Gwen out more than she already had would be the worst thing to happen today. "I was just called in to talk to the executives again."

Gwen said nothing. Silence reverberated.

"They said I filed a second sexual harassment complaint."

"Oh, Zoe." Gwen sighed heavily. "If you can get that paperwork, please send it to me, but if you can't, don't worry about it. I'll have my lawyers deal with it."

"They said..." Zoe had to take a deep breath. She pushed off the door and looked at her desk. It had been a safe space for her at one point. A place where she and Gwen had fucked, and it had been beautiful. Now she wasn't even sure if she could call it hers. "They said they haven't fired you yet."

"No, but it's coming."

That had been Zoe's fear. Especially with the way the conversation was going.

"I'm a liability now."

"Since the stalking has ramped up?" She already knew the answer, but she couldn't stop herself from asking the question. "I'm sorry. I shouldn't be making you talk about this."

"It's as much your problem as it is mine. Did they put you on leave?"

"No. But they did threaten to fire me because of the false claims."

"I'm so sorry."

Zoe blinked back tears. They stung her eyes. As much as she hated them, she couldn't stop them from falling. They curved around her cheeks to her chin, dropping off and disappearing into the ugly dark brown carpet. "It's not your fault."

"It is. I should have..." Gwen groaned. "I should have kept my distance better. I should have protected you more."

"You can't live in a vacuum. You deserve happiness." Zoe had never known truer words than those, and she hoped Gwen heard them and believed them. "You deserve to have a partner and fall in love and have a life."

"I do," Gwen whispered. "And so do you."

"I don't know what to do." Zoe sat on the edge of her desk and cradled her phone. "I don't know."

"You have to do what they tell you to, at least for now. Keep your head down. Maybe float your resume out and try to find a backup."

"They think you did it, you know." Zoe bit her lip. She hadn't meant to say that. But who else was she supposed to talk to? Nikki would just tell her she was stupid for even believing Gwen might not have been doing this. And despite her own wonderings, Zoe wanted to believe that Gwen was the victim.

"I know. I expected them to. There's enough proof against me, Zoe. You have to see that."

"But you didn't do it." *Did you?* She left that last part off. She couldn't force the words past her lips.

"Zoe, I was arrested. I've been in jail for three days, and I'm going to face a trial. Will I fight it? Yes. But you need to keep your eyes open. I'm a liability to everyone right now. I'm not worth it."

Oh, Gwen couldn't be more wrong. Zoe wanted to shout that from the rooftop, but she kept silent. If the police thought Gwen did it. If their bosses did. If Nikki did. Why was Zoe the odd one out?

"Go back to work, Zoe." Gwen's firm voice broke through her panic. "I'll talk to you soon. Keep your head down, do the work I know you're capable of doing, and you show them that you're worth everything you are."

"Will you come back to work?"

"I don't know. Right now, what I'm focused on is what's right in front of me."

"And what's in front of you?" Zoe closed her eyes, focusing on Gwen's voice. She couldn't stand to look at the empty office across from her, knowing that she was probably going to have to pack up all of Gwen's personal items and bring them to her, that she was going to be the one that would have to tell her goodbye.

"This lawsuit, the trial, and you."

"Me?" Zoe tensed.

"Yes. You."

What was she supposed to say to that? Zoe clenched her fist and stood up. She smoothed down her blazer and stopped in front of Gwen's office door. She was just about to speak when Gwen said, "Go to work, Zoe."

"Yes, Ms. Fudala." Hanging up, Zoe only had one thought. *Had she truly fallen in love with a stalker?*

twenty

BEST FRIENDS KNOW BEST

"Nikki." Zoe breathed out her name. She was practically in tears. They hadn't even let her leave work early, and Zoe had spent the whole day trying to focus and failing miserably. She'd debated texting Gwen multiple times, but there had been such a finality to their conversation that she didn't have the heart to try.

"What's wrong?" Nikki's voice was firm as it carried through the phone.

Zoe was instantly comforted—at least as much as she could be. There was one person on her side through all of this, and that was Nikki. She had been there through all of Zoe's troubles in the last three years. They were best friends.

"I can't even begin to explain on the phone. Come over tonight."

"When?"

Relief flooded her. This was exactly what she'd needed. Someone who had her back no matter what. "I'm leaving now."

"See you soon then."

Zoe was so lucky to have a friend who would drop everything just to help her. She hadn't been so lucky growing up to have friends like that. They always seemed to vanish as she changed jobs or moved to different places. The concept of a best friend for life, or even one that stuck around for more than a few years, was foreign. But Nikki was proving to be exactly that.

Packing up her office, making sure that she logged out and closed everything, Zoe left the building. As soon as she was outside, relief washed through her again. She just needed to escape. By the time she got to her apartment, Nikki was already waiting at her door.

"Thank God." Zoe opened her arms and fell into Nikki, wrapping her in a hug.

Nikki tightened her grasp, running her hands up and down Zoe's back and just holding her. Zoe closed her eyes and breathed in the comfort she had been longing for. This was perfect. Nikki wasn't Gwen, and in some ways, she was so much better. Nikki understood things that Gwen didn't. They had a different kind of relationship, and while Zoe longed to have that kind of relationship with Gwen, they weren't there yet. They were still in the fun stage of sex and lust.

And she wasn't sure they would ever get much deeper than that.

"What happened?" Nikki whispered.

Zoe shook her head and held a little tighter. It took her another few minutes before she felt she could straighten up and stand on her own. Nikki wiped at her cheeks. When had she started crying? Zoe had to take three calming breaths before she fished in her purse for her keys.

She led Nikki inside in silence. When the door was locked, Zoe wanted to collapse again. She'd never been the strong silent type, not like Gwen, but when she was in her boss's vicinity lately, Zoe didn't feel as though she could be the emotional one. Not when Gwen needed her to be sane and strong.

She immediately sat on her couch and collapsed onto it, curling her legs under her after she pushed her shoes off her feet. Nikki followed, staying close and setting a hand on her knee to offer comfort.

"Seriously, Zoe. You're freaking me out here."

Zoe shuddered. "I came into the office to another complaint that I apparently filed, but I didn't file it. I swear."

Nikki's face immediately hardened. The support Zoe had been hoping for wasn't entirely there anymore, but she had hope that Nikki would do what was best for her. That she would push aside whatever reservations she had in order to take care of Zoe because that's what Zoe really needed right then.

"I don't know what to do, Nikki. They've put her on leave, and I get that, but I'm left without a boss and in the middle of an investigation that I didn't actually start."

"Take a deep breath." Nikki tightened her grip on Zoe's knee. She flicked her dark brown hair over her shoulder revealing pearl drop earrings, ones that looked really familiar. Zoe parted her lips, but Nikki leaned forward. "You're not taking a deep breath."

"Right." Zoe's mind worked overtime. She really should just stop thinking for a minute and try to clear her head. She needed to listen to what her best friend was telling her. Nikki was someone she could trust. Doing as she was told, Zoe focused on her breathing and closed her eyes.

"This too will pass," Nikki said, her voice gentle and calming. "Everything will work itself out."

"I get that. I mean, I do, but this is all so insane." Zoe shivered, popping her eyes open to look at Nikki directly. "What would you do?"

"I think I would trust my gut instinct."

"Yeah? What's that telling you?" Zoe covered Nikki's hand, enjoying the physical comfort she desperately needed to center herself. If she didn't have it, then she'd be floating around in space, wandering on her own, and she'd no doubt come up with all the worst-case scenarios, which would only get her overactive imagination going again.

"I think she did it."

Zoe tensed. She bit her cheek and clenched her jaw. She wanted to move away from Nikki, but she couldn't make herself.

She was frozen in place, perhaps even time. Because what exactly did Nikki mean by that?

"I think you're blinded by your crush, Zoe, and I'm sorry to be the one to break it to you."

"B-break what to me?" Zoe barely made the words leave her lips. She was cold, clammy. Her entire body told her to get up and run, but she couldn't make herself move. Someone could come in, the stalker could come looking for her, and she wouldn't be able to run.

"With everything you've told me, I can't stop thinking that she's the one doing all of this."

"Doing what?" Zoe asked, but she already knew. The answer was on the tip of her tongue. Nikki had said it before, and she wasn't going to be the friend that Zoe wanted. But perhaps she was going to be the one that she needed.

"She's the stalker," Nikki whispered, leaned in, and locked her gaze on Zoe's face. Her eyes were wide, full of serious truth.

But it wasn't the truth.

It couldn't be.

Gwen was innocent.

"Listen to your gut," Nikki implored. "She was arrested for stalking, Zoe. People don't just get arrested for stalking without actual proof that they're doing something."

"She's trying to protect herself," Zoe whispered, but she honestly wasn't sure the words had left her lips.

"Look at the facts, sweetie." Nikki grabbed Zoe's hand hard, squeezing once before easing up. "Please look at everything that's happening."

"What facts?" Zoe was very nearly in tears. This was too much.

"Got paper and pen?" Nikki's eyes lit up, as if she'd been waiting for Zoe to actually give her the time of day and maybe give some credence to what she was saying.

Zoe's stomach twisted hard. Was she really doing this? Was

she really going to let Nikki try to convince her that everything she thought about Gwen was wrong?

"In the junk drawer."

Guess she was.

Nikki stood up and went to the kitchen, opening the drawer. Zoe closed her eyes and pressed herself into the couch cushion. She couldn't believe she was going to allow this to happen. She really couldn't. Her heart broke that she would even entertain the possibility that Gwen was the real stalker. How could a woman that busy and that organized even have time for something like that?

Clearly she had time to defend against it.

Shut up, Zoe! She chastised herself. Now she was making Nikki's argument for her.

Nikki sat next to her again on the couch, the cushion sinking with the weight of her body as Nikki pressed in close to her. Once again she brushed her dark brown hair behind her ear, and that pearl drop earring glistened in the light. Zoe frowned at it.

"Why did you dye your hair?"

"What?" Nikki frowned and faced Zoe directly.

"Why did you dye your hair? I never really asked that."

"Don't you like it?"

Zoe's stomach twisted sharply again. She wasn't about to tell her best friend that she hated the new hairdo, but she also still wanted the answer. It was such a change from Nikki's original blonde. "Yeah, I do. But why did you dye it?"

"Oh, I was just going back to my natural color." Nikki waved the comment off and put pen to paper.

Natural color?

Zoe frowned, but she didn't push. One problem at a time, and Nikki's new hair color was the least of her problems. In fact, it wasn't anywhere on the list.

"Let's start at the beginning. When did you even find out about 'the stalking'?" Nikki put the last two words in air quotes, as if to prove that it really wasn't happening.

Pulling her lip between her teeth, Zoe had to think back on it. "It was after we went to the winery."

"You both went?"

Zoe shook her head. "I went, and then she met me there. Something about being told to go even though she didn't want to. I don't know. I was a little tipsy at the time." Zoe's cheeks burned. She'd been more than a little tipsy, and Nikki would know that. But she didn't want to admit another fault and embarrassing moment out loud if she could avoid it.

"Right, so the winery." Nikki wrote it down on the yellow legal pad. "Which only came up because of the pictures, right?"

"Right." Zoe's cheeks heated. She wouldn't confess to Nikki that those pictures had also included one of her and Gwen together, that she had stashed that photo away in her desk so that no one would know. *Perfect.* It was still there. She hadn't actually taken it out and brought it down to the police station yet.

"So there were pictures of you and her together, right?"

"Yeah." Zoe clenched her fingers tightly into her palm, her nails biting into her flesh. "We work together, so yeah."

Nikki frowned and looked up at her. "But it didn't become a thing until after Gwen knew you were interested in her?"

"Knew I was what?" Zoe's stomach plummeted. "What does that have to do with anything?"

"Zoe." Nikki's tone was full of pity, and Zoe hated it. "Gwen didn't start telling you about her stalking until she figured out that you had a massive crush on her. This is all to turn you off from any kind of relationship with her."

"What? That makes no sense."

"Of course it does. You're not her type at all."

"Nikki, you're insane." Zoe curled tighter in on herself. "She wouldn't be doing this because of a crush."

"No? Then why would she stalk someone?"

"I don't know. Why does anyone stalk anyone? They're usually sociopaths."

Nikki paled. She pressed her lips together hard, the tip of the pen digging into the paper to the point that it ripped right through it. "She *is* a sociopath."

Cold washed through Zoe. Surely she would have noticed if Gwen had sociopathic tendencies. But nothing like that had ever come up. Gwen was a demanding boss, she rarely let people into her inner circle—well, at work anyway. But Zoe had been let in, hadn't she? They'd had sex, multiple times. Didn't that give Zoe some kind of internal viewpoint that others didn't have?

"I can't believe you can't see it!" Nikki's voice reached screeching levels. "She's using you. She's getting everything she wants—sympathy, victimizations—and you're playing right into it."

Was that really what it all was? Zoe clenched her muscles, the tightness in her chest increasing.

"She's manipulating you."

"She's not," Zoe defended, but even to her own ears it sounded weak. "She's struggling right now."

"Who isn't?" Nikki scoffed and ran her fingers through her hair. "Look, I'm not the asshole here. I'm just trying to help you see what's going on."

"Nothing is going on." Now she was lying? What was Zoe's next tactic? Melt into the couch and pretend she didn't even exist? She'd called Nikki over here to help her deal with the stress from the day and instead Nikki was yelling at her.

"Zoe." Nikki's tone softened. She must have noted Zoe's obvious discomfort. "I want to protect you. That's it. I'm worried about you."

Tears brimmed in Zoe's eyes. She'd gotten dragged into this drama in seconds flat, and she had no idea what to do next. That had been why she'd called Nikki. Help. She needed more help than she could even fathom.

"You could be in danger."

Except Zoe never felt like she was in danger when Gwen was around. No matter how many scares there had been, she hadn't been afraid for her own life. She'd seen that fear in Gwen, time and again over the last few weeks, but not for Zoe.

"She's the stalker, Zoe."

Zoe wasn't going to admit to that. Nikki's hand was back on her knee, and she leaned in trying to catch Zoe's attention. Pressing her lips hard, Zoe looked into Nikki's dark eyes. "It's a clusterfuck."

"Yeah, yeah it is." Nikki smiled a little. "Can you see my points?"

Nodding, Zoe tightened in on herself again. She could see exactly what Nikki was talking about, but that didn't mean that she agreed with it. The tension between them rose, Nikki's fingers digging into Zoe's thigh. The silence was thick with guilt, with fear, with disagreement.

Finally, Nikki sighed heavily. She swallowed. Zoe was riveted to every move. Something about Nikki tonight wasn't the Nikki she had expected or wanted. This wasn't the friend she needed.

"I'm scared I'll lose you," Nikki whispered.

Lose her how? Was Zoe pulling away because of her relationship changing with Gwen? Because of the trust growing between them?

"You don't talk to me anymore."

That was it. Zoe clenched her jaw hard and covered Nikki's hand again. "I'm so sorry. I didn't mean to do that."

Nikki nodded, her eyes falling closed. "I know you didn't."

"I'll work better to fix that."

"Thanks." Nikki gave a wry smile. "What are you going to do about your boss?"

"I don't know if there's anything I can do. I'm probably going to be put on unpaid leave like she is if I fight these harassment claims. I can't afford not to work. I need the income."

"You can always come live with me if it comes down to that."

As much as Zoe appreciated the offer, that was the last thing that she wanted. She clenched her jaw tightly and stared at their hands wrapped together. "It's not just that, this could ruin any future job that I try to get. I don't know what to do. One wrong move and all of it will unravel."

"I know you're not going to like what I have to say." Nikki's voice was soft, gentle.

"Which is what?" At this point, Zoe would take any advice she could get.

"I think you need to save yourself. Cut ties with Gwen and save yourself. No one else is looking out for you but me, and it's time you start doing that."

Zoe's stomach twisted sharply.

"You need to cut Gwen off."

As much as she appreciated Nikki's advice, Zoe knew one thing for certain. She couldn't—she wouldn't—leave Gwen out to hang on her own. Zoe would always be there for her. Whether it was naive of her to think that Gwen wasn't taking advantage of her, Zoe wasn't disloyal. She would stand by her boss no matter what.

"You're probably right," Zoe murmured, guilt eating away at her stomach. The wedge between her and Nikki grew significantly, and Zoe had no idea how to fix it. They were both stuck in their own opinions on this one, and one of them was going to have to give. Hopefully it wouldn't lead to the end of their friendship.

Zoe couldn't handle that, not with everything going on.

twenty-one

WHEN THINGS GET HEATED

Three days at work without Gwen was a lot. By the time Zoe dragged herself to her apartment she was exhausted, and the week had beaten her down so much. As soon as she had her key in and the door open, Zoe gasped. Her apartment was stifling.

Like sweat down her back instantly.

Like sauna level.

"What the hell?" Zoe shut and locked the door behind her, a habit she'd been sure to do since all the drama had started. She walked immediately to the thermostat and flipped it right off. It was set at ninety.

"How did that happen?" Zoe muttered before dropping her bags on the floor and stripping out of her jacket and her blazer. She could already feel the sweat forming along her skin, her cheeks on fire, and her head stuffy.

The knock on her door startled her. Zoe pressed a hand to her heart as she stared at it. It took her a few seconds to get her wits about her, but she made her way as quietly as she could to the door and peeked through the peephole.

Gwen.

Zoe immediately unlocked the door and opened it. She couldn't help the smile and relief that flooded through her at seeing Gwen standing there, dressed down but still looking stunning. "What are you doing here?"

"I thought we could talk."

Zoe opened the door wider and let Gwen walk inside, instantly regretting it when Gwen faced her with confusion. "Why is it so hot in here?"

Because you walked in. Zoe bit her lip. "I must have hit the thermostat accidentally when I left this morning."

Gwen was already stripping off her jacket and dropping it on the back of Zoe's old second-hand couch. "Are you sure it was you?"

"Yeah..." Zoe trailed off, distracted by the shifting of Gwen's body in her tight tank top. God, she was stunning. It had been days since they'd seen each other, longer since they had touched each other, but as soon as Gwen was in the room, Zoe wanted nothing more than to be near her.

"Zoe," Gwen chastised, a sly smile on her lips. "Are you sure you're the one who turned the heat up?"

"Yeah. Who else would it be?" Zoe managed to drag her gaze up to Gwen's pale eyes. She swallowed the lump in her throat that told her she wanted nothing more than sex and ordered all those old walls to come back up.

"You know who." Gwen crossed her arms as if suddenly chilled. Perhaps she was, though not by the temperature in the room. "She did it to me a few times years ago."

"Did she?" Zoe frowned and flicked her gaze back to the thermostat. "The door was locked when I got home."

"I'm sure she has a key."

That sent a chill right through Zoe. "We shouldn't be here then."

Gwen sent her a sharp look. "Did you honestly think she didn't? Or that she doesn't have a key to my condo?"

Zoe hadn't really thought about it. Gwen had been wrapped up in this stalking business for years. Zoe had only been introduced to it recently, and she had a lot of catching up to do on exactly what to look out for. "That must be terrifying."

Gwen closed her eyes in misery. "I thought we should talk."

"Okay." Zoe moved to the couch, sitting down even though it was still stifling inside. She probably should open a window or something, but with the serious look Gwen was giving her, she didn't want to ruin any chance that they would actually talk. Still, Nikki's words echoed in the back of her mind—Gwen knows what she's doing, Gwen is the stalker.

Gwen hesitated, but she did sit next to Zoe, her body still stiff. Had they lost the ease between them already? Zoe reached over and touched Gwen's hand lightly. "I'm sorry I can't offer you anything to drink."

Gwen waved her off. "I think alcohol is the last thing I need tonight, but thank you."

"Right. So what did you want to talk about?" Zoe reached up to her oxford shirt and undid the top three buttons. Her bra was already damp from sweat, and if she didn't take care of the oppressive heat soon, she was going to have to do a lot more laundry in the future.

Gwen's gaze dropped to Zoe's breasts, and she didn't move it back up. Intrigued, Zoe observed, watching Gwen's distraction, something she had never openly done before. She was always on point in her thinking and actions.

"See something you like?" Zoe asked, breaking the silence between them.

Gwen immediately looked her directly in the eye, her cheeks reddening even more than they already had, and it definitely wasn't from the thermostat issue. "Yes."

Zoe smiled, a warmth of pleasure hitting her at once. She hadn't expected Gwen to be so open with the compliments. She'd been so standoffish for years, and this was a different side that Zoe was loving getting to know.

"You should change your locks and not tell your super."

"I don't think I can do that," Zoe replied. "It's a violation of my lease."

"It's for your safety," Gwen responded as if there was no argument to what she was saying. "I don't want you to be hurt by this."

"Do you think that you'll hurt me?" Where had that question come from? Zoe had no clue, but after the week she'd had, she wasn't sure what to do next. She'd been stuck in a hell of having zero choices and just getting washed in whatever direction someone else decided for her.

"I know I will," Gwen whispered. She folded her hands tightly in her lap, as if preventing herself from touching Zoe in some way she shouldn't. "We shouldn't be doing this."

"Doing what?" Zoe wanted to smooth the pain that was so clearly written on Gwen's face. She wanted to kiss it away and make everything better, but that was impossible.

"I'm dragging you into this. She's been here. I know she has."

"Is that why you're so tense?" Zoe skimmed her hand down Gwen's shoulder to her fingers. "I might have just hit the thermostat—"

"Zoe," Gwen's voice broke on her name. She stared down at her hands in her lap, her face falling, her demeanor so downtrodden. Zoe had never seen her like this. What had happened in the last few days that she'd missed? She'd been so caught up in her own life that she hadn't done her due diligence to check in on Gwen when she really should have. "Don't lie to yourself about what's really happening here."

Zoe froze. She hadn't quite thought about it like that before. A drop of sweat slid between her breasts, tickling her skin. But she couldn't look away from Gwen's intense gaze. "Ms. Fudala..."

"That's what she wants. If we ignore the signs, then she can continue to do what she's always done."

"Which is what?"

"Make me crazy." Gwen let out a wry laugh. "Distract me. Disturb me. There are so many things..."

"Gwen," Zoe murmured. "You can't keep living like this."

"I know." Gwen reached up and swiped her fingers under her eyes.

Was she crying? Zoe couldn't quite tell, but she wanted to make Gwen feel as safe as possible. She ran her fingers gently against Gwen's shoulder, offering what support she could. Zoe leaned in slightly. "Does she make you feel crazy?"

"Every day." Gwen half laughed and half scoffed. "I don't even know what's real and what's not anymore."

"I'm real," Zoe answered quickly. Why did she have so much compassion for Gwen? Everything about this woman called to her. It had from the first day they met, but since they started a deeper relationship, Zoe had an even stronger pull to Gwen.

"You're the only real thing in my life right now." Gwen reached up cupping Zoe's cheek. Their gazes locked, Zoe's breath vanishing from her lungs with the sincerity in Gwen's gaze. "You're the only one I trust."

A heavy weight fell on Zoe's shoulders. *The only one?* How could anyone live like this? So utterly isolated. So desperate for help and companionship. And Zoe was all she had to rely on? "You don't have any family? Friends?"

"Not anymore." Gwen frowned again, her eyes fluttering closed. "Zoe, I don't want you to be hurt."

In all the time she had known Gwen, she'd never quite understood what levels of protection Gwen took for her. It wasn't just in the work levels—it was in the personal ones, too. This just proved that Nikki had to be wrong. Gwen couldn't possibly be callous enough to be a stalker.

"I'm not hurt." Zoe pulled Gwen into her chest, folding her arms around Gwen's shoulders in a hug that she didn't want to let go of. "I'm not hurt."

"She was here." Gwen's voice rattled.

"Yeah, but I'm okay. You're okay." Zoe stroked her fingers through Gwen's long brown hair. They stayed still for minutes on end, Zoe listening to Gwen's soft and steady breathing and holding on tightly.

Eventually, Gwen cleared her throat and shifted. She raised her chin, but didn't look Zoe in the eye. "I can feel her here."

"No one was here when I got home."

Gwen frowned. "She was in your apartment, Zoe. You're not safe."

Zoe's lip quivered. Gwen was right. If the stalker was focusing on her, then there was no telling that they weren't alone. Zoe hadn't actually checked the apartment since coming inside. She'd barely managed to turn the thermostat down before Gwen had shown up. Instead of saying that and adding more worry to Gwen's already immense pile, Zoe lifted Gwen's chin up. "Where would you feel safest?"

"Home."

"Then let's go home." Why did those words sound so normal falling from her lips?

"You'll stay?" Gwen looked at her, as if a lost little girl inside her was suddenly found.

"Yeah, Gwen. I'll stay if you want me to. Anytime, day or night, I'll be there."

Gwen sucked in a breath, pulling away slightly. She looked around Zoe's apartment, the heat still stifling. Gwen dropped her gaze back to Zoe's sweat-laden breasts. Her cheeks reddened. Zoe desperately wanted to know what was going through Gwen's mind.

"I'm not going to leave you." Did she really mean that? The words were out of her mouth before she could analyze them. Since when did she start taking these kinds of risks with Gwen? With anyone for that matter?

"Okay." Gwen tightened, shifting to stand. "Come home with me then."

"For sure." Zoe straightened her back as she stood. "Let me just get some stuff for tomorrow." She hated that she was still going to have to go into work in the morning, but at least for tonight she could make sure that Gwen was safe and well cared for.

Gwen went with her to the bedroom and the bathroom, trailing behind her as if she didn't want Zoe to be out of her sight for too long. Zoe packed up quickly, ignoring the fact that someone could be hiding in her closet. As they left, she made sure to lock the door and pocket the keys.

The car ride to Gwen's was quiet, but as soon as they were inside, Gwen's stress melted right off her. This was her safe space. Who was Zoe to deny that?

"Do you want some wine?" Gwen asked, gliding to the kitchen.

"Uh...sure." Zoe hadn't really wanted alcohol, but one glass wouldn't hurt. And if it was the mix that she'd made for the party, that would be even better. She was pretty sure the only reason she liked it was because of nostalgia.

They were seated in minutes, wine glasses in hands. Gwen sipped hers and hummed, her eyes closing and the last dregs of tension releasing from her body.

"Has it been stressful not working?" Zoe asked. "I can't imagine a workaholic like you is taking kindly to forced stillness."

Gwen chuckled lightly. "It's been a challenge, but I might have a few other things up my sleeves. And the lawyers are keeping me fairly busy."

"Any progress on that front?"

Gwen shrugged slightly, setting her drink on the table. "I don't want to talk about it tonight."

"All right." Zoe put her wine down, sad it wasn't their special blend. That was how she referred to it now, and she wouldn't ever stop.

"I wanted to talk to you about everything." Gwen found Zoe's hand, folding their fingers together. "But I'm not sure if I have the energy."

"You've had a trying time," Zoe said with understanding. She wouldn't ever stop giving Gwen what she needed, that much she believed wholeheartedly. Despite Nikki's warnings, Zoe wasn't sure that she could cut Gwen out of her life, that she could walk away without either one of them being hurt in the process. She wasn't sure she wanted to.

"So have you." Gwen's lips curled upward.

This melancholy from Gwen was so abnormal, and unease settled deep into Zoe's chest. She wasn't used to this, and that made her more worried than anything. Zoe lifted Gwen's hand and brought it to her lips for a gentle kiss. "Nothing I can't handle."

"I'm afraid you don't know the half of what you're in for."

"I can handle myself, Gwen."

"I love hearing you call me that." Pink tinged Gwen's cheeks, and this time Zoe recognized it instantly as pleasure, as a touch of happiness.

"Then I'll keep calling you that."

"I can't help but think that something bad is going to happen." Gwen settled into the couch, a forlorn look crossing her features.

"Even if it does, we'll figure it out." Zoe settled her head on Gwen's shoulder. "We always seem to figure our way out of problems. Remember when the caterer for the Grimsby launch was given spoiled chicken for the dinner? Or even better, when the sprinkler system went off for the Lucia launch and ruined all the decorations?"

"Oh God," Gwen moaned. "Yes, that was one of the worst days of my life." Gwen squeezed Zoe's fingers and dropped a kiss into her hair. "But you were there with me through it all."

"I was, and I will be again. I promise."

"Thank you."

"I'll always be there for you."

Fuck what Nikki had said. She couldn't be more wrong. This woman was strung tight with stress and fear. She couldn't be a stalker. She couldn't be the one behind everything. The arrest had to be false, and Gwen was going to come out the other side the victor. She had to.

If not, Zoe would follow her to the pits of hell and back.

Tilting her chin up, Zoe pressed a kiss to Gwen's cheek. When she turned, Zoe captured her lips in a soft embrace. Gwen curled her fingers into Zoe's hair, keeping the kiss light but steady. This had been what they were missing. The physical connection to the emotional one. Opening herself, Zoe pulled Gwen down on top of her. Tonight they would make love.

It would be so much more than fucking.

twenty-two

THE END OF THE ROAD

"What do you mean she was over here?" Nikki's sharp voice cut through the air.

Zoe turned sharply and froze when she heard it. Why was she so scared of her best friend? She'd honestly only come back to get another set of clothes so she could stay with Gwen that night. Zoe had held her all night while Gwen slept. In the morning, Gwen had admitted it was the first run of four-plus hours that she had slept in weeks.

"Hi to you, too." Zoe let Nikki into her apartment. The temperature was still the same as when she'd left it the day before, which meant it was probably just something that she'd hit on her way out that morning. No one had been in her apartment while she was gone to screw with her. Gwen was just paranoid.

"You let her into your apartment?"

"Yes." Zoe sighed. If Nikki had seen the look on Gwen's face, she would have let her in, too. Gwen had been flustered, broken, and exhausted. Zoe had to do something to help if she could.

"So you don't believe me then." Nikki crossed her arms and stood in front of Zoe's hallway, glaring.

"What?" Zoe shook her head. Had she missed something?

"You don't believe me that she's actually a stalker. She was arrested for it, for fuck's sake!" Nikki flung her hands out to the side, her cheeks turning red in exasperation.

"I think she's a victim, yes. But that doesn't mean she's innocent of everything, now does it?" It was the best Zoe could do, to lay blame in multiple places and perhaps ease Nikki's annoyance. She'd never seen her friend be this mad at her before.

"You're unbelievable, do you know that? What will it take for you to believe me?"

Was this only a matter of believing Nikki? She'd always been somewhat insecure about her role in Zoe's life. They'd had to teeter on the edge of what that meant for them in friendship, and Zoe had done her best to put Nikki's mind at ease. But she supposed with whatever new relationship was budding between her and Gwen, she had neglected Nikki.

That was probably exactly what this was.

Nikki felt left out.

"Oh, Nikki." Zoe took Nikki's hand and led her to the couch. Once they were both sitting down, Zoe looked deep into Nikki's brown eyes. "I'm so sorry."

Nikki frowned, her eyes tearing up. "I know you are."

"I should have realized that I wasn't paying enough attention to you. I shouldn't have abandoned you like that." Zoe covered Nikki's hand. "It's been such a shit show at work lately that I've completely forgotten that you have your own life and problems."

"We both have issues," Nikki said, her voice much calmer than it had been only moments before.

Zoe had done the right thing. She'd paused the argument so that the two of them could talk. She should have done this before when Nikki was so upset. "Tell me about what's been going on."

Nikki pursed her lips, her gaze not reaching Zoe's eyes. "I don't know."

"You know," Zoe pressed. She was going to have to work for this, make amends for the damage that she had caused. She'd done this before, countless times, in other relationships and in this one.

It would take some time and some effort, but it would all be worth it in the end.

Nikki tightened her jaw, breaking her hand free from Zoe's grasp. "I don't like Gwen."

"Really?" Zoe frowned. Nikki had never mentioned something like that before. She'd always been interested in what Zoe had to do at work, in her relationship with her boss, and her crush. Zoe's cheeks heated at that thought.

Nodding, Nikki folded her hands together. "I don't think she respects you, and with this newest development—"

"You mean her arrest?"

"Yeah. The arrest. I'm worried about you. That's all."

"Well, there's nothing to worry about because she's not really my boss right now. Gwen's been put on leave." Zoe glanced at the front door that she'd forgotten to lock. Gwen would panic if she knew that had happened, and Zoe really ought to be more careful, especially since it was proven she was a target of this stalker in some capacity.

"But you're still seeing her." Nikki seemed to want to get her point across, wanted Zoe to understand something, but she wasn't making clear what that something was. Was she?

"Gwen came over last night because she was scared, Nikki. I think it's reasonable for a woman in her situation to be scared. Hell, most women are scared to walk alone at night. Aren't you?"

"I suppose. But I still think she's guilty."

"Then we're going to have to agree to disagree on that one." Zoe's shoulders tightened. At this point, she wasn't sure they would ever come to an agreement on this front. Zoe covered Nikki's hand again. "I'm sorry if it felt like I wasn't listening to your concerns."

"But you're not. You said your apartment was hot. What if she was the one who had come in here and turned the heat on?"

"How would she have gotten my key?" Zoe gave Nikki a flat look.

"She probably tricked your super or your maintenance guy

into giving it to her. Hell, maybe she slept with them for it. I don't know."

Zoe pinched her face. "I don't think that happened."

Except Gwen had commented about Zoe changing the locks without her super knowing just to ensure her safety. So that had been something Gwen had thought about before, and brought up. Zoe never would have thought of something like that, and yet twice in two days it was mentioned.

"How else would the heat have been turned on so high?"

"Because I did it." Zoe rolled her eyes. "I don't have an automatic thermostat because management here is cheap as fuck, and so I have to turn it up and down every time I leave. I probably hit it or something. It wouldn't be the first time." Resting back into the couch, Zoe waited for whatever accusation Nikki had next.

Intuitively, Zoe knew this conversation was far from over.

But she also had a ticking clock that already started. She needed to get back to Gwen, or at least text her to tell her she would be running late so Gwen wouldn't worry. Because she would worry, especially after the thermostat incident last night.

"I'm so concerned about you," Nikki murmured, but she refused to look Zoe in the eye. She brushed her long box-dyed brown hair behind her ear, revealing the pearl drop earring she'd been wearing the other day.

A deep line creased in the center of Zoe's brow. "When did you get those earrings? They're pretty." She reached forward and ran her fingers over them.

"Oh." Nikki's cheeks flushed. "They're my grandmother's. I've had them for a while, just haven't worn them much until recently."

"Yeah, I noticed you were changing your style a bit." Zoe crossed her arms, then her ankle over her knee. She relaxed, hoping the change in conversation would ease whatever Nikki's tension was.

"Do you like it?" Nikki was suddenly sheepish.

"Of course I do." Zoe smiled at her. She didn't particularly care for it, but it wasn't her wardrobe or her changes, and so long as Nikki was happy with the changes, then she would be too. That was one of her best assets in life, being supportive to those around her. "I think you look beautiful."

'Thank you." Nikki scooted in closer. Her fingers were light on Zoe's thigh, as if she wasn't quite sure about setting them there or not.

Zoe covered Nikki's hand with a squeeze. They were finally on even footing again, or at least much closer to it. Still, Zoe wanted to finish up this conversation so she could get back to Gwen. They'd texted on and off throughout the day, and Zoe was pretty sure it had calmed Gwen's anxiety. It had also calmed Zoe's. Work had been stressful and slow without Gwen there to supervise and keep her busy. Unfortunately, they still had no idea when Gwen might be back.

"Did your crush on your boss ever go away? Or is that why you let her in?" Nikki flipped her hand and laced their fingers together.

Zoe stared at the touch, inwardly frowning and confused. Nikki had never really been one for physical touch, not like Zoe was. She'd accepted that early on in their friendship. So this change was startling.

"I'd say my crush changed more than went away. It's not the same as it was before, but so much has happened recently..." Zoe trailed off, still staring at Nikki's hand in hers. "I'm not really sure how to explain it."

"Then why did you let her in?"

"Because I'm loyal to her." That was true, even if Zoe didn't want to explain everything she and Gwen had been doing. From that almost-kiss on the couch to last night holding each other so they could sleep, something had distinctly clicked within her, moving from a boss-employee relationship to so much more. This wasn't just a distraction anymore, and Zoe wanted to find out where it was going.

"Does that loyalty go both ways?"

"What are you getting at?" Zoe finally asked, her tone sharpening. She tried to pull her hand from Nikki's, but Nikki's grasp tightened. Giving in, Zoe remained seated and still.

"She doesn't care about you like I do."

"I think you both care about me in different ways. I have a different relationship with each of you. That's normal."

Nikki sucked her lips into her mouth and sighed heavily. "I don't want her to take you away from me."

"Oh, Nikki. I'm not going anywhere." Zoe leaned against Nikki's side, putting her head on Nikki's shoulder. They were back to this insecurity that Nikki had. How would Zoe manage to make Nikki understand she was worth friendship?

"But you haven't really been around."

"I know. It's been... I don't even know how to describe what it's been, but it's been hard."

"That's when you need to rely on me."

"And I am." Zoe lifted Nikki's hand, the one clasped tightly around her own. "I'm right here."

Nikki frowned slightly, shifting to face Zoe more fully but still not releasing her hand. Zoe looked directly into Nikki's brown eyes and smiled at her, hoping that might ease the rest of the tension that was between them.

"What can I do to make sure you feel like you're still my best friend?"

Nikki's lips thinned. She dropped her gaze from Zoe's eyes, but she'd never been good at holding a gaze for long. Not like Gwen was. Nikki slid in closer, and before Zoe knew what was happening, their lips were pressed together. Zoe jerked back, her heart in her throat as she stared wide-eyed at Nikki.

"What are you doing?"

"I just... I thought..." Nikki's face went slack, her skin pale.

This had to be a nightmare, right? Zoe had never given any indication that she was interested in Nikki in that way. Had she? Her stomach roiled from the thoughts coursing through her brain in a panic.

"I thought we could..." Nikki sighed heavily, her eyes closing before she popped them open and moved in again. Their lips touched once more, but the feeling in the pit of Zoe's stomach only increased, that unsettled feeling that pushed her over the edge of discomfort.

"Nikki, stop." Zoe pulled back even more, leaning halfway across the couch just to get away from her friend. She had to get Nikki off this train of thought immediately. "I thought you liked men. You've never said anything about being interested in women."

Nikki shrugged slightly. "People change, right?"

"Yeah. I mean. Kind of? Not really. You can realize that you like women, that's fine. But you've never given any indication that you do or that you were curious and trying to figure it out. It's always been men for you." Zoe's heart raced. She tried to break her grasp free from Nikki's again, but Nikki wasn't letting up.

"I don't know. I think I like you. Don't you like me?"

"As my best friend," Zoe reiterated. She'd never seen Nikki as anything else. Nikki wasn't her type at all. "And if you like women, that's perfectly fine. I'm not going to shut you out because of that." Though kissing her randomly, twice, without asking was definitely something Zoe could walk away from. With her and Gwen, despite all the power imbalances, there had always been an understanding of consent. This was... Zoe didn't even have words for what this was.

"I'm sorry. I'm so sorry." Nikki let go of Zoe's hand and covered her face, turning to plant both feet on the floor.

"Don't be sorry. Nikki... it's flattering, really." Was it, though? At the moment, Zoe would say just about anything to help Nikki feel better about the situation. Anything to ease this awkwardness. "I just don't want to give you the wrong idea. I'm not interested in a romantic relationship with you."

"It's because of her, isn't it?" The venom in Nikki's words was clear.

"Her?" Zoe was taken aback by anger. She scooted backward

on the couch, planting her hands on the cushion as she stared wide-eyed at her friend. "Do you mean Ms. Fudala?"

"Of course that's who I mean. You like her instead of me."

"Nikki, I've always liked her, since I started working for her. Yes. She's my boss and a friend, and yes, I have romantic feelings for her." Zoe's mouth was dry, and she scooted back even farther. "I love you as my best friend. That's it. I don't think there could ever be more between us."

Nikki huffed and rolled her eyes. "I can't believe you."

She stood up sharply, her entire body a live wire ready to explode. Zoe stayed sitting on the couch but ready to pounce up if she needed to.

"How could you do this to me?" Nikki screeched. She jerked her fists down to her sides, bending over Zoe and getting in her face. "I can't believe you're choosing her over me."

Without another word, Nikki stomped out of the apartment and slammed the door behind her. Zoe held her hand up to her chest and blinked at the door. She needed to lock that. It was the only thought that ran through her mind. Whatever was going on with Nikki, she didn't know, but she was going to give Nikki time to cool off. In the meantime, she needed to lock that fucking door.

Now.

twenty-three

AND IT GOES LIKE THIS...

Zoe's heart still raced when she got to Gwen's, but she couldn't decide if it was anger or fear. What the hell was wrong with Nikki? She'd locked the door, packed her bag, and debated whether or not to call Gwen and tell her tonight was a bad idea.

But the thought of holding Gwen again, of wrapping arms around her to protect her was too much. She had to show up.

Knocking on Gwen's door, Zoe waited. She gripped her bag tightly and held it to her side as she waited. Where was she? Zoe had texted and said that she was on her way, but a quick glance at her phone told her Gwen hadn't even read the text yet.

"Where are you?"

Now Zoe's nerves were going for an entirely different reason. She looked around the hallway, wishing she still had a spare set of keys to Gwen's condo, but when she'd changed the locks, Gwen hadn't given Zoe a key. Or told her where a spare set was.

Shuffling her bag around, Zoe slid her phone out of her back pocket and checked it again. Still nothing. The worry etched its way higher in her stomach. Nausea threatened. Zoe clicked Gwen's name in her recent calls and waited as it rang.

"Come on... answer." Zoe gnawed on her lip, hanging on to every ring until the very end.

When Gwen didn't answer and it went to voicemail, Zoe tried again. But the second time, she was nearly in tears. She slid her phone in her pocket, frantic. Where was she?

Should Zoe call the police?

With a rogue stalker out there, what if Gwen was missing?

What if she'd been kidnapped?

"Zoe?" Gwen's voice rocked through her.

"Oh thank God." Zoe spun around and nearly dropped her bag to run to Gwen and wrap her arms around her. Relief flooded her, the tightness in her chest gone instantly. "I didn't know where you were."

"Zoe, I'm fine." Gwen stepped up closer to her, skimming a hand down her arm to her fingers and clenching them. "I'm right here, and I'm fine."

Gwen leaned in and pressed their mouths together sweetly. She cupped Zoe's cheek and pulled her in closer as she nuzzled Zoe's neck.

"I'm right here."

Zoe choked back a sob. What the hell was wrong with her? This whole thing must be affecting her more than she'd realized. Gwen wrapped arms around her, pulling her in so that her head rested on Gwen's shoulder. Zoe sucked in a sharp breath, closing her eyes.

This was real.

Gwen was here.

They were both perfectly fine.

"I'm so sorry," Zoe muttered. "I shouldn't be like this." But she didn't even try to move. Instead, she stayed right where she was and held on as tightly as she possibly could. Gwen was as much her safety as Zoe had been for Gwen. She didn't want to give this up. Zoe sucked in another sharp breath. "I don't know why I'm such a mess."

"Because this is stressful and ridiculous and completely unfair. I'm so sorry I dragged you into this." Gwen pulled Zoe's chin up and kissed her again. It was such a warm embrace, tender, and it was home.

When had Gwen become home?

"I'm not sorry," Zoe mumbled against Gwen's lips. "Never sorry for this."

She knew exactly what she meant by that, and she could only hope that Gwen understood the meaning. She wanted Gwen to know that there was so much more to this—to them.

Desperately, Zoe wrapped a hand around Gwen's neck and pulled her down. She deepened the kiss, sliding her tongue against Gwen's. The kiss went from sexy to sloppy. Zoe groaned and pulled back slightly.

"Tell me you're okay," Zoe asked.

"I'm fine."

"Tell me again."

Gwen hummed and nipped at Zoe's lower lip. "I'm perfect. Or I will be in a minute."

Diving back in, Gwen took control and pulled Zoe in. She melded their mouths together. She pushed Zoe against the door, smoothing her between the cold metal and Gwen's body. Zoe groaned. Where was this fire coming from? The passion?

Gwen had been distant at best since Zoe had bailed her out. But this was almost back to the woman Zoe had met, the woman she'd come to know in the last few months. Zoe still gripped her overnight bag tightly, lifting her hand up. The bag bumped against Gwen's side.

"Inside," Gwen commanded.

Her keys jingled in her pocket, and Zoe was mesmerized as Gwen quickly slid the key in the lock and let them inside. The click of the locks soothed the rest of Zoe's worry. Dropping her bag loudly, Zoe didn't wait as she pushed into Gwen and moved her backward.

Zoe walked Gwen toward the bedroom. She had her fingers at Gwen's shirt, pulling the buttons one by one as she went. Gwen had her hands in Zoe's hair, tangling the long locks as they continued to kiss. Just knowing that Gwen was okay, knowing that she was here and whole and in one piece was exactly what Zoe needed in order to feel alive again.

With Gwen's shirt pushed to the side, Zoe feasted on her breasts. She pulled at the button and zipper on Gwen's slacks and slid her hand between Gwen's skin and fabric. Gwen groaned. Zoe very nearly fell to her knees. In fact, that would be perfect.

Two more steps, and the back of Gwen's legs hit the bed. Zoe shoved her pants down and sunk to her knees, staring directly into Gwen's pale eyes. "Distraction?"

"Fuck me. Yes." Gwen spread her knees and put a hand behind her, holding herself upright.

That was all the demand Zoe needed. She nipped the insides of Gwen's thighs lightly, moving upward to right between her legs. She sucked in a sharp breath, the scent of Gwen's arousal hitting her at once. She longed for it, to taste Gwen upon her lips and tongue, to feel Gwen writhe under her skilled and now familiar touch.

"I'm okay, Zoe," Gwen murmured, her fingers digging into Zoe's hair and scraping against her scalp. "I'm not hurt."

Zoe wanted to believe her. She wanted to know what it felt like to trust that Gwen knew what she was feeling and that for tonight they were both safe. Zoe planted her mouth against Gwen, sucking and not even beginning to tease. They didn't need foreplay. They needed orgasm after orgasm that would throw them into oblivion, into a subspace, where stalkers didn't exist, where pain was no more, and where they were both authentically them.

Gwen put her foot on the edge of the bed frame, changing the angle. Zoe wrapped her arms around Gwen's hips and held on tightly. Zoe stayed against her, sucking, licking, teasing. Gwen groaned. She squirmed. She gasped. Zoe loved every single sound she made, and she clung to this—a memory she would never give up.

"I need you," Gwen stated on a sigh. "I'll always need you."

Hope lit in Zoe's chest. Was Gwen saying more than she had ever dared? Even through all the drama, through the lies, the deceit, the pain, the fear—had they actually found one another? Zoe pushed in more, her body vibrating with pleasure as Gwen undulated against her. Zoe's cheeks were wet, but when she opened her eyes and looked up, Gwen stared right back down at her. As if Zoe was her entire world.

"I need you, Zoe," Gwen whispered. "I'm so close."

Zoe wasn't going to stop now. If she could be the one to push Gwen into that space where pleasure consumed her, then that was right where Zoe was going to send her.

"Zoe." Gwen cried out her name as every muscle in her body tightened.

She didn't stop. Zoe kept her mouth against Gwen even when Gwen tapped her forehead, a sure sign that she wanted a break. But when Zoe didn't stop, Gwen cupped the back of her head and pulled her in tightly. Zoe's knees tingled, numbing, as she held on while Gwen cascaded through a second orgasm.

"Enough," Gwen barked breathlessly. It would be much more commanding if she didn't have her pants pulled to her knees and her cheeks weren't flushed with the aftermath of being spent.

Smiling, Zoe helped ease the rest of Gwen's clothes off before helping her to lie in the center of her rumpled bed. Zoe flopped down next to her, still fully clothed. She swiped the back of her hand across her mouth, grinning up at the ceiling.

"Zoe," Gwen chimed from next to her. She slid a hand along Zoe's stomach and up to her breast, covering it and giving a nice full squeeze. "Take off your clothes and touch yourself. I want to watch you. I want to see what I heard."

Zoe's nipples hardened instantly. Had Gwen really enjoyed that day? That phone call? "You want to watch me?" Zoe innocently asked.

"Oh yes." Gwen's voice dropped low. "I want to see how you touch yourself. I want to hear what sounds you make. I want you to imagine it's me touching you like you did that day after the winery."

Zoe shivered, goosebumps running all along her body. "I don't know if I can do that."

"Why on earth not?" Gwen sounded so perturbed by that fact. "You masturbate all the time. I know you do. I've seen the pictures." As soon as the words were out of her mouth, Zoe could see the regret cross her features. "I'm sorry. I shouldn't have brought that up."

"It's fine," Zoe said tightly.

"It's not. I..." Gwen pursed her lips, lazily lying naked next to Zoe. She blew a stray strand of hair from her face. "I'm not happy about the circumstances behind those pictures, please understand that. But I won't deny the fact that I have thought about them since. I would love to see more."

"Gwen..." Zoe trailed off, her cheeks so hot that she worried she would burn on contact with Gwen's fingers that fluttered over her lips. "Those photos are one of the most embarrassing things to ever happen to me. Not just embarrassing—violating."

"I understand. Truly I do." Gwen settled her hand against Zoe's arm. "You were violated."

"Yes, I was."

"And the phone call? The one where you forgot to...hang up?" Gwen looked Zoe directly in the eye. "What about that?"

"What about it?" Zoe bit her lip, her cheeks still hot.

"What did you feel when you knew I was listening?"

"Fuck," Zoe swore. She closed her eyes and covered her face with her hands. "Aside from disbelief and embarrassment?"

"Yes." Gwen walked her fingers up Zoe's body, over her breast, and slid in close so that her naked body pressed against Zoe's side. "Did it turn you on?"

Turning her head to look Gwen directly in the eye, Zoe held her breath. Honesty. That was all Gwen ever wanted from her. They could avoid, they could talk circles around the truth, but through all of this drama, from a stalker to distraction, Gwen had only ever demanded one true thing. Honesty.

"Yes," Zoe answered. She dashed her tongue against her lips and dropped her gaze to Gwen's mouth. "Yes, it turned me on. I touched myself again that night, thinking about you."

Gwen's lips pulled upward, a beautiful smile. "And what were you thinking about? Exactly."

Zoe's hands trembled as she pushed herself up to pull off her shirt. Gwen watched her with rapt attention. Zoe smoothed her hands over her breasts, then pulled her nipples until they were hard little nubs.

"Perfect." Gwen dropped her gaze over Zoe's body, a satisfied smirk on her lips. "What were you thinking about?"

"The way your skirt rode up your leg when you sat against the table." Zoe's voice was raspy. She pushed her jogging pants down her legs along with her underwear, shoving them off the bed with her foot. She brushed her fingers through the damp curls between her legs and bit back her groan.

"Do you always do that?" Gwen shifted on the bed, dipping the mattress with her weight.

"Do what?" Zoe gasped as she touched her engorged clit.

"Hold back before you give in and let go." Gwen smoothed fingers across Zoe's stomach, circling one finger around her belly button.

"Don't you do the same?"

"Not when it comes to sex."

Zoe snorted, trying to stay focused between the conversation and the soft touches. "We're going to have to agree to disagree on that one."

"What do you mean?" Gwen rested her full palm against Zoe's stomach right as Zoe slid two fingers inside herself.

Swallowing to try and keep her focus, Zoe searched for Gwen's eyes. "How long did you wait until you kissed me?"

"Too long." Gwen smiled, clearly understanding where Zoe was going with this. "But after that, I haven't held back."

"No, you haven't." Zoe bit her lip as she rubbed her thumb across her clit. Her eyes fluttered shut at the sensations running through her.

"Do you like this?" Gwen asked, her lips brushing Zoe's ear as she spoke. "Do you like thinking about me?"

"I always think about you," Zoe admitted. That was as close to the truth as she dared get. At least for now. They needed to put their current troubles behind them before Zoe would confidently say the other three little words that prickled in the corners of her mind.

"Oh, Zoe." Gwen dipped her head, covering Zoe's nipple with her mouth and tongue. She twirled her tongue in a circle before giving a definitive flick. She left Zoe's nipple wet as she moved to the other one, repeating the same thing to it. She kissed her way down Zoe's stomach to her hip as Zoe slowly continued the pressure against her pussy. "You never cease to amaze me."

Gwen followed Zoe's hand down with her own. She added a finger inside, right alongside Zoe's, before taking over the motion on her clit. Zoe flung both her hands above her head and clung on tightly to whatever she found there, the blankets clutched in her fists.

"Did you want me to touch you like this?"

"Yes," Zoe hissed, clenching her eyes tight. "Yes, I wanted you to fuck me, lick me, take me."

Zoe parted her hips and raised them up in the air slightly to improve the angle. Gwen curled her fingers inside her, pulsing them rapidly. *One. Two. Three. Four.* Zoe gasped. She moaned. She clenched her jaw and wrinkled her nose as she tried to hold on with everything she had.

"Don't hold back," Gwen murmured against her skin, the feather-light brush of her hair against Zoe's abdomen tickling her. "Let go."

Zoe grunted. She wiggled her hips. She focused her entire brain on nothing other than the sensations rolling through her, nothing more than the touches, the tingles, the brushes. Everything in this moment was perfect, just like it always had been between them.

They just understood each other.

"Gwen!" Zoe cried out, her back arching off the bed as a powerful orgasm burst through her. She bit her lip hard as she let the feelings flow through her, into her, consume her.

"Perfect. Beautiful. Stunning."

Zoe wasn't sure if she heard Gwen correctly, the buzzing in her ears was too loud. But they lay pressed against each other until their bodies cooled. Every once in a while, Gwen would lean in and kiss her.

"What are you thinking about?" Zoe finally ventured to ask.

Gwen gave her a wry smile. "That I want a shower."

"I'm not going to be offended by that." Zoe winked.

"Don't be." Gwen kissed her nose. "I just want to ease the stress from today off my shoulders."

"Then by all means, take a shower. I find them a safe place of refuge, too."

"You won't mind?" Gwen asked.

"No. I'll even give you your space and only think about hot water sluicing over your body once or twice."

"Once or twice?" Gwen gave her a disbelieving look.

"All right, the entire time you're in there." Zoe gave her a cocky grin.

Laughing, Gwen lifted up on her elbows and kissed Zoe firmly. "Next time, you can join me."

"I'll hold you to that."

Gwen walked saucily, fully naked, with swaying hips and a grin over her shoulder, out of the bedroom. Zoe shifted on the mattress, pulling a pillow under her head as she relaxed and closed her eyes.

The sound of a door opening caused her to furrow her brow. Frowning, she popped open her eyes to see what Gwen had forgotten, and froze.

"Say a fucking word, and I'll kill you."

twenty-four

DON'T GET IN HER WAY

Zoe's entire body stiffened. Her heart raced, and her eyes were wide. She stared at the woman across from her, the one coming out of the closet, the one who looked wild and crazy. Her dark brown eyes bulged. Her pearl drop earrings were askew and caught in her box-dyed brown hair.

"Nikki," Zoe whispered. Her stomach dropped. "It's you?"

"Of course it's me." Nikki wrinkled her nose and scooted to the bedroom door, shutting and locking it.

Zoe watched every move Nikki made as fear coiled its way through her like a snake. She had brought the enemy right to Gwen. Everything in this moment and beyond was her fault.

Gwen.

She was in the shower, trying to relax, cleaning herself up. She was vulnerable. She had no idea—

"Why did you have to get in my way?"

"Excuse me?" Zoe shot back, her eyes widening.

Nikki came closer, bending over the bed. The sharp knife in her hand shone in the light from the nightstand. Zoe gulped, pushing herself deeper into the mattress as if to get away. She'd never seen Nikki like this, so unhinged, so dangerous. Zoe held her breath, casting her gaze at the door.

Surely Nikki would know exactly where Gwen was. She would know exactly what they had been doing. Zoe had to protect Gwen. That was the only thought she'd had. She'd brought this insanity upon both of them, but Gwen didn't deserve it. Gwen hadn't asked for this.

"Shut up!" Nikki growled.

Except, Zoe hadn't said anything. She shuddered as Nikki's hot breath brushed across her skin. Zoe stayed as still as possible, her entire body on edge as she waited to see just what would happen next.

"You shouldn't be here." Nikki grabbed Zoe's arm harshly and twisted it.

Pain ricocheted through Zoe's body and up her arm into her shoulder. She cried out as it hit her chest. Nikki jerked back and slapped the back of her hand across Zoe's cheek. The sound cracked through the room.

If Gwen were there, she would try to stop this.

She would do something.

Zoe should do something. She started to get up, but Nikki shoved her back down. She took a zip tie from her back pocket and wrapped Zoe's hands together in front of her body, pulling it sharply. Zoe hissed.

"What are you doing, Nikki? I thought we were friends."

"We were *never* friends," Nikki spat. She grabbed the blanket and threw it over Zoe's body. "Cover up. You look disgusting."

Zoe wanted to whimper. She wanted to cry out and warn Gwen that Nikki was here, that something bad was happening, but there was no way that Gwen would hear her in the shower. Zoe had no way to warn her.

Grasping the edge of the blanket, Zoe pulled it over her body. While she felt less exposed, she felt even more in danger. Moving swiftly wasn't going to be a choice anymore. Tears stung Zoe's eyes, and she had to work hard to hold back her sob.

"Shut up!" Nikki hissed, glancing at the door. "If you ruin this for me, I'll suffocate you. You won't mess this up!"

"What do you want?" Zoe had to keep her talking. If they were still talking when Gwen finished her shower, then she might hear them when she came in. It might be the very warning that Zoe was looking for.

"Nothing from you. All you had to do was one thing. And you couldn't even do that!" Nikki was back, standing over her with a menacing look.

She looked possessed.

Terrified, Zoe stared into Nikki's eyes as they flicked back and forth and all over the room. "Did you come straight here?"

"Of course I did, you idiot. I had to get here before she came back."

"Right." Zoe bit the inside of her cheek. She didn't want to make Nikki any angrier than she was. She might do something no one wanted.

"So you love her?" Zoe asked.

Nikki flipped around on her, her eyes wild, her hair a mess. Zoe's fear ratcheted up a notch. Nikki came close, leaning down so her breath raced across Zoe's face. "I don't love her."

"Then why are you doing this?"

"I'm going to *be* her." Nikki straightened her shoulders and smoothed her hands down her outfit.

Everything clicked. The hair dye. The earrings which she undoubtedly stole from Gwen. The new clothes she's been buying and wearing. Were any of those stolen from Gwen? Zoe had so many more questions.

"W-when did you meet her?" Zoe finally settled on one.

Nikki furrowed her brow. "Don't you remember me telling you the story?"

"I don't." Zoe bit the inside of her cheek again, hard. She needed something to help keep her centered, to help keep her wits about her. "Tell me again."

"We met in the elevator." Nikki's voice sounded distant, like she was telling a story she had told so many times before that it was rote memory. "She was so kind, holding the door for me."

Zoe waited with great anticipation for the rest of the story. For a meal, for a conversation, for something, but Nikki didn't continue. She didn't elaborate.

"Did you go on a date?"

"No!" Nikki nearly screamed and then jerked with a start as she stared at the bedroom door. "She's coming."

Moving swiftly, Nikki grabbed a roll of duct tape that Zoe had somehow missed. She ripped off a chunk before shoving Zoe's discarded underwear between her lips and taping over her mouth.

"Shut it. I don't want her to hear you."

A tear fell from Zoe's eye, sliding down her cheek to disappear into the mattress. Gwen had no idea what she was walking into. She was going to be thrown into this insanity with absolutely no warning.

Gwen's bare feet padded on the floor as she came closer. Every breath Zoe took was so loud in her ears. Her stomach swam with fear. Would Nikki kill her? Would Nikki torture her first? Surely if Nikki wanted to become Gwen, then Gwen would have to cease to exist.

"Zoe, I—" Gwen stopped short.

Her eyes widened. Her cheeks were pink from the shower, her hair wet around her shoulders. Her gaze landed on Zoe before she immediately shifted to look Nikki directly in the eye.

"Who are you?" Gwen's voice suddenly stopped as Nikki swung the wrought iron lamp and crashed it into Gwen's head.

Zoe screamed, the sound muffled by the gag. She pushed herself up to watch as Nikki caught Gwen and slid her to the floor in a lump. Nikki put her hands under Gwen's armpits and dragged her around to the side of the bed so Zoe could see her fully.

"Pathetic," Nikki mumbled. "I'll be so much better than her."

Blood oozed from the side of Gwen's head and down her face. Nikki had hit her hard. Hard enough that it could probably kill her. Zoe sniffled, trying to remain as focused as possible. Right now, she was the only one who could get them out of this. She was the only one who could save them.

But she was bound and gagged.

Nikki bent over Gwen, zip tying her hands behind her back and then zip tying her feet. She kept the robe tight around her body. Nikki kicked her. She repeatedly pummeled Gwen in the abdomen, in the head, anywhere she could reach. Her grunts grew louder and louder as the force of her blows increased.

Zoe screamed again, making a racket to get Nikki's attention. Finally, Nikki spun around to face her. She went from annoyance to pure rage in an instant. Where had all of this been hiding? Nikki slammed her fist into Zoe's side, hard, knocking the wind from Zoe's lungs.

"You should have listened to me. You should have just left her alone."

More tears fell from Zoe's eyes as she listened to Nikki's rants. She had to stop this somehow, but they were both tied up, Gwen was unconscious, and Zoe had no idea what to do. She couldn't reach her phone. It was in her pants pocket on the floor on the other side of the bed. Gwen's phone was somewhere— Zoe had no idea. Was there an alarm? Surely Gwen had an alarm installed. Except they hadn't turned anything off when they'd come in.

Zoe turned her head to look at Gwen again, to check on her and make sure that she was okay. Gwen's eyes were locked on hers. Nikki paced at the foot of the bed, not paying attention to either of them. Gwen slowly moved her gaze from Zoe to the nightstand. Her lips trembled as she did it again.

Zoe looked at the nightstand. Was there something in there? A phone? A panic button?

Gwen looked so pale. The blood she was losing had to be too much. Her lips trembled again, and she mouthed one word.

Gun.

Zoe winced. She was going to have to do it. This was going to be her only option. She nodded her understanding, but then she was left with panic that she had to figure out how to get the gun from the drawer and get Nikki to stop this insanity.

She looked back at Nikki, watched her pace and mumble to herself. This had to be unplanned. They had to have triggered something for her to escalate this quickly. It must have been the kiss. Nikki must have been watching them. Zoe shuddered at the thought. She'd been violated before, but it was nothing compared to this.

Checking on Gwen, Zoe made sure that she was still with her, but her eyes were closed again. Her chest rose and fell in a steady rhythm, but it was slow. They didn't have much time. Nikki stopped suddenly. She spun around and faced Zoe with fire in her eyes.

"I didn't want to have to kill you."

Zoe whined in the back of her throat. She wished she could talk, that she could say anything that would help ease Nikki's discomfort and calm her down so that they didn't have to do this. Zoe didn't want to die tonight, and she certainly didn't want to watch Gwen be murdered right in front of her eyes either.

"But I have to. I can't have you knowing..." Nikki trailed off. "I can't have you acting a fool when I take her place at work."

Work? Did Nikki really think she could walk into the office and no one would be the wiser? God, she was a fucking lunatic.

Nikki shook her head as she stood over Zoe. Hands wrapped around Zoe's neck, pushing down and strangling her. Zoe flung her arms up, her legs out. She pushed against Nikki, trying to break her hold as she gasped for air and choked on the fabric in her mouth. Her eyes burned from tears and lack of oxygen.

This was it.

This was the moment she was going to die.

Thank God she wouldn't have to watch Gwen die.

Biting down hard on her cheek, Zoe closed her eyes and pushed with everything she had against Nikki and toppled her over onto the floor. Scrambling up, Zoe desperately tried to get her hands to work on the flush drawer to the bedside table, but she couldn't get her fingers into the edge to pull it open.

Something hard hit the back of her head. Zoe fell to the floor in a heap. Her eyes were blurry, bright lights popping in front of her vision. She couldn't make it stop. Her head ached, her muscles were sore. Bile rose up in her stomach and moved into her throat. It was so hard to keep it down.

"You bitch!" Nikki screamed, her voice reverberating through Zoe's skull.

Her last chance.

Zoe pushed up on her knees and pried the drawer open. Inside was a handgun, perfectly laid. She snatched it up, pressing her hands around the handle and whipping around to face Nikki. Tears streamed down her cheeks as she pressed her back into the nightstand.

She wanted to tell Nikki to stop.

She wanted to ask why Nikki was making her do this.

She wanted so much.

Nikki stared at her, a flash of fear in her gaze before it was quickly masked. She rolled her eyes. "Come on, Zoe. We both know you're too chickenshit to do that. In three years, you never made a move on your boss until she caught you fucking yourself."

Zoe wanted to yell at her to shut up, but she couldn't. She groaned around the gag and aimed the weapon right at Nikki. She wasn't going to let Nikki out of her sight if she could. She silently begged Nikki to stop so she wouldn't have to do this. But in the back of her mind, she knew that there was no other option.

"Shoot me already!" Nikki screeched.

Zoe pulled the trigger.

twenty-five

ALL IT TAKES IS ONE

Nikki collapsed to the ground.

Zoe sat, her back pressed against the cold nightstand, the gun held in front of her, still aimed at Nikki's motionless body. Had Zoe killed her? Did she even hit her? She'd closed her eyes when she pulled the trigger so she had no idea. She'd never fired a weapon before.

With no idea how long it had been, Zoe finally forced herself up on her knees. She scooted across the hardwood floor to Nikki, peering over her to look at her face. Her chest still rose and fell, so she wasn't dead. Her mouth was open, her eyes closed, and a pool of blood formed along her stomach.

Nikki was still alive.

Keeping the gun in her hand, Zoe stood up and stepped over Nikki's still form. She found her pants, snagged her phone out of her pocket, and called the police immediately. She didn't want to look at Nikki. She didn't want to see if she was still alive or not, or to witness the aftermath of the fact that Zoe had shot her!

"911, what's your location?"

Zoe's voice caught in her throat. *Shit.* She still had the gag. She couldn't talk. She couldn't tell them anything yet. Fuck. How could she be so stupid? Trying to talk around the gag, Zoe made odd sounds as tears streamed down her face again.

"What's your location?" the dispatcher repeated.

Zoe reached up and dug her fingers into the duct tape. She ripped it from her face and gasped for breath. Her heart raced a mile a minute as she snagged the phone and held it up to her ear. She rattled off Gwen's address, twice, just to confirm with the police that they had the right location.

Help was on the way.

But until then, she was stuck dealing with everything on her own.

She wanted to cry. She wanted to scream out her frustrations. She managed to put the phone on speaker and set it on the mattress, letting the dispatcher talk to her through everything that was happening, not willing to hang up so long as she was able to.

With the gun back between her fingers, Zoe walked over to Nikki and touched her leg with her toes. She sucked in a sharp breath when Nikki didn't move.

"She's not waking up," Zoe said over her shoulder to the phone.

"Okay."

"I shot her." Zoe's voice broke on the last word. "I have a gun, and I'll put it down when they get here, but I'm not risking it until then."

Was this really all over?

Zoe stepped around Nikki and found Gwen. She ran the backs of her fingers against Gwen's cheek, hoping that she'd wake up. Her eyelids fluttered, and Zoe could make out the barest sliver of her blue eyes. Zoe's heart skipped. She raced back to the bed for the phone and brought it to Gwen and put it on the floor.

"My b—" Zoe stopped. She was buck naked, Gwen was in a robe, she couldn't say boss. "My girlfriend is hurt."

"Where is she hurt?" The dispatcher asked.

Zoe sucked in a breath. "She was hit on the back of the head, and it looks like she hit something else when she fell down."

"All right. Ambulances and police are coming. They should be there in a few minutes."

The relief that washed through her was palpable. Zoe touched Gwen's cheek and tried to get her to open her eyes even more. *Come on, Gwen. Don't do this now.* Zoe choked back a sob. She wished her hands weren't still tied together so that she could cup Gwen's cheek. Bending down, Zoe kissed her forehead and sucked in a breath, the scent of shampoo lingering in her wet hair mingled with the hard iron scent of blood.

"Ma'am!" The dispatcher said loudly. "Is the door locked?"

"Yes," Zoe whispered. She pulled back and looked down at Gwen.

"Can you unlock it?"

Zoe didn't want to leave Gwen's side, especially when she was unconscious and Nikki was only a few feet away. But she had to let them in. She needed help. All the help. Zoe pushed onto her feet, jumping over Nikki before she ran to the front door and turned all the locks. She opened it and raced back to Nikki and Gwen. Luckily, neither one of them had moved.

Well, not so lucky.

Gwen was scaring her. Zoe was on her knees in front of Gwen again, soothing fingers over her arm and trying to wake her up. "Gwen, come on. Open your eyes."

"Zoe, did you unlock the door?" the dispatcher asked forcefully from the phone.

"Y-yes. Gwen's not waking up." She sounded so worried, her voice wavering.

Nikki's leg jerked, then her arm. Zoe moved away and scrambled for the gun again. She wasn't going to let this change get by her. She wasn't going to let Nikki get the upper hand. She bit her lip as she pointed the gun at Nikki and just waited.

For her to move.

For her to speak.

Anything that would indicate the first bullet hadn't done enough. Zoe shivered. She wasn't willing to take her gaze off

Nikki even for a second. Nikki curled in on herself, her breathing increasing as she groaned.

"She's waking up!" Zoe shouted, hoping the dispatcher would hear her and do something about it. Not that she could. But this woman was the only reason Zoe didn't feel alone.

"Stay calm, Zoe. The police should be there in two minutes."

Hadn't she said that more than two minutes ago? Zoe shuddered, keeping her hands raised and the weapon pointed directly at Nikki. If she had to shoot again, she would. She wouldn't let anything else happen to Gwen. Zoe swallowed down the bile that rose in her throat.

"They're almost to the door."

Zoe clung onto every single word the woman said. Nikki jerked again. Another groan exited her lips. She was moving and making noise. Shouldn't Gwen be doing that? Shouldn't Gwen be moving and waking up already? Why wasn't she?

"Police!" The male voices reverberated around the room.

"Bedroom!" Zoe shouted back.

As soon as they entered the room, she dropped the gun and raised her hands, still zip tied, above her head and sucked in a sharp breath. Her eyes blurred over as they took control of the situation.

She was safe.

They both were.

Finally.

Zoe collapsed against one of the officers, who wrapped her in a blanket. She choked back a sob until she managed to catch sight of Gwen. There were so many people in the bedroom. Cops filled every available spot while they restrained Nikki and applied pressure to the wound in her upper stomach.

Radios went off nonstop as people talked over each other. Zoe didn't want to look at Nikki. She scooted as close to Gwen as she could, and when they lifted Nikki's body onto the backboard and took her out of the room, Zoe clung to Gwen's hand. The police officers let a second medical team in, and they immediately sliced through the zip ties holding Gwen's hands and moved her to lie flat on her back, pulling Zoe off of her.

Zoe shivered as they wrapped her in a rough wool blanket that came from somewhere. She wasn't even sure. They cut her wrists free, but mostly let her sit there and watch everything happening. Gwen and Nikki were far more injured than she was, so they were being cared for first.

It was chaos in there, and Zoe wasn't sure what was happening, but they seemed to know what they were doing. The police went about everything like ants in a hill, organized chaos. Zoe huddled on the edge of the bed until Gwen was moved out on a gurney, leaving a pool of blood on the floor in her wake.

Zoe very nearly vomited at the sight. She'd never seen that much blood in her life, and the fact that it was coming from Gwen? She couldn't even fathom how bad that cut was on the back of her head.

"Head wounds bleed more than normal, don't they?" Zoe asked no one in particular.

"They do," a kind officer answered. When Zoe looked up into dark brown eyes and a mass of blonde hair, Zoe sighed. This officer, whatever her name was, would be her saving grace tonight.

Zoe closed her eyes slowly, feeling safe for the first time in months. She'd ignored how much danger she was in, but it was impossible to do that now. Not with blood, not with gun residue on her hands, not with the aches in her body and the energy drained from her.

"Will she be okay?" Zoe asked, not sure if the officer knew who she was even talking about, but hoping she would. Everything around her moved in slow motion, and it was getting harder for her to focus on the people in the room.

"I don't know," the officer said. "I hope so. She looked okay to me."

"You mean you've seen worse."

"Yeah." The officer let out a wry chuckle. "Let's get you into the living room, okay? Out of here."

Zoe nodded, but she didn't answer right away. The officer helped her to stand up, wrapping an arm around her back as they started to walk out of the bedroom. Zoe's head was so light, as if she was about to float away and the only thing that was holding her to the ground was the officer next to her. She shook her head slightly when her vision blurred to try and get it back in focus.

What was happening?

It must be from the rush of adrenaline. Zoe clung to the officer, walking like a drunken fool into the next room. They set her on the couch and then the woman disappeared. There were even more people out here, if that was possible. Zoe rested her head back on the couch and closed her eyes, her heart racing.

It was over.

That was the only thought filtering through her brain. Well, other than the one where she was wondering how Gwen was. Gwen worried her. Not only the fact that she was injured, but this entire process. Zoe wanted to help her through everything, to be right next to her. But it was clear that she had to stay there and answer some questions before they would let her go.

Zoe took in a deep breath, but it was so hard to breathe. Her chest was constricted. Her head still felt like it was floating away from her body. Zoe sunk into the couch even more and held herself as still as possible. Was it normal for the world to spin when she knew she was sitting still?

"I brought you some water." The voice sounded so distant.

Try as she might, Zoe wasn't able to lift her hand to reach for the glass that she assumed was somewhere in front of her. Because she couldn't even bring herself to open her eyes to look for it.

"Zoe?" The officer sounded worried now. "Zoe, open your eyes."

Try as she might, Zoe couldn't force herself to speak. Something loud was said, but she couldn't focus enough to make out what the words were. She let the couch consume her, hold her in its caress because there was nothing else that would do that.

"Zoe. I need you to open your eyes. Where are you hurt?"

The panic was there, just not in her. Zoe couldn't even figure out what to say. She wasn't hurt. Gwen was, and Gwen should be the focus of their attention.

"Shit."

Cold fingers against Zoe's face and then her body. She was floating. She let the darkness surround her even more fully than before. This was exactly what she needed. The dark, sweet embrace of nothingness.

twenty-six

COLLATERAL DAMAGE

Zoe wanted to cry when Gruzska pulled her into the conference room again. Her first day back at work after a week off and a short stay at the hospital was nothing significant. Except the tension she'd expected to have eased was still there. The office was quiet as hell, and Gwen still wasn't at her desk.

She dragged her feet as she walked inside and plopped heavily into the seat. She probably should have waited longer before returning. Her mother had yelled at her for that, too. Then again, her mother didn't even know the half of what had happened in the last few months.

Nikki.

How had Zoe missed all of the signs that her best friend was stalking her boss? That she was no friend at all, but only trying to get closer to Gwen? Every time she thought about it, Zoe was nearly in tears. And now was not the time to cry.

The executives looked at her with pity plainly filling their gazes. Would they finally be on her side? Why couldn't they just have believed her from the start? The fact that they insisted that she was lying, that they ignored her cries for help, didn't sit well with her. And here she was, once again trying to explain everything.

"I have a police report, if you'd like it," Zoe started straight out on the defensive. They hadn't listened to her before, so there was no reason for her to assume that they were going to listen now.

Gruzska seemed surprised by that. He raised a bushy eyebrow in her direction. "And what will be in it?"

"Ms. Fudala was being stalked. The harassment claims that you think I filed are a part of that case."

"Ms. Fudala was being stalked, not you."

"I was collateral damage." Zoe folded her hands in her lap, tightening her fingers as she tensed. This was exactly as she expected it to go. Nothing was more terrifying than sitting in this meeting and knowing no one would hear her. "There is a confession that the reports weren't made by me."

Gruzska pursed his lips, but he didn't answer. Probably because to do that would be to admit that there was a security issue with their systems, which was a bigger problem. One they could in theory avoid if Zoe didn't make a fuss over it all.

"When will Ms. Fudala be welcome back to work?" Zoe knew for a fact that it would be a few more weeks at the very least. Gwen still wasn't out of the hospital yet. The blow to her head had been hard enough that she wasn't quite released yet. Though they did expect that to happen soon.

Zoe had been working endlessly on organizing cleaners in the condo now that the police were done with it. She wanted it as clean as possible so that Gwen wouldn't have to see what it looked like after everything that had happened.

"That's for us to discuss with her," Sandra stated.

Of course. Why had Zoe expected any different?

She shivered and grasped her hands tighter. It was impossible to get anything out of these three, wasn't it?

"There's still the matter of the harassment claims." Sandra's lips thinned. "We need to deal with what happened."

"Nothing happened," Zoe reiterated. "The claims are

completely false. Ms. Fudala has never done anything untoward to me. I promise you. She's been absolutely professional."

Except she hadn't. Zoe hadn't either. They'd had sex in the office with Gruzska in the damn room with them. Everything had been consensual, but that wouldn't matter to them. It really shouldn't matter to them, even if it did to Zoe. A pit formed in the middle of Zoe's stomach. She was going to struggle to make this right because she couldn't. And that knowledge was becoming too much for her.

This was one battle that she wouldn't win.

"We're still investigating the circumstances surrounding the claims, and until the investigation is complete, Ms. Fudala will remain on leave."

Zoe sucked in a sharp breath. "Fine."

"We will meet with you again soon."

Frankie, Sandra, and Gruzska all started packing up the papers they had in front of them as if they were going to leave. A surge of anger reached the front of Zoe's head, and she couldn't hold back any longer.

"You don't want to know about Ms. Fudala? You haven't asked about her at all." Her palms were on top of the table, and she froze, halfway standing and halfway sitting. "Don't you care about her?"

"Of course we do," Frankie stated, his voice soothing. "But we can't talk to you about her."

"Bullshit." Zoe sneered. "She's my boss, so I know way more than you might think. Ms. Fudala was stalked for over a decade by a cunning asshole." Zoe stood up, flinging her hand out in front of her. "You have never believed her about what was going on, and that almost cost her her life. It almost cost me mine! Either start believing us when we tell you something is happening or continue to be the scourge of society."

Without waiting for another beat, Zoe left the conference room. That had not been what she'd expected. She stomped her way back to her office and slammed the door shut, locking it. She wanted to pick up everything on her desk and throw it across the room, but that was impossible. She wanted to do something to release the anger that was consuming her.

She hadn't allowed herself to be angry.

Not since everything that had happened. Waking up, alone, in that hospital bed was one of the scariest things she'd ever experienced. Finding out that Gwen was okay but struggling had been another blow. She hadn't done enough. She hadn't figured it out fast enough. She'd led Nikki straight to Gwen.

Fuck.

She needed to leave. She couldn't stand to be in this building anymore. Rapidly putting in a request for time off, Zoe snagged her purse and walked out of the office. If they got mad at her for it, they could suck a dick. She should have waited longer to come in again. She should have taken more time to bolster and prepare herself for what was going to come.

But she hadn't.

Instead of going home, Zoe went straight to the hospital. She had made that trip so many times in the last few days that she knew it by heart. As soon as she got there, she checked in as a visitor, got her sticker, and walked straight to Gwen's room.

"Hey," Gwen said as soon as Zoe stepped in, a huge grin on her face that immediately fell. "What happened?"

"Nothing." Zoe shook her head, trying to mask the discomfort. She should have worked better at that before coming for a visit, but she'd needed to see Gwen to calm down. The pull to her had been much stronger than she'd expected and this had been the first thought in her mind.

"After everything we've been through, don't lie to me." Gwen patted the bed, and Zoe slid onto it. Gwen took her hand, smoothing her thumb over Zoe's skin in a gentle pattern.

Tears threatened to break and fall down Zoe's cheek. She'd been doing so much of that lately. She hated it. But this was something else. The compassion she heard in Gwen's voice, the strength she still had after everything was what broke her.

"They still don't believe me."

"Who?" Gwen asked.

"Gruzska and the others."

Gwen hummed, squeezing Zoe's fingers firmly. "I take it you had a follow-up meeting with them."

"Yes, and it's apparently not the last. I'm so sick of it, Gwen. How can they still have their heads buried in the sand after everything?"

Frowning, Gwen reached up and cupped Zoe's cheek. She brought her in closer, pressing their lips together in a sweet embrace. Zoe sucked in a sharp breath when Gwen brought her back in for another kiss. Zoe would have liked to say that the first kiss made all the difference, but it didn't. She had to work double time to even focus on the second. By the time Gwen kissed her a third, she was slightly more at ease. The fourth and fifth kisses were much better, and the tension that had ridden in Zoe's shoulders vanished.

"That's better," Gwen murmured, her voice low and satisfied. "Gruzska is worried about his company, nothing else. This isn't a personal matter for him. It's a professional issue, and by professional standards, I'm a risk."

"Gwen, you've been the perfect boss."

"No, Zoe, I haven't." Gwen leaned back in the bed, her hand still holding Zoe's, but her face hardened. "I haven't been the perfect boss, and if you really think about it, you can see that too."

A deep line creased in Zoe's forehead. Surely Gwen was being too hard on herself, wasn't she? They'd never had an issue working together. Sometimes Gwen was a bit harsh, but that was only when she was stressed. Zoe could easily have the same reaction.

"We're in a relationship," Gwen supplied.

Zoe's frown increased in intensity. "So?"

"You're my personal assistant, Zoe. It's inappropriate on so many levels." Gwen squeezed her hand one last time before pulling back. "Gruzska can't dismiss the complaints because there's an ounce of truth to them. And because they're not the first ones that have been filed against me."

"What?" Zoe jerked back, already missing Gwen's steady hand in hers.

"Whether it was Nikki or not, I won't know, but I've had these complaints filed against me before. They never amounted to anything because I hadn't done anything, but now I have."

Zoe pulled her lip between her teeth and gnawed on it. She stared down at Gwen's fingers before reaching for them. She needed the touch to center herself. She didn't want to give that up, no matter what Gruzska and his minions ended up deciding about Gwen's fate.

"I broke the rules in a spectacular way." Gwen didn't seem worried about what she was saying at all. In fact, she looked damn pleased with herself. "When they find out, I won't be surprised if they fire me."

"What?" Zoe jerked back. "This is your career."

"It is. But I made certain choices, and I fully understand the consequences."

"Gwen." Zoe rubbed her lips together. She looked Gwen over. She seemed so much brighter than she had in the last couple of days. Her color was back in her cheeks, her eyes were sharp, and there was something behind her gaze that Zoe couldn't quite name. Not yet. "I don't even know what to say right now."

"You don't have to say anything. I'm fully aware of what's going on, and I have no doubts that there will be some major changes as a result of the conversations happening right now."

"Are you leaving?"

"No, not yet anyway." Gwen reached for Zoe's hand and squeezed. "But I do have some good news. I am leaving one thing."

"What?" Zoe was so close to tears. She couldn't imagine going to work without Gwen there, without her presence in the offices, telling her what to do and their deep brainstorming sessions.

"I am leaving this bed today." Gwen grinned broadly. "They're working on my discharge papers as we speak."

Zoe jerked slightly. "Are you serious?"

"Yes. Want to take me home, Zoe?"

"Yes!" Zoe leaned forward and threw her arms around Gwen's neck, tugging her in tightly for a hug. She was so careful of the back of her head with the stitches still in. "I'm so happy for you."

"Me too. I can't wait to sleep in my own bed." Gwen's body stilled.

Zoe understood what she was thinking, and she held Gwen even more carefully than before. "We'll figure that out, okay? We'll go back to your place and see how comfortable you are, and go from there."

"Okay," Gwen whispered, wrapping her arms around Zoe's back and hugging her. "I need to talk with Friendly tomorrow."

"That asshat?"

Gwen snorted and kissed Zoe's cheek before pulling back. "Yes, unfortunately. He's still in charge of the case for now, and he needs to do another interview with me. I believe he talked to you already?"

"Yeah." Zoe wrinkled her nose. "He's still an asshat."

"Yes, but at least now we can prove that we were right." Gwen winked, smiling again.

Zoe wasn't sure when the last time was that she'd seen Gwen smile this easily and this readily. In fact, Zoe wasn't quite sure she'd ever seen Gwen this relaxed before. But the question pinged in the back of her mind—was this the calm before the storm? Gwen had been stalked for twelve years, that kind of stress and trauma didn't just vanish because people believed her or because the stalker was currently in custody. Or would be shortly when she was released from the hospital.

Zoe hadn't told Gwen that, and she'd assumed that someone

had. They hadn't discussed it either. But Nikki was in the same hospital that Gwen was still in. Floors away and with a guard, unable to get up and walk, but having Nikki in such a close proximity was terrifying. Still.

When would that go away?

Zoe stared down at Gwen's hands again, the veins bulging on the top of her hand, the dark spots from one too many days in the sun when she was a kid. Swiping her thumb across it, Zoe plastered on a smile. "We were right. And that's something I'll always hold close."

"Yes. Let's." Gwen settled into the bed. "I'm so ready for a more comfortable bed than this one."

Zoe giggled. She understood the sentiment. The two days she'd spent in the hospital were plenty for her. Going home had been a different story, however. She'd barely slept since returning home, even though she'd had the locks changed immediately and added in some secondary locks. She hadn't found much rest, even with the knowledge that there was no way Nikki could harm her.

This involved more than just a breach of trust with Nikki. She'd used people in Zoe's life against her, repeatedly. She had trusted others, and they had flat out failed her. Zoe pushed that to the side, however. Right now her focus needed to be on Gwen. They needed to figure out what would happen next.

And Zoe could only hope that whatever was between them didn't end. At least not yet. But there was a niggling fear that came running back into her mind. This had only been for a distraction to start with. This had only been for Gwen's benefit. Now that the drama was seemingly over, the tension valve had been released.

But where did that leave them?

"Zoe?" Gwen's voice was firm.

"Yeah?" Zoe jerked her chin up, finding immense amounts of compassion in Gwen's gaze.

"Stop overthinking."

Grinning, Zoe leaned in for a kiss. Just that simple touch would remind her of everything that was at stake. "Yes, Ms. Fudala."

Gwen's scoff was the perfect response.

twenty-seven

THE FIRST DATE

"Come to dinner with me," Gwen's smooth voice filtered through the phone into Zoe's ear.

She knew she shouldn't have answered, not while still in the office, not while Gwen was still on leave and supposed to have no contact with anyone, not while the harassment claims still hadn't fully been taken care of. But Zoe couldn't help it. Gwen had called.

"Sure. When?"

"Zoe," Gwen cooed through the phone, a lift in her voice that Zoe hadn't heard in quite some time. "This is a date."

"A date?" Zoe frowned. Why would they go on a date? They hadn't exactly decided if this relationship would continue, although they had consistently talked everyday about non-work things for weeks now. Hadn't they? Were they in a relationship?

"Stop overthinking." Gwen had a lilt of laughter in her tone. "Come over tonight."

"To your condo?"

"Yes."

Could she walk in there? With all the memories of everything that had happened, Zoe wasn't sure that she had the bandwidth to be in the condo with Gwen again. She'd already done it and that had been hard enough. Gwen had been strong through everything, but Zoe hadn't wanted to go into the bedroom, not at all.

"Can we just go to my place?" It was the safer option, wasn't it? Because while Nikki had been inside her apartment, nothing detrimental had happened there. No in-person attacks, no blood pooling on the floor and death threatening.

"Sure, if that would make you more comfortable."

Gwen sounded...annoyed? No, that wasn't the right word for it. Zoe tried desperately to listen to her tone and figure out exactly what Gwen was thinking and feeling that she wasn't saying. She was notorious for not speaking her mind, but Zoe usually had such a better read on her than this. Maybe she was losing her touch.

"Zoe." Gwen chuckled. "I know you're nervous, but we'll talk tonight, okay? I'll bring dinner with me."

"Okay."

"And it's nothing bad, I promise you."

"Okay." Zoe gnawed on her lip and stared at the open door to the office. "When?"

"As soon as you get off work. I'll be waiting for you."

"Perfect." Zoe sighed, a smile already on her lips. She loved how Gwen had been keeping her informed of where she was going and when, ever since Nikki had burst in on them. It seemed they both enjoyed that at least for now. It meant there was backup if they needed it.

Someone would know.

They wouldn't be left in the same situation they had been in, with no one to call.

"See you soon." Gwen hung up.

Zoe stared at the clock on her computer screen. She had thirty minutes until the end of the day. When had that happened? Because she swore she'd just gotten back from lunch, and the amount of work she'd done also indicated that she'd just gotten back from lunch. She'd been struggling to focus for ages though, ever since they'd put Gwen on leave. Zoe supposed it was a good thing that her workload had been light since then.

Starting the process of packing up, Zoe went through the motions. Everything had been so quiet in the office that it was almost unnerving. She slung her bag over her shoulder, logged out of her computer and then turned it off—a habit she wasn't sure she'd ever break since Nikki had someone hack into it—and double checked the doors were locked before she left for the day.

This time, however, when she left the building, Zoe had a lightness to her step that wasn't there before. She was going to see Gwen—for a date. This was as official as they had dared to get so far. Yet the conversation at the hospital still lingered in the back of Zoe's mind. Gwen had expected the harassment claims. They'd happened before. And there was an ounce of truth to them this time.

This proved that, didn't it?

Zoe and Gwen were in a relationship now. They were *dating*. They essentially had been before this, but they hadn't put boundaries on it yet. Now they were defined, or at least they were going to have that defining conversation, weren't they?

True to her word, Gwen was at her front door when Zoe got there, two paper bags in her hands as she waited. Zoe smiled, relief washing through her just at the sight. She both loved and hated that Gwen was able to do that to her.

"Hey." Gwen's lips curled upward, her entire face relaxing as soon as she looked Zoe over.

Maybe they did that for each other?

"Hey," Zoe answered, leaning in and stealing a kiss. She pressed Gwen against the door but kept the embrace soft and generous. This wasn't the time to entice Gwen into something else. They really did need to talk first. There was still so much left unsaid. "So what's for dinner?"

"Other than you?" Gwen's deadpan look was perfect.

Zoe snorted lightly as she put her new key into the lock. Even though Nikki was still in jail, she didn't fully feel safe yet. There was still too much going on, considering everything, and she was pulled into the police investigation in ways she really didn't want to be. Is that what Gwen wanted to talk about tonight?

It must be. She wouldn't want to talk about their relationship.

They set everything up at the coffee table and leaned back into the couch with plates held up. Zoe's shoulders were solid rocks of tension. She had thought that had gone away, but she was wrong. It had only gotten better for a few minutes. Now it was worse. She grimaced. She needed to relax, if only so that Gwen wouldn't be tense.

Finally, Gwen broke the silence. "They're going to find out about our relationship."

"What do you mean?" Zoe's eyes bugged out, and she put her fork on her plate, unable to take another bite until she knew more.

"Think about it. We were interrupted. That will hit the news, but it'll be in the police reports as well. When this goes before a judge, everything is going to come out and Gruzska and the others will know."

Mulling that one over, cold washed through Zoe. Everyone would know who she had slept with, that she'd had sex with Gwen, probably multiple times, and there would be no denying the sexual harassment claims. "Right. I hadn't thought about that."

Gwen hummed and took another bite. "I figured you might have buried your head in the sand on that one."

"How?"

"Because you don't like conflict." Gwen gave her a wink before putting her plate onto the coffee table, half-eaten. "And you avoid it as best as you can."

Well, that was true, but it still unnerved Zoe that Gwen knew her so well. For the last three years of working for her, she had figured that Gwen hadn't paid much attention to her beyond the things that Zoe did for her. Then again, the last few weeks of whatever was going on between them should have proven otherwise.

Gwen paid attention.

A lot of attention.

"Okay, so then what's happening?" Zoe shoved a forkful of food between her lips. She wasn't being forceful because of anger, she told herself that several times before giving in. She was doing it because she was scared.

Gwen slid a hand over Zoe's thigh. "My lawyers are going to see what's happening with the police case and what the district attorney decides to do before we make any definitive moves, but they're planning on suing Nikki, amongst a few other people."

"Other people?" Zoe's eyes went wide again. She put her plate next to Gwen's, giving up on the ruse that she was actually eating and enjoying her dinner.

"The management in my building for starters. They gave access to Nikki when they shouldn't have. They're also considering suing Friendly and the police department depending on how botched the investigation really is."

"Oh." Zoe gnawed on her lip again. "I guess that makes sense."

"Twelve years of this, Zoe. I lived with her stalking for twelve years, and it wasn't until you that she was caught." Gwen slid Zoe a beautiful smile. "I'll be forever grateful to you for that."

"She nearly gave you a brain aneurysm, literally."

"Not literally." Gwen had a quirky look on her lips. "But if it hadn't been for her, I wouldn't have allowed myself to get so close to you in the first place."

"You wouldn't have held back from other relationships either," Zoe pointed out.

Gwen couldn't deny that one, so she didn't. She scooted in closer and rested her head on Zoe's shoulder. She took Zoe's hand in hers, folding her fingers around Zoe's. Gwen's breath was a light flutter against Zoe's neck. "I have never felt so safe with someone as I have with you."

"Gwen," Zoe whispered, dropping a kiss into Gwen's hair. "I haven't exactly kept you safe."

"Sure you have." Gwen tilted her chin up and kissed Zoe's neck. "More times than you can count."

Zoe was going to disagree with that one until her dying day, but she really didn't want a fight right then either. And there was that avoiding conflict thing Gwen had pointed out. Cringing, Zoe relaxed and eased into Gwen's soft touch. "So what does the lawsuit mean for us?"

"Nothing," Gwen answered instantly. "Our relationship as it moves forward is completely separate from that."

"Are you sure?"

"Yes." Gwen kissed Zoe's neck again, this time also hitting the underside of her chin.

Zoe groaned lightly, her eyes fluttering shut. Gwen had such a way with touches like this, a way to make Zoe relax even when she didn't want to. "Do that again."

"Yes, ma'am." Gwen chuckled lightly as she pressed another kiss to Zoe's chin, then behind her ear, then the corner of her lips. "I don't want us to stop whatever we've started."

"I think I love you." Zoe's voice was so soft. As soon as the words left her lips, however, she tensed sharply. What the fuck had she just said? As realization dawned, Zoe buried her face in her hands. "Oh my God!"

"No, don't do that." Gwen sat up a little and pulled Zoe's hands from her face. She kissed her knuckles before kissing her wrists. "Don't take it back."

"I can't believe I just said that."

Gwen's lips bowed. "Of course you can't, because it's not a thought you've fully formed yet."

Embarrassment was the only thing Zoe felt right now, and Gwen wasn't making it any better. She wanted to crawl in a hole and bury herself until she figured out what to do about the situation, how she could get out of it, or at least figure out if what she'd said was what she actually meant.

"You've never said anything you didn't mean," Gwen kissed Zoe's cheek.

Was Gwen a mind reader now? Zoe sank even farther into the couch, but she knew she wasn't going to get out of this one. Gwen pushed up on her knee and moved to straddle Zoe, sinking onto her lap as she leaned forward and put her hands on Zoe's cheeks.

"Look at me, Zoe."

"I don't want to." Zoe pouted and clenched her eyes shut. She couldn't believe she had just said that. It changed everything they were doing, and there was no going back now. Gwen couldn't tell her to take a hike without Zoe being devastated.

"Please." Gwen smoothed her thumbs along Zoe's cheek bone and then down her neck and over her collar bones. She used touch to center Zoe, and they both knew exactly what she was doing. She'd done it before. Zoe had done it for her. "Please look at me."

Prying one eye open, Zoe stared into Gwen's face, her rounded cheeks, her bright blue eyes, the hint of flush in her skin. She looked so alive, so happy, so perfect. Then again, Gwen always looked perfect. Out of habit, Zoe grabbed onto Gwen's hips and held her tightly.

"I love you," Gwen said so simply, as if it didn't take any effort for the words to slide from her beautifully full red lips. "I love you, Zoe."

"No, you don't."

"Don't be an idiot right now, silly girl." Gwen winked and shifted, the heat from between her legs pressing into the top of Zoe's thigh. There was a gentle rub and movement, like she was already working herself up. Was she? "You can't tell me what I feel or don't feel."

"I know," Zoe whispered, trailing her palms upward to cover Gwen's breasts and massage them lightly before sliding her hands around Gwen's back and pulling her in closer. "I know I can't."

"And I'm telling you that I love you." Gwen pressed a kiss right in front of Zoe's ear and took in a sharp breath. "I love when you touch me, when you look at me all shocked when I say or do something you don't expect. I love how protective you are."

"Anyone should be." Zoe allowed her eyes to flutter shut, and she tangled her fingers into Gwen's hair, moving in for a swift kiss. "Everyone should see how amazing you are."

"Not everyone thinks that I am. But I'm so happy that you do." Gwen kissed Zoe's cheek, pressing kiss after kiss against her skin as she worked closer to Zoe's lips. "If you do love me, if you don't take that back in regret, then I'm so happy that you do. I don't want anyone else but you."

Humming, Zoe finally pressed their mouths together, this time deepening the kiss as she tangled their tongues together. Warmth and love filled her, taking control of every doubt that she had, every lingering fear and worry, and smashing it. Zoe sucked in a sharp breath when Gwen pressed her crotch down hard on Zoe's leg, definitely hot, definitely wet.

Were they really doing this?

"Gwen," Zoe murmured against Gwen's mouth. "I love you."

"Perfect." Gwen dove back in for another kiss. "You make me so happy, silly girl."

Zoe grinned as they continued their embrace. She felt so comfortable, sitting with Gwen in her lap, snogging her boss, touching her. This wasn't just about sex and distraction anymore. It might have been that the first time—but if Zoe really thought about it, even that first time had been about so much more. They had come together using distraction as an excuse, and both of them had their minds blown by the connection they'd found.

It really shouldn't have surprised them. They'd worked together for years, they knew each other so well, they loved each other before they'd started any kind of romantic relationship, and this had just expanded on that. Zoe moved swiftly, pressing her arm against Gwen's back and flipping her down onto the couch cushions so Zoe hovered over her.

"Are you sure?"

"Yes, I'm sure." Gwen brushed Zoe's hair behind her ear and smiled up at her. "I'm always sure when I make decisions."

"Very true." Zoe kissed her again, hard this time. "You might have to move though."

Gwen laughed hard, the sound rocking through her as Zoe kissed her way down Gwen's chest, over her clothes, to her breasts, and then back up to her mouth. "I'm already working on selling the place. I can't—" Gwen gasped when Zoe used her teeth against the soft skin of Gwen's neck. "—As much as I want to stay there and prove I can, I can't."

"You're welcome here."

"I'd already planned on sleeping here tonight."

"Thank fuck." Zoe kissed Gwen hard. "Because I don't plan on letting you out from under me until you're thoroughly fucked."

Gwen's moan was all the response Zoe needed. She pulled up Gwen's shirt and pressed a multitude of kisses against the hot skin of her belly.

"You ready for that?"

"Yes," Gwen hissed. "Yes, show me how much you love me."

twenty-eight

DEALING WITH THE FALLOUT

Zoe twirled the tip of her tongue all over Gwen's stomach before sliding back up to kiss her lips. This was the first time they'd had sex since that night, and it was harder than she'd imagined to push the images of Nikki's attack out of her mind.

But this was something she wanted to do.

Something she was determined to do.

If they couldn't sleep at Gwen's or even stand to be there, that was one thing. But Zoe wouldn't let Nikki ruin what was between them. Zoe kissed her way back down to Gwen's stomach, taking her time to settle into the fact that they were going to have sex again.

This time they were safe.

Nikki was still in jail, and they were here, safe and protected from anything bad. Scraping her teeth across Gwen's tender skin, Zoe smiled as Gwen moved and wiggled against her. They both wanted this it seemed, for something between them to intensify and their connection to grow deeper.

"Tell me," Zoe breathed, not realizing just how out of breath she was. She really needed to focus on that and make sure that she was staying in the here and now.

"Tell you what?" Gwen raised her hands over her head and

grasped onto the arm of the couch. Her gaze was direct and strong as she looked down at Zoe lying between her legs.

"Tell me if you need to stop or if I need to move or if something doesn't feel right, okay?" Zoe fought back tears. Where the hell had those come from?

"Zoe." Gwen surged upward. She immediately wrapped her arms around Zoe's shoulders and pulled her in for a tight hug. Zoe buried her nose in Gwen's neck and held on with everything she had. Gwen was her safe place—that much she'd known for months now. This woman held space for her to be worried and upset and never condemned her for it. "Zoe," Gwen murmured again, stroking Zoe's hair down her back.

"I'm sorry." Zoe blinked hard, trying to shake herself out of whatever mood she'd been dropped into.

"Don't be sorry." Gwen kissed her cheek, then her nose, then her lips. "This is all so very new to us."

Maybe Gwen didn't understand. Zoe frowned. This wasn't because of a declaration of love, this was because of Nikki, and the consequences of everything she had done to Gwen. Well, not just to Gwen, but to both of them. Nikki had violated Zoe repeatedly since she'd thought she and Gwen were—Zoe whimpered. What the hell was wrong with her?

"This isn't because I love you," Zoe finally made the words out. She pushed away from Gwen and wiped her eyes, which were thankfully dry. "That's not new."

A line creased in the center of Gwen's forehead, and it was adorable. Zoe smiled, though she knew it didn't meet her eyes.

"What do you mean?"

"I've loved you for years, Gwen. Years." Zoe grinned fully. "This isn't about that. This is because of her."

"Say her name." Gwen's face hardened. "I know her name now, and I want to hear it. She's not just a figment."

In awe of Gwen's strength, Zoe folded their hands together and settled her head on Gwen's shoulder. "This is because of Nikki."

"Nikki is a cunt."

"What?" Zoe jerked up and stared at Gwen in shock. "Did you really just say that?"

"Yes, and I'll never apologize for it. That woman tormented me for twelve years. No one believed me but you. She got into my head. She is the worst possible person on this planet, and I won't give her a break or be nice about it."

"I get that," Zoe said softly, now running her fingers over Gwen's shoulder and arm to try and soothe her. "I'm sorry I brought her up."

"Don't be." Gwen looked Zoe directly in the eye. "She hurt us, in more ways than physically. The physical injuries are the easiest to deal with. These emotional scars are going to last a lifetime. I can't sleep in my own bedroom, Zoe."

"That's why you're here." Realization dawned on Zoe. She was such an idiot. Trying to seduce Gwen when they weren't ready.

Gwen sucked in a sharp breath. She curled her fingers around Zoe's cheek and then drew her in for a quick kiss. "Yes, that's why I'm here. But I'm also here because you are safe. You are love. You are hope. Zoe... silly girl..." Gwen smiled broadly, the pain from seconds before vanishing into the ether. "You're why I'm here, and I want you."

Confused, Zoe frowned. "You what?"

"I want you. I've always used sex as a distraction, but I didn't realize how much better it would be with someone who cared about me after the distraction was over." Gwen lifted Zoe's chin and kissed her again, this time lingering. Her lips were wet, smooth, hot. She pushed into Zoe and took more of the kiss.

Zoe tangled her fingers in Gwen's hair and held onto her tightly. She sucked in a breath when Gwen nipped her lower lip and then nibbled her way down Zoe's neck to the top of her breasts, nibbling through Zoe's shirt.

"I want you, and I want this." Gwen kissed Zoe's lips again.

"If you don't want to have sex right now, please tell me and we can stop, but I plan on staying here all night."

Zoe hummed, dropping her forehead onto Gwen's shoulder and closing her eyes. "This is the first time all week I haven't been looking over my shoulder for her. I'm safe with you."

"We're safe together." Gwen rubbed the back of Zoe's neck, pushing into the tense muscles until they eased.

Zoe finally lifted her head. Then she stood up and held out her hand. "Let's do this."

"Are you sure?" Gwen asked.

"More than ever."

When their fingers touched, a spark of arousal lit between Zoe's legs. They'd never connected quite like this before. This was raw honesty, and oh how she loved it. As soon as they stood by Zoe's bed, Zoe wrapped her arms around Gwen's waist and pulled her in for a long kiss.

She took her time with this one, making sure her heart and head were in the right place before dropping her hands to the edge of Gwen's shirt and lifting it up over Gwen's head. The black lacy bra contrasted sharply with Gwen's skin, bringing out the smooth lines of her breasts, and the goosebumps that rose up now that her skin was exposed to the air.

"You're so beautiful," Zoe murmured as she delicately ran her fingers over the top of Gwen's breasts, back and forth over the skin reverently. "Not just your body, but your mind, your heart."

"I don't need accolades," Gwen answered, but she didn't reach up to stop Zoe either.

Grinning with humor, Zoe laughed lightly. "Oh, I think you do, and I think you deserve them time and time again. Get on the bed, Gwen."

"Anything you say, boss." Gwen's eyes glittered as she sat on the edge of the bed and undid the zipper and clasp on her pants. She pushed them down her legs along with her thong, smiling as she used her toe to flip them into the air before they landed in a pool on the floor.

All right. They were really doing this. Zoe stripped off her shirt and pants, clambering onto the bed on top of Gwen. Their mouths connected in a fire and urgency that Zoe had thought was long gone from their evening. Something about that pause, about talking about their fears and worries, made this even better.

When Gwen arched her back as Zoe pressed her thigh between Gwen's legs, Zoe unsnapped her bra. As pretty as it was on her skin, Zoe wanted full access to everything. She wanted them to be unhindered by the world tonight. She tossed Gwen's bra over the side of the bed and immediately covered Gwen's nipple with her mouth.

Gwen hissed and pressed hard against Zoe's thigh, hissing again. Zoe couldn't keep the smile from her lips, the happiness that soared through her. This was so much better than any time before. She pulled off of Gwen's breast with a pop before moving to the other one. Gwen hummed and rocked her hips up and down against Zoe's thigh, giving herself as much pleasure if not more than what Zoe was getting just from being this close and touching her.

Zoe lavished Gwen's breasts, the soft skin of her chest and stomach. She wanted this to be slow and easy, a coming together after a time of upheaval that very nearly destroyed what was just budding between them. Zoe maneuvered her hand between them, sliding her fingers through Gwen's damp hair between her legs, against her slick folds, finding her swollen clit and just pushing on it.

Gasping, Gwen's eyes fluttered shut. "You have such a way with your hands, silly girl."

Zoe bit her lip as she stared down at Gwen, beautiful as ever, sprawled against the sheets on her bed. Her eyes were closed, and her entire body slack from tension and worry, though she was certainly filled with arousal, considering Gwen was barely holding still as she writhed against Zoe, begging for more.

Giving in, Zoe slid her pointer and middle fingers inside Gwen, feeling the heat surround her, the tightness of her pussy.

Zoe sucked in a breath and pressed the heel of her palm against Gwen's clit and leaned in. The pressure was simple, and Zoe barely moved, but it made Gwen go wild beneath her. Zoe was going to make Gwen come so many times that she wouldn't be able to walk. Gwen would be stuck snuggling with Zoe until morning—not that either of them seemed to want anything else.

"Zoe," Gwen breathed her name heavily. She hadn't stopped moving, her hips rotating in a circle, her feet planted into the mattress as she lifted up slightly. "How do you always do this to me?"

"Do what?" Zoe leaned down and trailed small kisses against Gwen's neck and collarbone. She moved to the tops of Gwen's breasts but avoided her nipples, wanting to tease only so much at a time. She wanted to drag this out.

"Make me want you so much." Gwen wrapped her arms around Zoe's neck and brought Zoe's mouth up to meet hers.

The kiss was passionate. It was filled with desire and dreams. Zoe could taste them if she closed her eyes. They weren't just her dreams, they were Gwen's mixed with hers, a full mingling of their lives, intertwining together. Zoe didn't want to break the embrace. This was one of the holiest moments she had ever experienced in her life.

Gwen's moan filled Zoe's chest and locked them together. Zoe pulled her hand between Gwen's legs back slowly and pushed in slightly, increasing the pressure before relieving it. Gwen gasped and pushed her shoulders into the bed.

"Don't stop doing that." Gwen looked right up in Zoe's eyes. "Don't ever stop loving me."

"Never," Zoe murmured and moved in for another kiss. This time she kept it quick and once again trailed kisses down Gwen's neck.

Zoe moved her hand faster, but tried her best to keep the pressure the same. Gwen rolled her hips in time with Zoe's movements, her body suddenly jerking. It was a sure indication that she was getting closer to orgasming than before. Zoe longed to see

Gwen come apart underneath her, to fall apart just so that Zoe could catch her. Zoe curled her fingers slightly, changing the sensation for Gwen in a way she hoped would get them both right where they wanted.

Gwen cried out. She reached up behind her, finding the pillow to grasp onto as her body contorted and her hips rose up, her shoulders pushed down, and her feet dug into the mattress. Gwen flung an arm around Zoe's back and clutched onto her, bringing their bodies together as she careened. It was the most beautiful thing Zoe had ever seen. This was Gwen, completely unhindered, with nothing holding her back. This was Gwen bare, vulnerable, broken, and sewn back together—or at least in the process of it.

Zoe lay next to her, running soothing fingers over Gwen's skin and pressing soft kisses anywhere she could easily reach. She waited patiently for Gwen to come back around, to find her voice and her body again. Finally Gwen looked up at Zoe, her big blue eyes full of love and nothing else.

"Silly girl, did you really think you could take me out with one orgasm?"

"Not at all." Zoe grinned, her cheeks heating.

When had she taken to Gwen's forwardness with sex talk? It was something she'd come to love and appreciate, even if she wouldn't start saying those things herself right away. Maybe she would get there someday. But not today. Today she would just appreciate Gwen for all that she was and everything they gave to each other.

"But you know what?" Zoe leaned in and nuzzled against Gwen's cheek. "The night has just started."

"You know what?" Gwen answered, a smile in her tone. "You're right."

twenty-nine

SECOND CHANCES AT THE WINERY

"Are you ready?" Gwen's smooth voice filtered through Zoe's ears, warming her, along with the smile on her lips.

"Absolutely."

Zoe stepped out of Gwen's car on the crisp October Saturday. It had been nearly impossible to wait the two weeks to come, but Gwen had suggested it as a date day and Zoe'd jumped at the opportunity. Then again, the memory of walking drunk and wanting so much to lean in and kiss Gwen was a cold shock to her system.

But she could actually do that now.

Without consequences.

Grinning, Zoe walked around the car and snagged Gwen's hand with her own, folding their fingers together as they turned toward the main entrance to the winery. She couldn't believe this had become her life in the last few weeks.

They were on a date.

A real, true, proper date.

Zoe had never done a relationship so backward before, but perhaps that's exactly what needed to happen for the two of them to end up together. They walked toward the front of the winery, and Zoe could feel Gwen stiffen, the muscles in her shoulders and arm tightened.

Slowing her step, Zoe tugged Gwen back slightly until they were looking into each other's eyes. "She's not here."

"I know." Gwen bristled, and Zoe could tell that she was trying to brush off the concern.

"Gwen." Zoe squeezed Gwen's hand a little harder, making sure that she had Gwen's full attention. "She's not here."

"I know that, silly girl."

Zoe smiled at the sweet nickname. Gwen hadn't been able to stop calling her that on and off, but this was the first real time she'd done it since they'd gotten back to the real world. At least, Zoe had. Gwen was still on leave from work.

"I know you know that." Zoe listed forward, pressing their lips together with a smile. "But your body doesn't know that yet. You're tensing up."

"Shit," Gwen mumbled, her eyes casting down in embarrassment. "How do you even notice that?"

Zoe shook her head slowly. "I've been observing you for years. I think I was bound to get something right eventually."

"Fair." Gwen dragged in a deep breath, holding it in her lungs for a five count, and then released it slowly. She did it two more times before she nodded to herself and then made eye contact with Zoe. "I suppose you should ask this time."

"Are you ready?"

"Yes." Gwen moved in, pressing their lips together firmly. This kiss was different from the one before, the taste of passion in it that Zoe could never ignore with Gwen. But this time, it was front and center. "We can explore that later."

"Yes, please."

Laughing seductively, Gwen kissed Zoe's cheek then started toward the winery. They walked hand in hand together. This time felt so different than the last. Zoe had been nervous the first time she'd been there, wanting to impress her boss and make sure that she picked the best wine for the party.

But this time she was relaxed. She didn't need to impress anyone, and they weren't there for work. This was time solely for them, so they could get to know each other better. Without a stalker hidden in every dark corner.

Zoe made sure to stay as close to Gwen as possible. They climbed into a vehicle for a tour of the winery. Zoe was attempting to listen to the man tell her all about the grapes they were growing, but Gwen's fingers sliding along the inside of her thigh were so damn distracting. Gwen pressed one finger firmly, then dragged it up toward Zoe's crotch before suddenly lifting it and releasing all the pressure. Then she did it again. And again.

Clenching her jaw, Zoe raised an eyebrow at Gwen. This was a level of flirtation that she hadn't expected. Gwen had been so meek the other week that Zoe had wanted to take everything as slow as they possibly could just to make sure that Gwen was in the right state of mind.

Zoe leaned over, her lips brushing against Gwen's ear when she murmured, "What are you doing?"

"Nothing we haven't done before," Gwen responded, a lilt of fascination in her tone.

Zoe was envious of that. Public sex, and public displays of affection, weren't something she was used to. Clearly, Gwen felt otherwise. Between the party, the elevator ride up, the little sexual exchange with the mirror, and sex in the office—Gwen was obsessed with pushing the boundaries of what could be considered normal.

Gwen turned her cheek, pushing Zoe's mouth against her. Her skin was so hot, and her scent overwhelming. Zoe shivered, her nipples hardening in her bra and under all the layers of clothes she'd worn to stay warm this time of year. Gwen slid her fingers higher, repeating the same pattern but faster until she reached the apex between Zoe's legs and immediately backed off.

"We're at the winery," Zoe protested.

"Yes." Gwen turned her cheek even more, pushing Zoe's nose

practically into her neck. "And as you said before, Nikki is nowhere nearby."

Relief flooded through Zoe. Was this Gwen with no holds barred? She leaned in, pressing her nose into the hot skin at Gwen's neck, and then she dared to do the unthinkable. Three months ago, she never would have thought herself capable of this.

But now?

Her world was so different.

"She's locked in a jail cell," Zoe murmured. Then she dashed her tongue out again before scraping her teeth.

Gwen hissed, then moaned in pleasure. "Today is for us, not her."

"It is." Zoe winced. She couldn't stop herself from thinking about tomorrow, as much as she might want to and as much as it seemed Gwen wanted her to. Tomorrow would bring them back to work—well, Zoe back to work. She had to believe that with the arrest and trials and the charges being dropped against Gwen that she would be allowed back to work soon enough.

Which would leave them where?

"Aren't we supposed to be paying attention?" Zoe asked. It was her way of pulling back, of connecting to this moment and what their future might be. They hadn't really talked about that since everything had happened.

Zoe would support Gwen no matter what, through thick and thin. With the pressure and tension of how their physical relationship had started, with the beginnings of their emotional relationship just starting, Zoe was worried about what any change might bring.

"Hmm, I am. Aren't you, silly girl?"

Again that nickname sent a shiver of pleasure coursing through her. Zoe couldn't get enough of it. She nipped at Gwen's earlobe before pulling away and rolling her eyes. "You're insatiable some days."

"Most days," Gwen corrected. "But you've known me for

years now. Does it really come as a surprise to you that when I know what I want, I don't stop until I get it?"

Zoe's jaw dropped, then her mouth went dry at the thought. Gwen wanted her. But there was something else Gwen was hinting at. Zoe just couldn't quite figure out what that was.

"What do you mean?"

Gwen sighed. She moved her hand, taking Zoe's and curling their fingers together. The space between them was palpable, but it didn't feel wrong. In fact, this was what Zoe had been looking for. She wasn't ready to jump into finger fucking in the back of the tour vehicle.

"I'm not going back to work."

"What?" Zoe's eyes bugged out, and she clenched Gwen's hand hard.

"I quit."

"You don't quit," Zoe countered. "I've seen you do anything to get what you want. You don't just quit."

Gwen's lips quirked up in the corner at that. Zoe knew she was right. Gwen had never quit anything in the time they had worked together, and Zoe suspected that had been her pattern for far longer. Just look at how long she'd fought against an unknown foe.

"Why are you quitting?" Zoe looked directly into Gwen's eyes, so unsure but needing an answer.

"So many reasons." Gwen patted the top of Zoe's hand and leaned back in the seat as the driver took them into another part of the vineyard.

"Tell me."

"Your harassment complaints weren't the first ones, I told you that." Gwen dashed her tongue across her lips, staring out into the fields surrounding them. "But I want them to be the last. As long as I've worked there, it hasn't been the greatest job. I've put up with a lot. I was afraid."

"Afraid of what?" Zoe's heart went out to her. She could only imagine what Gwen had been fearful of for the last twelve years.

Gwen swallowed hard, closing her eyes. "I was afraid no one else would take me. Not with that history, not with Nikki, not with who I am."

"You're amazing at your job."

"Which I think is the only reason they didn't fire me." Gwen gave Zoe a wry smile. "But with your complaints they don't have a choice. I'd rather quit before a termination ends up on my record."

"You can't leave me," Zoe whispered, her gaze falling to their connected hands.

"I'm not leaving you." Gwen turned sharply, cupping Zoe's cheek. She stared directly into Zoe's eyes, Gwen's wet with unshed tears. "I'm *not* leaving you."

Why was Zoe clinging to her like this?

Zoe had never felt so bonded to someone before, not like this. Even Nikki, with three years of friendship—despite her recent betrayal—she hadn't felt like this. And how could Zoe even begin to trust someone after what Nikki had done to her?

Tears spilled down her cheeks, piling one on top of the other. She couldn't see straight. Her eyes burned, her nose stopped up. This was the emotional fallout that she had been waiting for, the moment of recognition of how fucked up this whole situation was.

Gwen shushed, dragging Zoe in to press her head against Gwen's shoulder. Gwen stroked her fingers through Zoe's hair, down her back, over her shoulders. She said sweet nothings, most of which Zoe barely recognized and knew she'd never remember. Still, it was Gwen's steady tones, her rhythmic breathing, the glide of her fingers that held Zoe exactly where she was.

"How do I trust myself?" Zoe whispered, finally. She knew Gwen had no context to even begin to answer the question, but Zoe wasn't sure she could add more to it at the moment.

Gwen kissed Zoe's cheek and hugged her close. "I don't know how to help you with that. It'll take time, but it's something you have to do on your own."

Zoe shook her head and closed her eyes. "But you're leaving."

"Just from work, silly girl. I'm not leaving you."

Zoe gasped in a snot-filled sob. "I can't keep going to work without you. You're the entire reason I'm there."

"Then leave Gruzska."

"What?" Zoe jerked back, wiping her hands along her cheeks. Had Gwen really said that? What did she mean by it? "I can't just quit. Not without another job—"

"Come work for me." Gwen brushed her thumb along Zoe's lip. "Nothing has to change except the location."

"You don't have another job."

Gwen gave her a small smile. "Do you really think I would quit without a backup plan? I'm starting my own company. I've been preparing to do it for years, and now's the time."

"Your own company?"

"Yeah. My own marketing firm." Gwen's eyes lit up, that passion Zoe had seen in her for years coming back into her gaze. Her cheeks reddened slightly as she pushed loose strands of hair behind her ear. "We can keep doing this."

"No, we can't. Everything will be different." Zoe clung to the familiarity. With as much chaos as she had faced in the last few months, she couldn't stand to put one foot into another change. She needed that consistency to keep her head on the right way. Didn't she?

"It will," Gwen agreed. "But different isn't bad."

Zoe wasn't sure about that. She sniffled, wiping her nose with the back of her hand, and she closed her eyes against the burning tears. "I don't know if I can do that."

"Think about it." Gwen wiped the tears from her cheeks. "That's all I'm asking for."

Zoe wanted to say yes. She really did, but the thought of being part of a startup, the thought of leaving her job when she had no one else to support her with everything that had happened, the thought of what she would do to even pay rent next month nearly sent her into another full blown panic.

"I didn't want to bring this up today."

"Why not?" Zoe sniffled again, but she seemed to be getting a better hold of herself. Gwen wasn't pushing for an answer, not that Gwen ever did. She really did have time to think about this. Wasn't there some rule about not making major life decisions within six to twelve months after a major traumatic event?

Stalker popping out of the closet after you fuck your boss counted as a major traumatic event, right?

"Zoe," Gwen chastised lightly. "Calm your racing thoughts."

"Sorry." Zoe bit her lip, and suddenly she found her hands in Gwen's again. This place was warm. This place was perfect. It was perfect because it was real and because it came with good and bad.

"I want today to be easy." Gwen blew out a breath as they pulled back up at the winery. Zoe had missed the entire tour. "I want today to be simple."

"Gwen..." Zoe trailed off, realizing for the first time in weeks that she hadn't even thought to call her Ms. Fudala. "Nothing with you is simple."

Gwen gave a little smile, her cheeks tinged with a blush. "I think you're right."

When Zoe stepped out of the vehicle, Gwen was right there. Gwen wrapped her arms around Zoe's middle and pulled her in, their lips pressing together in a deep kiss. Zoe struggled to keep up, her mind swirling with thoughts, her body on fire with sensations. Gwen nipped at her lower lip, humming as she said, "That's my silly girl."

And Zoe melted.

Again.

thirty
PACKING UP

"We need you to pack up Ms. Fudala's personal items." Gruzska stood in the doorway, as if entering the office would taint him in some way.

Zoe had barely had a moment to sit down before he'd shown up. She couldn't imagine finding out this way that Gwen was leaving. With her lips parted, surprise still filling her chest even though she'd known it was coming, Zoe nodded slightly. "Yes, sir."

"Please have it done by the end of the day."

"I understand."

He left.

The wake of chaos that Zoe had felt as soon as Gwen had dropped the bomb that she'd quit intensified. She stared at her phone on her desk, half-tempted to text Gwen and tell her what happened. But she would already know, wouldn't she? Zoe sat in a cold sweat, still unsure of what to do next.

She was startled when someone new stepped into the office, someone she'd never seen before. He carried boxes with him that he stacked next to the door before walking out without another word.

"Jesus."

Zoe was so on edge. Hadn't the entire Nikki situation been enough? She would think that now that Nikki had been arrested and was still in jail, she would feel safer. But she didn't. Gwen wasn't the only one struggling with that.

This office wasn't the balm she wanted it to be anymore.

This was where she'd met Gwen, where she'd met Nikki, where she'd inadvertently brought the two of them closer together because of her damn trusting nature. Zoe bit her lip hard when the next set of boxes hit the ground.

Right.

She had a job to do.

Zoe snagged the first box and packed it up. She started in Gwen's office, in one corner, and she stacked the full boxes by the door. It was lunch time when the man came back to take away the boxes Zoe had packed and add more to the pile for her to build and pack. This was going to take her all day, and Gwen was trusting that she wasn't going to forget anything that was hers.

Turning on soft music, Zoe got into the zone. She didn't want to be here later than she had to be, and she certainly didn't want to still be packing tomorrow. She needed to get this done today.

But the office was so empty.

She'd thought it had been missing something before, but with Gwen's personal things gone, with the books that she'd proudly kept on her shelves packed away, with her desk drawers empty and the pictures on the walls gone, Zoe couldn't deny it. This was empty.

She had nothing left here.

Biting her lip, Zoe taped the last box shut and stared at her handiwork. Her back ached and her arm muscles were sore from lifting all day. She checked her phone and saw a couple missed messages from Gwen, checking in and apologizing that Zoe had to be the one to pack it all up.

They wouldn't even let her in supervised to do that.

Zoe bit the inside of her cheek and sent off a quick reply.

When she emerged from Gwen's interior office into her own, she stopped short.

What the hell was she doing here?

There was nothing left for her here. They would move her to another office, one that she would hate. She wasn't interested in this industry. She'd only been interested in working for Gwen, which left her where exactly?

Biting her lip, Zoe looked at the extra boxes still leaning against the door.

She couldn't, could she?

She'd never been so bold before. But perhaps throughout all of this, Gwen had taught her a few life lessons. Swallowing the lump in her throat, Zoe moved swiftly. She built up three boxes, and she shoved every personal item of hers into them before the gentleman came back to take the last box with him.

"Is this it?" he asked.

"Yeah." Zoe put her hands on her hips and surveyed the room. "Yeah, that's everything."

Zoe sat in her office chair. This was the right decision. She wasn't even sure when the choice had solidified in her brain, but it was very clear that it had. She was leaving.

Turning her computer on one last time, Zoe opened a blank document and wrote up her resignation. With it printed and in an envelope, she grabbed her purse and walked directly to Gruzska's office. She wasn't even permitted inside to see him.

Biting her lip, she stared at his admin and handed the resignation over. "Everything of Ms. Fudala's is cleared out of the office. As are all of my personal belongings."

She looked confused.

"Here." Zoe handed over the notice. "It's effective immediately."

Zoe didn't wait. She turned on her toes and started toward the elevator. She dropped her badge with security and walked out of the office building for the last time. The weight that had been on her shoulders lifted immediately.

The drive home was easy.

When Zoe unlocked the door to let herself inside, Gwen sat on her couch and looked up at her oddly. "What are you doing home so early?"

Never before had Zoe thought that simple question would ease her the way it did. She wanted to hear the simplicity every day. Smiling, Zoe dropped her purse by the door and shucked her jacket. Gwen hadn't taken her eyes from Zoe's face, and when Zoe sat down and snagged Gwen's hands, pressing a kiss to her lips, she grinned.

"I quit."

"What?" Gwen's brow furrowed. "I thought—"

"I couldn't do it anymore. I can't work there without you." Zoe wanted to melt into Gwen's body, be held by her. "I'm not going back."

"Zoe..." Gwen trailed off.

"I want to work with you." Zoe laced their fingers together, bringing Gwen's knuckles to her lips. "That's all I want."

"Are you sure?"

"More than ever." Zoe smiled as Gwen's lips curled up, the realization dawning between them. "I love you."

Gwen surged forward, their mouths connecting. Zoe's eyes fluttered shut, her heart racing. Gwen cupped the back of her head, pulling Zoe closer as her mouth opened, as their tongues tangled. Zoe lost herself in the kiss. She pushed up on her knees, practically moving into Gwen's lap.

"If you ever want a different job—"

"Shut up, Gwen." Zoe nipped Gwen's lower lip and then pressed kisses down her neck. "I can't imagine working for anyone else."

"With me." Gwen swallowed. "You'll be working with me."

Zoe sucked in a sharp breath. It was a distinction, one that she hadn't fully thought through. But she was trusting her gut. Gwen had never done anything wrong by her, and Zoe had to believe that everything would work out in the end for the both of them.

"Zoe," Gwen whispered, planting a kiss on Zoe's cheek. "We have to talk a minute."

Groaning, Zoe pulled back slowly. She just wanted to be wrapped in Gwen's arms, to live there a little bit longer each and every day. "I don't know where they're delivering all your stuff, but my stuff is with it. I figured you wouldn't mind."

"I don't mind. It'll be delivered to my condo tomorrow."

Zoe kissed Gwen's lips one more time. "Then what else is there to talk about?"

"I sold my condo."

Sitting back with a thump, Zoe looked Gwen over. "You did?"

Gwen nodded slowly. "I did. I didn't think it would sell so quickly, but I took the first offer. Not practical, I know, but I can't..."

"...go back there," Zoe finished for her. She understood. They'd been staying at Zoe's apartment since the attack, and Zoe loved having such easy access to Gwen that she wasn't sure she could go back to any other way of living.

"Yeah. I'm looking for somewhere to move temporarily, until I can decide what I'm doing next."

"I thought you'd already decided." Zoe furrowed her brow in confusion. Gwen always came with ideas, and then plans attached to those initial ideas.

Gwen shook her head, water in her eyes again. "It may surprise you, but it's been difficult to make decisions through all of this. With the trial looming..." Gwen trailed off, and Zoe could tell she was having to pull herself back together.

Zoe waited patiently, not wanting Gwen to feel pressured to share if she wasn't ready for it.

"...with the trial looming, I feel like we're in a stalemate until something is decided."

"But you quit your job. You sold your home."

"I know." Gwen's lips thinned. "Those were things I had to do."

"So what do we do now?" Zoe brushed her fingers along

Gwen's hand, then up her arm, trailing a pattern back and forth. She wanted to give as much comfort as possible. This was a tough time for both of them. They were in the midst of a legal battle, and Zoe had no idea how any of that even worked. She'd never been involved in something like this before.

"We rebuild ourselves." Gwen snagged Zoe's fingers, bringing them to her lips for a tender kiss. "We start fresh."

"What does that mean, though?"

"I don't have answers for you." Gwen looked torn. "I wish I did."

Zoe's lip quivered. She really had to be okay with not being okay, with not having the answers. That was something she had never been good at. Especially when it came to the direction her life was taking. Yet even without answers, she was comforted by her decision.

Her phone rang, vibrating in her pocket. Zoe hesitated before she pulled it out, seeing the number and grimacing. "I should have known they'd call."

"Call?" Gwen furrowed her brow. She took the phone and looked at the number before handing it back. "What happened today?"

Zoe sighed, silencing the phone call. "I spent all day packing up the offices, and every single item that I put into a box was a reminder of what I was losing. And it wasn't a job. It was you." Zoe swallowed hard. "I love you, Gwen. And I can't stand to work for someone who is such an asshole to their employees, someone who doesn't believe people who have worked for them for years. What they did was unconscionable."

"What they did was protect the company," Gwen countered. "That's exactly what they should have done."

"No. It's not." Zoe bit her lip when her phone buzzed again. "They should have believed you!"

Zoe was adamant that Gwen needed to understand her. She was so tired of Gwen letting everyone walk all over her. Gwen was strong, one of the strongest women Zoe knew, and she deserved to have the world hear and believe her no matter what she said. Because she wouldn't lie. She hadn't lied.

Gwen canted her head to her side. She touched Zoe's hand lightly and pressed their fingers together before tenderly running her fingers up and down Zoe's arm. Now who was doing the comforting?

"They should have believed you," Zoe said firmly. She wasn't going to give this one up.

"It would have been amazing if they had. But they didn't." Gwen looked directly at Zoe. "And I can't fault them for their disbelief. Not now anyway. Maybe in a few years when all of this is behind us."

"Behind us." That's right. They were still in the middle of everything, and Zoe was still having to deal with all of the strings being tied up. But would they tie up nicely? "There's so much going on."

"I know." Gwen gave her a small smile. "But I think we can handle it together, don't you?"

"Some days." Zoe's phone buzzed again. Gruzska. Again. She wrinkled her nose at it. "I suppose I should take this."

"I'll go to the bedroom to give you privacy."

"No. It doesn't matter at this point." Zoe swiped her thumb along the screen and waited for the call to connect. In a fit of confidence, she put the call on speaker. "This is Zoe."

"Zoe." Gruzska sounded annoyed. "I need an explanation."

"Actually, sir, I don't think you do." She cringed at her use of the salutation. She had wanted to be strong, and yet she still sounded like a meek secretary, like he'd always treated her.

"You can't just quit effective immediately."

"I can, and I did." Zoe slid her gaze over to Gwen, who leaned back in the chair, crossed one long leg over the other and looked as if she were the cat who caught the canary. She seemed damned pleased with herself, but why?

"No. You can't."

"Mr. Gruzska. I can quit effective immediately, and I did just that. And no, I don't owe you an explanation."

He sputtered. "We need an exit interview."

Zoe hummed, keeping her eyes locked on Gwen's.

Gwen raised an eyebrow, her lips slowly curling up. Was she enjoying this little display?

Zoe bit her lip as she leaned closer to Gwen, sliding her free hand along Gwen's thigh. "If you want an exit interview, I'll schedule one with your secretary. I would like Frankie Cohen to be present."

"This is unacceptable."

"No, I don't think it is." Zoe moved her hand up Gwen's leg, hitting her hip and spreading her fingers out to stretch down between her legs.

Gwen hummed and spread her legs. Damn. She did like the public part of this, didn't she? No wonder she was so comfortable with Zoe's little masturbation episode on the phone. It probably turned her on.

"Would you like me to schedule it?" Zoe brought the phone closer and set it on the cushion of the couch next to Gwen as she slid onto her knees in between Gwen's legs.

"Any way I can convince you to stay on?" Was that desperation in his tone?

Zoe looked up at Gwen and mouthed the words, *Desperate much?*

Gwen replied silently, *He always is.*

Gwen's gaze glittered with amusement as she ran her fingers through Zoe's hair and over her lips.

Answer him. Gwen mouthed.

"No." Zoe breathed relief. This was the right decision. She had no doubts about it now. Whatever happened with her and Gwen, she would figure it out, but she needed to get out of that office. She needed to be someplace that trusted her, that believed her. It wasn't about the fact that they didn't believe Gwen. It was because they had ignored her. They had chosen to believe lies instead of their *valued* employee.

"What can I do to entice you to stay on?"

"You can't." Zoe reached for the button on Gwen's pants, pulling it free before slowly lowering the zipper. "I quit, effective immediately."

"Zoe." Now he sounded as though he was pleading. "This won't be good for your future."

"I disagree." Zoe dropped a kiss against the rough fabric of Gwen's pants, on the inside of her thigh. Her skin was so warm through the fabric. "The perfect decision for my future is to leave your company."

"Zoe—"

"Nope. You don't treat your employees fairly. You don't listen to or believe them. I only stayed because of Gwen Fudala, and now? There's no reason for me to be there." Zoe placed another kiss on Gwen's leg.

Gwen hissed in response.

"You're a shitty boss," Zoe added.

Gwen moaned.

Interesting.

Zoe nipped this time. She took far too much pleasure in the fact that Gwen was absolutely getting off on this. Leaning up on her knees, Zoe skimmed her hands upward, palming Gwen's breasts through her shirt. Gwen covered Zoe's hands, making sure Zoe stayed right where she was.

"I'm not coming back to work for you," Zoe stated firmly. "And you know what? Fuck the exit interview."

Gwen moved swiftly, learning forward and taking Zoe's mouth in a heated kiss.

Zoe pulled back with a grin on her lips and a giddy feeling in her chest. "See you never, Mr. Gruzska."

thirty-one

HUNG UP ON YOU

The phone call ended. Zoe double checked before she plowed back into everything she was doing to Gwen in that moment. She was pretty sure that Gwen wouldn't have minded keeping Gruzska on the phone, but Zoe wouldn't have been able to do it. She'd been embarrassed enough by one phone call.

Then again...look where it had landed her.

Face first in Gwen's pussy.

Chuckling, Zoe reached up and slid her fingers under the edge of Gwen's pant line. She jerked her elbows back and pulled the material down. Gwen eyed her gleefully, raising her hips up to help as Zoe continued to pull the fabric down her body. She stopped when the material got to Gwen's knees and dove right in.

She had been waiting for this.

And the phone call, combined with Gwen's obvious pleasure at what was happening, spurred Zoe on more than she had expected it to. She'd liked it. Zoe didn't hesitate or wait. She pressed her face right into the crook between Gwen's thighs and opened her mouth.

Gwen's clit was hot, moist, ready for Zoe's taking.

Hissing, Gwen slid her hips forward on the couch cushion

and leaned back. Her fingers threaded into Zoe's long hair, tightening as she raised up, her knees effectively capturing her in place.

"Fuck," Gwen grunted.

Zoe laughed again, the sound rolling around in her chest as she sucked hard. She wanted to get Gwen as close as possible to coming, and then she was going to pull back. Zoe was going to tease this out for as long as she could, edging Gwen through a mind-blowing orgasm.

Gwen groaned. Her thigh muscles tightened. Zoe clapped her palms down on top of them, pushing down to hold Gwen in place. She sucked and teased with a fervor she never had before. Gwen pulled her face in closer, then pushed back, as if she was still trying to direct everything they were doing.

But Zoe knew better.

This was her time to lead. Gwen had gotten all hot and bothered by the fact that Zoe had taken control. By the fact that Zoe hadn't let herself be walked all over, and that was sexy. A shiver ran through Zoe's body, hardening her nipples. She rubbed her thighs together, already worked up over what she knew was happening.

Gwen grunted, her hips jerking. Zoe pushed her back into the cushion and kept her mouth in place. She wiggled one hand free and found the edge of her pants, undoing them before she slid her hand between her skin and panties, finding herself soaked. Zoe moaned, closing her eyes and focusing on Gwen's body while she played a gentle rhythm against herself.

"So sexy," Gwen murmured, brushing Zoe's hair to the side to see her face better. "Amazing."

Zoe said nothing as she continued to move her tongue along Gwen's clit. When she flicked Gwen's clit with her tongue, Zoe flicked her own with the tip of her finger. She had to hold back the groan and concentrate. Doing this in tandem, while brilliant at first, might be the end of her. She wasn't sure she'd be able to concentrate long enough to keep everything going like she wanted to.

Sucking in a sharp breath, Zoe pushed her face in harder. Gwen cried out, lifting completely off the couch for a brief second. Zoe pushed one finger inside herself up to her knuckle and pushed against herself with her thumb and that finger, rocking her hips into her hand.

"Fuck," Gwen muttered, losing herself.

Zoe jerked back suddenly, not wanting Gwen to come just yet. Gwen's eyes widened, and she looked Zoe over head to crotch, her lips curling upward in a seductive smile when her gaze landed on Zoe's fingers still in her pants, still playing with herself.

"You know exactly what a woman wants, don't you?"

"Some days," Zoe teased back, breathless. "And I'm sorry to tell you, but you're going to have to wait for it today."

Gwen hummed satisfaction. "Then what next, silly girl?"

"You get to watch me for a bit." Zoe leaned back on her knees, still covered by her clothes. The only thing Gwen could see was the movement of the back of her hand in her pants and the look on her face. Yet, Gwen seemed enraptured.

Zoe rocked her hips up into her hand, keeping her eyes on Gwen. When Gwen's cheeks reddened, when her breathing increased, Zoe lowered her gaze to right between Gwen's legs, finding her pussy still wet from her mouth. Zoe shuddered, her movements hitching as her body pooled pleasure into the vat that was her nerves. She struggled to keep her breathing even. She panicked trying to stay upright.

Gwen moved swiftly, wrapping arms around Zoe's back and holding her up as she tightened. Her orgasm rushed through her, taking over all of her senses. She was just about to pull her hand away, but Gwen covered Zoe's fingers through the fabric of her pants.

Gwen whispered into Zoe's ear, "Ride through it."

Gasping, Zoe slowed her movements and played out her pleasure, twitch by twitch as it shot through her body. She couldn't see anything. It was so dark. All she could feel was Gwen against her, her nerves electrified, her breath rasping, her heart racing, her cheeks on fire.

"Gwen," Zoe murmured, dropping her forehead to Gwen's shoulder.

"I'm right here," Gwen whispered, dropping kisses all over Zoe's head and cheeks. "I'm right here."

A gentle emotional warmth rushed through Zoe, and she reveled in it. She hadn't felt this safe, this at peace, in ages. Zoe collapsed into Gwen's arms. She stayed there, tears stinging her eyes. Happiness. Contentment. Love.

"I love you." Gwen kissed her ear. "I love you," she said again on a sigh.

Zoe turned her face up, pressing their mouths together. This embrace was home. She'd never been so complete before this. Gwen eased the kiss into gentleness, away from desperation. They stayed there, mouths together, hearts racing, bodies holding each other up.

She never wanted to move. Zoe wanted to stay right in the circle of Gwen's arms for the rest of her life if she could manage it. Cupping Gwen's cheeks, Zoe drew in a sharp breath and bolstered herself. They weren't done yet, and she still wanted to finish what they had started. Trailing her fingers down Gwen's form, Zoe found the edge of Gwen's shirt and lifted it over her head.

Gwen smiled, her eyes alive with mischief and joy. Zoe would take that look over any other look any day. This had been what she'd wanted for years, and finding it in her boss, finding it in someone she'd had a secret crush on for years was completely unexpected.

Zoe unhooked Gwen's bra, shoving it away. In a swift move, she twisted Gwen around so she was on her back, Zoe hovering over her. Grinning down, Zoe wrinkled her nose. "Are you ready for this?"

"Anything with you."

Melting, Zoe leaned in and kissed Gwen brightly. She pushed

Gwen's pants down until they were at her ankles and then tugged them off sharply. Gwen, bare and beautiful, was laid out before her, ready for the taking. Zoe hummed, pressing a sweet kiss to Gwen's raised knee before leaning in, the fabric against her skin scratchy. But she didn't want to be naked just yet. She wanted the full experience of Gwen's body, diving into everything that was Gwen's pleasure in this moment.

Zoe scraped her teeth against the inside of Gwen's thigh lightly, enjoying the little jump she got as a reaction. Gwen sucked in a sharp breath and laughed a little.

"You're good at teasing tonight."

"I have three years of teasing to catch up on."

"Then by all means." Gwen raised her hands above her arms and locked her eyes on Zoe's. "Don't stop."

Zoe didn't. She bent over Gwen, trailing kisses along her skin one after the other. She brushed her nose into Gwen's damp curls and then moved away again. Gwen's breath hitched.

"Do whatever you want to me, silly girl."

Zoe planned on it. She wrapped her arms around Gwen's legs and pulled her in. Once again, she found her face buried. Gwen was heaven. Her scent surrounded Zoe, filling every one of her senses. Her flavor hit the back of Zoe's tongue, sliding down her throat and becoming the only thing that Zoe could taste.

Letting her eyes flutter shut, Zoe focused all her attention on Gwen. She slid her tongue slowly, flicking Gwen's clit right at the end. Then she did it again, repeatedly. Zoe took her time, bringing Gwen closer to orgasm but never pushing her over that edge.

Like before, she wanted this to last as long as possible.

Tonight was solely about them. It was about new and fresh starts, moments where they indulged in each other and who they had become for each other. Zoe knew that she would give Gwen everything that she had—she'd done that for years. She'd never expected to find that Gwen was already doing the same for her.

Sighing, Zoe pressed kisses on the sensitive skin right where Gwen's leg met her hip. She pulled Gwen in closer, the edge of her ass resting on Zoe's knees. Gwen's hair was a halo around her head, her eyes locked on Zoe's face.

"I'm all yours," Gwen whispered.

Yes, yes, she was. Zoe couldn't ask for more than that.

Zoe started with two fingers, sliding them knuckle deep without a word. Then she pulled them out, a tedious pace that she knew would annoy Gwen to no end—or at least annoy her body. Gwen was craving everything Zoe would give her. Zoe could see it in her eyes, in the tremors in her legs, in the hitch in her breath.

"Zoe..." Gwen trailed off.

This time, Zoe curled her fingers when she pulled back. Gwen gasped, her hips jumping up. Zoe got a thrill out of it, knowing that she was the cause. She waited until Gwen was on the verge again before pulling her hand away and replacing it with her mouth.

"You're torturing me," Gwen murmured.

Exactly, Zoe thought. Maybe Gwen could get a little taste of her own medicine, of how tempted Zoe had been for the last three years, how tortured she'd been watching Gwen from afar.

Zoe dipped her thumb right into Gwen before pulling out. Then she circled Gwen's anus in tight circles.

"Yessssss," Gwen hissed. "Yes, do that."

Wonderful. Zoe waited still. She wanted to make sure that Gwen was ready for her. She continued to tease before sliding her thumb in slowly. She waited for the muscles to relax against her intrusion, teasing Gwen with her mouth at the same time. Gwen pressed her heel into the carpet and pushed up, seeking Zoe to go deeper.

Giving Gwen what she wanted, Zoe pushed in more. She'd wanted to try this several times throughout the time they'd been together, and she had a feeling Gwen would be receptive to it. But now, when they both trusted each other fully, was the perfect time and place for it. Zoe sucked hard as she pushed her thumb in as far as she could make it go.

Gwen moaned.

Zoe wasn't going to hold back any longer. Her patience had worn out, and she wanted to see how hard Gwen would come all over her, how much Gwen would let loose now that there was nothing holding her back. Zoe sucked on Gwen's clit hard, harder than she ever had before.

Gwen dug her fingers into Zoe's hair, scraping her nails along her scalp and tugging the strands of hair. Gwen cooed. She groaned. She said nonsense as she rocked her hips into Zoe's mouth, fucking Zoe's face as much as Zoe fucked her.

"Zoe!" Gwen gasped. "I'm there."

Zoe held on, not changing anything about what she was doing as Gwen's entire body tightened in intense pleasure. Wishing she could see Gwen's eyes, her face, every change in her body as she held onto this moment, Zoe held still. She wanted to give Gwen everything that she could.

Staying with Gwen through the orgasm, until Gwen couldn't stand it anymore and pushed Zoe away, was the most beautiful thing Zoe had ever experienced. She kissed her way back up Gwen's body, pressing her lips gently to Gwen's hardened nipples. When Zoe kissed Gwen's lips, it was lazy, wet, and full of sluggishness.

Had Zoe really managed to screw Gwen's brains out?

That was something she had never thought would happen. Humming, Zoe kissed Gwen's neck and her chest as Gwen's breathing calmed. She was completely in love with this woman. With her strength. With her audacity. With her control and compassion. Zoe flicked her tongue across Gwen's nipple and then blew air on it, smiling to herself.

She could entertain herself with Gwen's body for hours. In fact, that was exactly what she wanted to happen tonight. They could talk about the future tomorrow. Tonight was for them, right now, in this moment and nowhere else.

"Fuck," Gwen breathed out finally, a little laugh at the end. "Why haven't you done that earlier?"

"Confidence," Zoe answered easily. Meaning she had none, and she hoped that Gwen would understand her lack of explanation on that front. If she'd had confidence, she wouldn't have waited for a drunken masturbating phone call to make a move on her boss.

Even then, she hadn't been the one to make the move.

"You can do that to me anytime you want." Gwen arched her back, stretching her muscles.

"If you think I'm done, then you better think twice."

"Oh?" Gwen locked her gaze on Zoe's, amusement flashing through her eyes. "And if we're not done, then what's next?"

Zoe grinned wickedly. She took her time as she purposely slid her hand right down Gwen's chest, over her belly, and between her legs. She didn't give Gwen a second as she plunged three fingers right into her. Cocking an eyebrow up at Gwen, Zoe waited for the reaction.

Gwen tensed and shook her head with a laugh. "Don't stop now that you've started."

"Wasn't planning on it."

"Good." Gwen's lilting laughter died quickly when Zoe started a brutal pace.

She wasn't ever going to give this up.

Never.

epilogue

TO THE FUTURE

"Guilty."

The word reverberated through Zoe's head, slinging away and then coming back like a boomerang. Gwen's hand was warm in Zoe's as they stood for the final verdict. Her heart raced. She'd expected this. The district attorney had told them it was looking good. While Nikki had fought the charges, she'd eventually seemed to give up.

Gwen stood stoically, barely moving. Turning slightly, Zoe leaned into Gwen's side. When Gwen's light blue eyes locked on Zoe's, her lower lip quivered. Relief flooded Gwen's face, her cheeks going slack, her shoulders dropping, a rush of air leaving her lips.

Zoe swiftly moved in, wrapping her arms around Gwen's back and tugging her in for a hug. Zoe held her. They held each other. Standing in the courtroom, the other people around them, everything faded. This moment was about them and everything that had ultimately brought them together.

The rest was a blur. Nikki was escorted from the room. Zoe refused to look over. She didn't want to see Nikki in handcuffs, the devastation she must feel, knowing what was going to happen. Zoe didn't want her heart to break again.

"Come on," Gwen murmured into Zoe's ear. With a firm hand on Zoe's back, Gwen guided her out of the courtroom and into the hall.

They stepped outside into the cooling September air. It had been almost an entire year since Nikki was arrested, and in that year, they had both found peace. Still, the trial, the conviction—it had brought everything up again. Zoe savored every touch Gwen gave her.

Zoe sucked the cool air into her lungs, holding it in her chest. "I was pretty damn sure they were going to find her guilty, but hearing it..."

"It's relief," Gwen supplied. "Absolute relief."

"Yeah." Zoe turned her head to look into Gwen's eyes. "It's so strange."

"It's been a long time since we've been at peace."

Nodding, Zoe agreed. She moved in and pressed their lips together quickly. "What now?"

"Now we have a meeting with Athena."

"I meant for us." Zoe clung to Gwen's arm. She wanted answers to questions she didn't even know how to form.

Gwen dropped her hand to Zoe's, twisting the engagement ring around her finger. Zoe needed that reminder, whether Gwen meant to do it on purpose or not. She had made it a habit as soon as she'd put the ring on Zoe's finger three months ago.

"We know what our future looks like, silly girl."

"Right." They did know. They were getting married in six months. Their business was thriving, with multiple clients having moved from Gruzska to them in the last few months. Working together was amazing, and Zoe loved being more involved in the business than she had been before.

Gwen moved in and kissed Zoe right on the corner of her mouth. "Come on. Athena's waiting for us. I already texted her."

When the hell had Gwen managed to do that? Zoe held on tightly to Gwen's arm as they walked together toward the parking garage. It wasn't much longer until they were seated on a couch in

Athena's office. This woman was formidable, and quite honestly, she scared the living shit out of Zoe.

"I'll file first thing in the morning." Athena sat in the chair, one ankle crossed over the other. Her clothes were on point, and covered every inch of her skin except hands and face.

Zoe clenched her jaw. "We're really doing this?" she whispered.

Gwen clutched her hand still. "Yes. I'm not going to stand for someone else to be treated the same way I was."

"I get that, but this...this is only going to drag out what just ended." Zoe soothed her fingers up and down Gwen's arm, hoping that her comment wouldn't start a firestorm of tension and anger.

"It will." Gwen's lips thinned. She turned from Athena to face Zoe. "But what's another year or two to me? I've already been fighting this battle for thirteen years. If my extra one or two prevents someone else from experiencing it? I think that's worth it."

Love filled Zoe's chest. This was who Gwen had been under everything, and Zoe had fallen completely in love with her. Lifting their joined hands, Zoe kissed Gwen's knuckles. "Then we fight to the bitter end."

Athena nodded sharply, pulling papers over. They spent the next two hours going through exactly what was going to happen next. Zoe was going to have to ask Gwen for a recap, because she knew she only understood half of what was discussed. At best, it was half. Legalese wasn't her forte.

By the time they got home, Zoe was ready to collapse into the couch and resurface in the morning. Gwen, apparently, had a different idea. She started spouting off work things, asking if Zoe had done them yet. Narrowing her gaze, Zoe cocked her head at Gwen and squinted with pursed lips.

"If you don't sit down with me, I'm going to hog-tie you and tongue-fuck you until you can't think about anything else."

Gwen froze in the middle of pulling the tie on her jacket. Her eyes locked on Zoe's, her cheeks pale. "We have a lot of work to do."

"One, there's always a lot of work. Two, today is not the day to do it." Zoe was going to remain firm in this decision.

"The launch is next week."

"It is," Zoe countered. "And my previous comment stands true. If you don't sit down with me on this couch, I will make you."

Scoffing, Gwen pulled her jacket off and threw it over the arm of the couch. Zoe could see the anger winding through her a mile away. They were so comfortable together now, in tune with each other, and Zoe knew she'd be able to bring Gwen around.

Gwen plopped onto the couch, but she still held a stiffness in her shoulders. Zoe longed to soothe it away, to push those knots out, to ease Gwen back into the amazing woman Zoe knew she was. This day had taken a lot out of them, whether or not Gwen wanted to admit that.

Zoe immediately took Gwen's hand in hers, tightening her grasp. She pressed her cheek to Gwen's shoulder and took deep breaths. Zoe knew, without a doubt, that just her proximity to Gwen would do what they needed. It had taken her a bit to put two and two together, but realizing that a simple touch or thirty seconds of closeness would make the world a brighter place for Gwen, Zoe wouldn't ever deny them that.

"I can't believe it's over." Gwen's words were soft, barely above a whisper.

This was what Zoe had been waiting for.

"I don't know what to do now."

"I get that." It had been why Zoe had asked the question earlier in the day. What did their future look like now that this big bad enemy was gone?

"Athena says the civil suit will take maybe a year depending if people want to settle or fight it." Gwen tightened her grasp on Zoe's fingers. "We'll be seeing a lot more of her for a while."

"I suppose so." Zoe turned and kissed Gwen's cheek. "It's a new battle now."

"It is. One that's not as scary."

"They believed you, Gwen." Zoe moved away slightly so she could see Gwen's face. "You were believed."

Tears trailed down Gwen's cheeks. She shook her head, biting her lip. Zoe knew she was at a loss for words, that for the first time in thirteen years, all of her experiences were validated. Gwen swallowed hard and blew out a breath.

"You were the first."

"But not the last," Zoe countered.

"No, not the last." Gwen moved in and pressed their mouths together.

"Never the last. And this next battle? We've got this together."

Gwen cupped Zoe's cheek, pulling her in for another kiss. This one deepened. Their tongues tangled, mingling with the salty tears that still trailed from her eyes. Zoe hummed and pulled Gwen down on top of her as she fell onto the couch cushion.

"Always together," Zoe breathed the words out when Gwen kissed down her neck. "Never alone again."

"I love you," Gwen said, kissing Zoe's nose. "I never thought anyone would be able to love me with everything."

Zoe smiled up at her. "You aren't your baggage. It just helps to make you who you are."

Gwen smiled. "Silly girl. Can't you just take a compliment."

"Nope." Zoe grinned broadly, wiggling a leg free so she could wrap it around Gwen's hips and pull her in closer. "Can you?"

"You're amusing."

"I try to be."

Gwen nipped at Zoe's lower lip, sucking it into her mouth. Zoe groaned, her body already gearing up. From the sudden release of tension to this? She would take it any day.

"You going to fuck me or not?" Zoe teased, purposely moving her hand down Gwen's chest, over her breast, and between their bodies to press against her.

Hissing, Gwen dropped her head to Zoe's shoulder. "I think I could use a good distraction today."

"Not a distraction," Zoe countered. "Love. And orgasm!" Zoe tagged on at the last minute.

Chuckling, Gwen pressed their mouths together. "That'll be the name of my memoir."

"Oh Jesus." Zoe's cheeks heated. She wasn't the greatest with words. But Gwen's mouth against hers pulled her from that spiral and brought her right back to this moment. This was for them and no one else. This was the reminder of what pulled them together, but it wasn't their whole story.

It never would be.

~

Thank you so much for reading this book! This was a labor of love and the story went from a flash fiction piece of about 250 words to a short story of just under 10,000 words to a full length novel. I have loved getting to know Zoe and spending so much time with her.

If you'd love to stay connected, please sign up for my newsletter and send me an email!

about the author

Adrian J. Smith has been publishing since 2013 but has been writing nearly her entire life. With a focus on women loving women fiction, AJ jumps genres from action-packed police procedurals to the seedier life of vampires and witches to sweet romances with an age gap twist. She loves writing and reading about women in the midst of the ordinariness of life.

AJ currently lives in Cheyenne, WY, although she moves often and has lived all over the United States. She loves to travel to different countries and places. She currently plays the roles of author, wife, and mother to two rambunctious youngsters, occasional handy-woman. Connect with her on Facebook, Instagram, or Ream.

shameless expectations

Escaping the past is hard. Living in the present is harder.

Monti Schroeder is on a quest for peace. She has been since the moment she was born, but peace has remained elusive. Living as a nomad, she takes work where she can get it. When her sister calls with a favor for her neurotic boss, Monti agrees for a few extra bucks. What Monti finds when she arrives is a woman just as broken as she is. And no matter what, she can't leave Athena to flounder on her own.

Athena Pruitt has made it through the last twenty-two years with one rule. Avoid everything uncomfortable. Her house has become her prison, and she is desperate for respite. Unable to handle physical touch, she's wary when her personal assistant hires a "special" masseuse who can help. But Monti isn't a typical massage therapist.

Each day, each massage, each moment Monti and Athena spend together they unravel just a little more. With wells of trauma and pain filling both to the brim, just what will happen when their vessels break?

Will Monti find peace? Will Athena learn to live without shame? Will they both mend their brokenness beyond repair?

also by adrian j. smith

Romance

Memoir in the Making

OBlique

Love Burns

About Time

Admissible Affair

Daring Truth

Indigo: Blues (Indigo B&B #1)

Indigo: Nights (Indigo B&B #2)

Indigo: Three (Indigo B&B #3)

Indigo: Storm (Indigo B&B #4)

Indigo: Law (Indigo B&B #5)

When the Past Finds You

Don't Quit Your Daydream

Love Me At My Worst

Inside These Halls

Maybe Someday

Crime/Mystery/Thriller

For by Grace (Spirit of Grace #1)

Fallen from Grace (Spirit of Grace #2)

Grace through Redemption (Spirit of Grace #3)

Lost & Forsaken (Missing Persons #1)

Broken & Weary (Missing Persons #2)

Young & Old (Missing Persons #3)

Alone & Lonely (Missing Persons #4)

Stone's Mistake (Agent Morgan Stone #1)

Stone's Homefront (Agent Morgan Stone #2)

Fantasy/Science Fiction

Forever Burn (James Matthews #1)

Dying Embers (James Matthews #2)

Ashes Fall (James Matthews #3)

Unbound (Quarter Life #1)

De-Termination (Quarter Life #2)

Release (Quarter Life #3)

Beware (Quarter Life #4)

Dead Women Don't Tell Tales (Tales of the Undead & Depraved #.5)

Thieving Women Always Lose (Tales of the Undead & Depraved #1)

Scheming Women Seek Revenge (Tales of the Undead & Depraved #2)

Broken Women Fight Back (Tales of the Undead & Depraved #3)

Deep Sounding Chaos (Love, Tails & Battle Wails #1)

Printed in Great Britain
by Amazon

55535713R00175